Dedalus European Classics
General Editor: Mike Mitchell

The Mystery
of the
Sintra Road

Eça de Queiroz

The Mystery of the Sintra Road

Translated by Margaret Jull Costa & Nick Phillips

Dedalus

ARTS COUNCIL ENGLAND
Supported using public funding by

Published in the UK by Dedalus Limited,
24-26, St Judith's Lane, Sawtry, Cambs, PE28 5XE
email: info@dedalusbooks.com
www.dedalusbooks.com

ISBN printed book 978 1 909232 29 7
ISBN ebook 9781 909232 60 0

Dedalus is distributed in the USA & Canada by SCB Distributors,
15608 South New Century Drive, Gardena, CA 90248
email: info@scbdistributors.com   web: www.scbdistributors.com

Dedalus is distributed in Australia by Peribo Pty Ltd.
58, Beaumont Road, Mount Kuring-gai, N.S.W. 2080
email: info@peribo.com.au

Publishing History
First published in Portugal in 1870
First Dedalus edition in 2013
First ebook edition in 2013

Translation copyright © Margaret Jull Costa & Nick Phillips 2013

The right of Margaret Jull Costa & Nick Phillips to be identified as the translators of this work has been asserted by them in accordance with the Copyright, Designs and Patents Act, 1988.

Printed in Finland by Bookwell
Typeset by Marie Lane

This book is sold subject to the condition that it shall not, by way of trade or otherwise, be lent, resold, hired out or otherwise circulated without the publisher's prior consent in any form of binding or cover other than that in which it is published and without a similar condition including this condition being imposed on the subsequent purchaser.

A C.I.P. listing for this book is available on request.

The Author

Eça de Queiroz (1845–1900) is considered to be Portugal's greatest novelist. Dedalus has embarked on a project to make all his major works available in English in new translations by Margaret Jull Costa.

Published so far are: *The Mandarin, The Relic, The Tragedy of the Street of Flowers, The Crime of Father Amaro, Cousin Bazilio, The Maias, The City and The Mountains,* and *Alves & Co.*

The Translators

Margaret Jull Costa

Margaret Jull Costa has translated the works of many Spanish and Portuguese writers. She won the Portuguese Translation Prize for *The Book of Disquiet* by Fernando Pessoa in 1992 and for *The Word Tree* by Teolinda Gersão in 2012, and her translations of Eça de Queiroz's novels *The Relic* (1996) and *The City and the Mountains* (2009) were shortlisted for the prize; with Javier Marias, she won the 1997 International IMPAC Dublin Literary Award for *A Heart So White*, and, in 2000, she won the Weidenfeld Translation Prize for Jose Saramago's *All the Names*. In 2008 she won the Pen Book-of-the-Month Club Translation Prize and the Oxford Weidenfeld Translation Prize for *The Maias* by Eça de Queiroz.

Nick Phillips

Nick Phillips is a New Zealander with a passion for the Portuguese language and the literature of Portuguese-speaking countries. His collaboration with Margaret Jull Costa on the translation of *The Mystery of the Sintra Road* mirrors the co-authorship of the original novel.

Contents

Prefatory Letter to the Publisher	9
Doctor ***'s Account	15
The Letter from Z.	59
From 'F.' to the Doctor	65
Z.'s Second Letter	92
The Tall Masked Man's Account	97
The Revelations of A.M.C.	186
Her Confession	222
The Concluding Revelations of A.M.C.	271
The Final Letter	280
Afterword	281
Two Authors : Two Translators	288

Prefatory Letter to the Publisher of
'The Mystery of the Sintra Road'
Prior to the Publication of a Third Edition in 1884.

One summer evening fourteen years ago, while sitting before our respective cups of coffee in a café in the Passeio Público and slowly succumbing to the melancholy of Lisbon as it dozed off to a tearful pot-pourri of tunes from Verdi's *I Due Foscari*, we made up our minds to *do* something and make a loud enough noise to wake the whole place up, with said noise taking the form of an extraordinary novel to be sent blaring out across the Baixa from the dizzy heights of the *Diário de Notícias*.

To that end, without plan, without method, without training, without qualifications, without style, merely huddled round the 'glass tower of the Imagination', we began to concoct this book, one of us in Leiria, the other in Lisbon, each equipped only with a ream of paper and a fund of good humour and audacity.

It seems that Lisbon really did wake up, out of kindness perhaps or curiosity, for, having read *The Mystery of the Sintra Road* in the pages of the *Diário de Notícias*, its citizens then went out and bought it as a book. And today, gentlemen, you send us the proofs of a third edition, asking us what we think of that work written all those years ago, a time we recall now with great nostalgia.

The happy reign of João VI had already ended. Obliging Garção, merry Tolentino, and much-mourned Reis Quita had all passed away. Beyond the Passeio Público, which, like the rest of the country, had been evacuated by Junot's troops, it fell to M. Octave Feuillet to stimulate our imaginations. The name Flaubert was unknown to writers of popular serials. Ponson du Terrail cried out in the wilderness of minor journals and lending libraries. M. Jules Claretie published a book entitled… (well, no one nowadays can remember what it was called) of which the critics so movingly wrote: 'Here is a work that will endure!' In short: we were young.

What do we think today of the novel we wrote fourteen years ago? We think – praise the Lord! – that it is quite atrocious, and that neither of us, whether as novelist or critic, would wish its like on anyone, not even on our worst enemy, because it contains a little of everything that a novelist ought not to include, and almost everything that a critic would wish to see removed.

We will spare you – so as not to make matters worse by filling three volumes – the enumeration of all its faults! We shall draw a discreet veil over its masked men of various statures, its mysterious doctors, its fair-haired English captains, its dangerous countesses, its tigers and elephants, its yachts on which are hoisted white linen and lace handkerchiefs like flags of fantasy, its sinister glasses of opium, its elegant corpses, its romantic costumes and, finally, its horses spurred on by riders in pale-grey capes who disappear into the dust of incredible adventures as they gallop through Porcalhota and off into the distance!

All these things – though pleasant, invariably sincere and even, on occasions, moving – are displeasing to their now more mature creators, who long ago averted their gaze from the misty horizons of sentimentality in order to devote themselves to the patient, humble study of the stark realities of their own street.

Why then do we allow the reprinting of a book, which, being entirely imagined and invented and based not at all on real life, goes entirely counter to our campaign in favour of analysis and objective certainty?

We consent because we believe that no workman should be ashamed of his work.

Legend has it that Murat, when King of Naples, ordered the old riding-whip he had used as a chasseur in Napoleon's army to be hung in the throne room, and that he would often point first to his sceptre and then to the whip, saying: 'That is where I started.' This glorious tale only confirms us in our view – not, of course, that we are applying it literally to ourselves. As thrones, we still have the same old chairs we sat in fourteen years ago, with no ornamental canopy to cover us; and our greying heads have not, as yet, been encircled by any crown, be it of laurels or of Naples.

It is a source of modest satisfaction that, since we finished this book, we have not ceased to labour, not even for a day, not until now, with its unexpected reappearance in a third edition, a guise it wears with an impudent air of triumph that rather suits it!

Then, as now, we wrote honestly, that is, as well as we could; and it was perhaps that love of perfection – our artistic integrity – that explains the public's warm feelings for this book of our youth.

There are two more reasons for this new edition.

The first is that the reprinting of this book – which was quite unlike any other when it first appeared – may contain, for a generation greatly in need of it, a useful lesson in independence.

Far from being inventive, audacious, revolutionary and

iconoclastic, the younger generation that followed us seem servile, imitative, copy-cat and altogether too deferential to their teachers. New writers nowadays cannot take a step forward without stepping into someone else's footprints. Such pusillanimity makes their work seem hesitant and dull. To those of us on our way out, the upcoming generation gives the impression of having emerged from the cradle already old and to be entering the writerly profession on crutches.

We long ago burned the letters from our first romantic excesses, but we want those from our intellectual extravagances to remain. At the age of twenty, one should be irreverent, not, perhaps, in order to make the world progress, but at least to stir it up a little. There is time aplenty in old age to be prudent, correct and sedentary.

In art, the waywardness of the young and their rebellious resistance to tradition is indispensable if new life is to be breathed into inventiveness, creative power and artistic originality. Preserve us from literature that lacks the spark of youth! For like old people who have gone through life without ever having experienced the shock of a single adventure, there will be nothing in it worth remembering. Furthermore, for those who, in their maturity, were wrenched by duty from the pleasures of spontaneity and forced into the harsh, sad, mean land of exactitude, where, instead of the splendour of heroic deeds and the beauty of passion, they find only shrivelled characters and wretched feelings, for them, it would be a great comfort to be able to hear once in a while, on sunny mornings, along with the returning Spring, the golden bee of fantasy buzzing in the blue, as it used to do in the good old days.

Our other reason for not rejecting this book is that it remains a witness to the close collaboration of two old men of letters, whose friendship has lasted for twenty years in the midst of a crumbling society. And while that may not be a triumph for our intellect, it is a source of sweet joy for our hearts.

Lisbon, 14 December, 1884.
Yours in friendship,
Eça de Queiroz
Ramalho Ortigão

Doctor ***'s Account

I

To the Editor of the *Diário de Notícias*

Sir,
I am placing in your hands my personal account of an extraordinary affair in which I became involved in my capacity as a doctor, and I ask that you publish – in whatever way you deem appropriate – at least the substance of what I set before you.

So grave, so veiled in mystery, so seemingly steeped in criminality are the events I am about to describe, that I feel it is vital to make the facts available to the general public, as a way of providing the only key to unlocking what seems to me a truly horrifying drama, even though I was only present at one act, and know nothing of the preceding scenes, nor how it may end.

Three days ago, I was travelling back to Lisbon from the outskirts of Sintra in the company of F., a friend of mine, at whose house I had been staying for a few days.

We were riding horses kept by F. on his estate and which were due to be returned to Sintra by a servant who had set off for Lisbon the previous evening.

It was late afternoon as we crossed the moors. The melancholy of both the hour and the place coloured our mood, and we gazed silently about us as we trotted slowly along.

About halfway between São Pedro and Cacém – at a

The Mystery of the Sintra Road

deserted spot whose name I do not know because I so seldom pass that way – we came across a coach stopped in the road.

It was a coupé, painted dark green and black and drawn by a pair of chestnut horses.

The coachman, who wore no uniform, was standing in front of the horses with his back to us.

Two fellows were bent over the wheels on the side of the coach we had to pass, and seemed to be intently studying some detail of the steering mechanism.

A fourth individual, also with his back to us, was standing near the ditch on the other side of the road, where he appeared to be looking for something, perhaps a stone to place beneath the wheel.

'It's all down to the disgraceful state of this road,' observed my friend. 'The axle's probably broken or else a wheel's come adrift from the hub.'

By this time, we were passing between the three men I mentioned, and F.'s conjectures had barely left his lips when the horse I was riding veered suddenly and fell to the ground.

The man beside the ditch, and to whom I had paid little attention, being too engrossed in studying the stationary carriage, had caused my horse to fall by snatching at its reins and tugging as hard as possible, while, simultaneously, driving the animal in the opposite direction with a hefty kick to its flank.

My mount, an inexperienced yearling that handled poorly at the best of times, slipped and tumbled over when it made that rapid, enforced about-turn.

The unknown man gave another tug at the reins to make the horse get up and, while helping me to my feet as well, he asked with some concern if I had hurt my leg, which had remained pinned beneath my horse when it fell.

The Mystery of the Sintra Road

He spoke in the modulated tones of the educated. The hand he offered me was smooth and delicate. A black satin mask of the kind used at masquerades covered his face, and I seem to recall that he wore a narrow black crêpe band about his hat. As demonstrated by the way he had caused my horse to fall, he was an agile and extremely strong young man.

I sprang to my feet and, before I could utter a word, I saw that during the time it had taken for me to be unseated from my horse, a scuffle had broken out between my companion and the other two individuals who had been pretending to examine the wheels and who also had their faces covered with masks like that of the man I have already described.

You may well say, sir, that this is pure pot-boiler fiction, worthy of Ponson du Terrail! But that is because life, even on the road from Sintra, can at times seem more like a novel than artistic verisimilitude can tolerate. But I am not creating art, I am recording facts.

Seeing one of men grab the bridle of his horse, F. had forced the man to let go by dealing him a blow to the head with the handle of his riding crop, which the other masked man immediately managed to wrench from his hand.

Neither of us was carrying a weapon. Nevertheless, my friend had pulled from his pocket the heavy key to the main door of his house in Sintra and, digging his spurs into his horse, he was stretching out along its neck as he attempted to use the key as a weapon to strike the head of the masked man still holding the bridle.

The fellow, however, kept a firm grip on the rearing horse with one hand, drew out a revolver with the other, and pointed it at my friend's head, saying calmly:

'Steady now!'

The man whom F. had set upon with the riding crop had

felt obliged to sit down for a few minutes, leaning against the carriage door, visibly dazed but not wounded, for F.'s riding crop was made only of light whalebone with a handle of plaited horsehair. The man had now got up from the ground and put his hat back on.

By this time, the assailant who had felled my horse and helped me to my feet was also holding a pair of small silver-handled pistols, the kind the French call *coups de poing* and which can pierce a door at thirty paces. He now cordially offered me his arm, saying affably:

'It seems a far more sensible option to accept the seat I have available in the carriage than for you to continue on horseback or to have to walk from here to the pharmacy in Porcalhota dragging a bruised leg.'

I am not readily intimidated by a show of weapons. I know what a gulf lies between threatening to fire a gun and actually doing so. I could move my bruised leg easily enough and F. was riding a strong horse; we are both of us robust types; we could perhaps have held out for another ten minutes or a quarter of an hour, during which time it was highly likely, on such a heavily frequented stretch of road, that some other travellers would arrive and help us out.

I must confess, though, that I felt greatly intrigued by the very unexpectedness of this strange adventure.

There was nothing in our previous lives to suggest that anyone would want to exert pressure on us or threaten violence.

For reasons I cannot satisfactorily explain, it did not seem to me at the time that the people surrounding us had robbery in mind, far less homicide. I'd had little chance to observe them closely and had only heard them utter a few fleeting words, but they appeared to me to be decent people. Considering these events calmly, I realise that my conjecture was based on various disparate details, which, however glancingly, I had made an unconscious attempt to analyse. For example, I remember that the lining of the hat belonging to the masked man whom F. had lambasted with his riding crop was made of pale grey satin. The one who had pointed the revolver at F. was wearing a pair of pewter-grey gloves fastened with two buttons. The one who had helped me up had very narrow feet shod in patent leather boots; his close-fitting nut-brown trousers had adjustable tabs at the waistband; and he was wearing spurs.

Notwithstanding my inclination to give up the fight and get into the coach, I asked my friend – in German – if he thought we should resist or surrender.

'Surrender! Surrender!' said one of the strangers gravely. 'So that we can save precious time! Please come with us! One day you will know why we donned these masks and why we ambushed you. We give our word that tomorrow you will be safe in your homes in Lisbon and your horses will be back in Sintra two hours hence.'

After some reluctance, which I helped to overcome, F. dismounted and climbed into the coach. I followed him.

They gave us the most comfortable seats. The man who had been standing in front of the pair of coach-horses now roped together our two mounts; the one who had made my horse stumble climbed onto the coachman's seat and took up the reins; the other two joined us in the carriage and settled into the seats facing ours. Then they closed the wooden blinds covering the side-windows of the carriage and drew a green silk curtain across the inside of the front window.

At the moment of our departure, the man who had taken up the reins tapped on the window and asked for a cigar. The other two men passed him a straw-work cigar box, and he tossed the mask he had been wearing through the same opening. Then we set off at full speed.

As I was getting into the carriage I thought I caught a glimpse in the distance of a horsedrawn omnibus and a cabriolet approaching from the direction of Lisbon. I don't think I am deluding myself when I say that the occupants of these coaches must have seen our horses, one of which was grey and the other chestnut, and may perhaps be able to identify both the carriage in which we were travelling and the person who served as our coachman. As I mentioned earlier, the vehicle was green and black. The polished mahogany blinds had four narrow oblong slits at the top, in the form of a cross.

I do not have time now to write the rest of my story and still be able to despatch this letter by today's mail. I will, therefore, continue later. And I will reveal, if you have not already guessed it, my reason for concealing both my own identity and that of my friend.

II

24 July, 1870

I have just seen the letter I addressed to you published in full on the page reserved for popular serials. In view of this, I will try to ensure that any future letters do not exceed the space available in that section of the newspaper.

I neglected to date my earlier letter, thus leaving it unclear as to when exactly we were ambushed on the Sintra Road. It was Wednesday last, the 20th of the current month of July.

I will move on swiftly to tell you what took place in the carriage, omitting no detail and trying to reconstruct our conversation, as far as possible using the actual words.

The carriage set out towards Sintra. I assume, however, that it made a number of wide detours along the way, so smoothly done that we did not even notice any sudden variations in the speed and pace of the horses. Only certain perceptible climbs and descents led me to suppose this, although we continued to travel along a smooth macadamised road. Moreover, there were slight changes in the amount of light filtering in through the green silk curtain, indicating to me that the coach was changing its position relative to the sinking sun.

Their clear intention was to confuse us as to which route we were taking, and the fact is that only two minutes after setting out, I would have been quite unable to say whether we were travelling from Lisbon to Sintra or from Sintra to Lisbon!

The light inside the carriage, though dim, was enough for us to be able to make out certain objects, for example, I could read the numerals on my watch. It was a quarter past seven.

The stranger opposite me was also looking at his watch, but he failed to put it back in his waistcoat pocket properly and it fell out again almost immediately and remained hanging on its chain in full view for some time. It was a very singular watch that could not easily be mistaken for any other and which, when I describe it, will be instantly recognisable to anyone who might have seen it before. The lid was made of smooth black enamel, with, in the centre, underneath a helmet, a gleaming gold coat of arms.

We had only been travelling for a few minutes when the man seated opposite F., the one who had urged us so vigorously to accompany them, said to us:

'I hardly need say that you can have every confidence as regards your personal safety.'

'Of course,' my friend replied. 'We are not in the least worried. I hope that you will do us the justice of believing that we were not coerced into coming by fear. Neither of us is such a child as to be terrified by the sight of your black masks or your firearms. You have just been so kind as to assure us that you mean us no harm. We, for our part, ought to advise you that were your company, at any point, to become disagreeable to us, nothing would be easier than for us to tear off your masks, smash the blinds and invite you, in the presence of the first coach that happens by, to hand over your weapons before placing you in the custody of the first parish law officer we meet. It seems right to me, therefore, that we begin by respecting the friendly feelings that have brought us together. Otherwise we would all become grotesques: you the terrifiers and we the terrified!'

While F. was saying these words with an air of cheerful good will, the man he was speaking to seemed to become increasingly angry. He was compulsively joggling one leg up and down, meanwhile resting one elbow on his knee, stroking his beard and looking intently at my friend. Then, leaning back as if he had changed his mind, he said:

'Yes, you're right and perhaps, in your shoes, I would do and say the same.'

Then, after a brief pause, he continued:

'What would you say, gentlemen, if I were to prove to you that this mask, which you choose to see as mere burlesque, is, rather, confirmation of the seriousness of the matter that brought us here? Imagine if you will, one of those amorous liaisons of which there are so many. A married woman, for example, whose husband has been away travelling for a year. This lady, well known in Lisbon society, is pregnant. What is to be done?'

There was a silence.

I took advantage of the brief pause that followed this somewhat primitive exposition of the problem to declare:

'Send the husband a deed of separation in law. Then, if she is rich, she can go off to South America or Switzerland with her lover. If she is poor, she can buy a sewing machine and slave away in a garret somewhere. That is the fate of women, both rich and poor alike. Anyway, death comes quickly enough in such circumstances, whether in a villa on the shores of Lake Geneva or in a rented room in Rua dos Vinagres. One dies just the same, of consumption or tedium, worn out from work or pining away in paradise.'

'And the child?' enquired the masked man.

'The child, since he is both outside the family and outside the law, is a poor wretch whose misfortune derives in large part from a society that remains unable to define the responsibilities of the clandestine father. If the parents are as hopeless as the law and have to resort to ambushing people on the Sintra Road in order to ask them what they should do, the child would be better off being left at the gates of a foundling hospital.'

'You speak as fluently as any distinguished philosopher. As a physician, however, you are perhaps forgetting that in this situation, there is a small formality to comply with before you leave the child on the foundling wheel: you first have to bring him or her into the world.'

'That is for the specialists. You have not, I believe, brought me here in that capacity.'

'You are mistaken. It is precisely because you are a doctor that you are here. It is precisely because of your medical skills that we ambushed you on the Sintra Road and are now taking you in secret to give succour to someone in need.'

'But I am not a practitioner.'

'That doesn't matter. You are not in practice: so much the better for us. We will not be inconveniencing any patients by having you abandon them for a few hours while you pursue this adventure with us. You qualified in Paris and even published a thesis on surgery that attracted much attention and drew high praise from the Faculty. Let us pretend, therefore, that you are going to help at a birth.'

My friend F. began to laugh:

'But *I* have no medical qualifications nor have I published a thesis,' he said. 'Would you care to tell me what role *I* am to play?'

'You want to know the reason why you are here? Well, I shall tell you.'

At this point, however, the carriage came to an abrupt halt and our companions, startled, sprang to their feet.

III

I heard the sound of our coachman jumping down from his seat, followed by that of the two lanterns being opened one after the other and a match being struck on the steel rim of the wheel. Then I heard the spring on the little door that you close after lighting the candles and a faint creaking as he adjusted the lanterns on their stands.

I did not initially understand why we had stopped to carry out this task when night had not yet fallen and we were travelling along a good road.

It can be explained, however, as a precautionary measure. Our coachman preferred not to have to stop where there might be other people about. If we were to pass through a village, the lights being lit in the streets – and which we would be able to see through the curtain or the cracks in the blinds – might give us a clue as to our whereabouts. By lighting the lamps early, any such discovery would be thwarted. As we passed between buildings or high walls, the projection of the bright light from the lanterns onto those walls and its reflection back into the coach would make it impossible for us to know whether we were driving through a village or along a well-lit street.

As soon as the lanterns were lit and the carriage had set off again, the masked man who had promised to explain to F. the reason why he had been chosen to accompany us, proceeded to do so:

'Imagine I am the lover of the lady whom I described. The matter is known only to three friends of mine, close friends, childhood playmates, comrades from university, constant companions, each of us ready to make whatever sacrifice that friendship might demand. Alas, none of those friends is a doctor. We had to find one and, at the same time, ensure that my secret would not be passed on to other people, whoever they might be, a secret that involves a man's love and a lady's honour. My child will probably be born tonight or tomorrow morning. Since no one must know the identity of the mother or even suspect, by some clue, who she might be, it is vital that the doctor does not recognise the people he is speaking to or, indeed, the house to which he has been taken. That is why we are wearing masks and why you gentlemen must allow us to keep the shutters closed and the curtain drawn, and also why we will blindfold you before you leave the carriage and enter the house we are going to.' He turned to face F. and continued: 'Now do you understand why you are here? We could not prevent you from accompanying your friend from Sintra today, nor could we postpone this visit or leave you at the point on the road where we kidnapped the doctor. You would easily find some means to follow us and discover who we are.'

'Most ingenious,' I observed, 'but you clearly have little regard for my discretion.'

'To entrust someone with someone else's secret is to betray the owner of the secret,' the masked man countered.

F. agreed wholeheartedly with this point of view and said so, praising the masked men's spirit of romantic adventure.

The very sincerity with which he spoke these words appeared to trouble the stranger somewhat. It seemed to me that he had expected it would prove far harder to persuade us and so was rather put out by F.'s sudden acquiescence. He who had always been ready with a prompt retort and a glib word now found himself unable to respond to the confidence invested in him, and from then until we reached our destination, he kept a silence that must have weighed heavily on his normal talkative, expansive self.

It should be said, however, that shortly afterwards, the coach left the macadamised road on which we had been travelling and continued along what was either a local road or a short cut. The ground was stony and potholed. Given the jolting of the carriage – which, under the expert hand of the driver, continued to proceed at a gallop – and the racket made by the wooden shutters banging against the window frames, conversation was well nigh impossible.

At last, we turned onto a smooth road. The carriage stopped for a second time, and the coachman climbed quickly down from his seat, calling:

'Coming!'

He returned shortly afterwards and I heard someone say:

'They're taking some girls to Lisbon.'

The coach proceeded.

Could it be some kind of customs barrier near the city? Perhaps our driver had made up a plausible excuse so that the officials would not come and open the carriage door? Would the phrase I had overheard be intelligible to my companions?

I cannot say for certain.

Soon afterwards, the carriage drove onto some kind of paved area and two or three minutes later, it stopped. The coachman knocked on the window:

'We're here,' he announced.

The masked man, who had not uttered a word since the moment I mentioned earlier, took a handkerchief from his pocket and said to us with some embarrassment:

'I do apologise for this, but that's how it must be!'

F. leaned towards him and the fellow put the blindfold over his eyes and I, in turn, was blindfolded by the man opposite me.

The Mystery of the Sintra Road

We then climbed down from the coach and were led by our companions into a house and down a corridor. As far as I could deduce from the way in which we had to stop and make way for someone coming in the opposite direction, it was clearly a very narrow corridor.

'Shall I take the coach?'

'Yes, do,' answered the voice of our guide.

We paused for a moment. The door through which we had entered was locked, and the man who had served as coachman went on ahead saying:

'Let's go!'

We shuffled forwards, went up two stone steps, then turned to the right and reached a staircase. It was an old, steep, wooden staircase covered with a narrow carpet. The steps were very worn and their once sharp projecting edges had grown smooth and round. Along the wall beside me ran a cord that served as a banister; it was made of silk and, to the touch, felt little used. The air was damp and had the musty smell common to uninhabited houses. We climbed eight or possibly ten stairs, turned left at a landing, climbed yet more stairs and stopped on the first floor.

No one had said a word, and there was a sombre quality to the silence that enveloped us like a cloud of gloom.

I heard the carriage moving off and felt a sense of dread, a childish anxiety.

A key turned in a lock, we crossed the threshold and the door was locked again behind us.

'You may take off your blindfolds now,' said one of our companions.

I uncovered my eyes. It was night.

One of the masked men struck a match, lit five candles in a bronze candelabra, picked it up, went over to a piece of

furniture covered by a travelling rug, and lifted the rug.
 I could not contain my shock and let out a cry of horror. There before me lay a man's dead body.

IV

I feel exhausted and on edge as I write to you today. The obscure affair in which I find myself involved, the ill-defined sense of danger surrounding me, the tension as I try to divine the truth behind this adventure, the sudden disruption to my normal, sedate routine – all this is creating a state of unhealthy agitation that I find hard to bear.

As soon as I saw the corpse I asked abruptly:

'What does this mean, gentlemen?'

The tallest of the masked men replied:

'There is no time for explanations. Forgive us for having misled you, but, please, doctor, take a look at this man! What's wrong with him? Is he dead? Is he sleeping off some narcotic?'

He spoke these words in a voice filled with such urgent, anxious supplication that, given the entirely unforeseen nature of the situation, I went over to examine the corpse.

It was lying on a chaise longue, its head on a cushion, its legs casually crossed at the ankles, one arm bent and resting on its chest, the other hanging loose, the motionless hand touching the floor. There was no sign of a blow, a bruise or a wound or any sign of bleeding; there were no signs of choking or strangulation. The expression on his face did not indicate suffering, convulsion or pain. His eyelids were lightly closed, as if he were asleep. He was cold and deathly pale.

I prefer not to give a detailed account of what I found on the corpse. That would mean overloading this brief narrative with scientific explanations. Even without a thorough examination, and the supporting data that only close analysis or a post mortem can provide, it appeared to me that the man was under

The Mystery of the Sintra Road

the now fatal influence of a narcotic.

'What did he drink?' I asked, out of purely medical curiosity.

I was not thinking at the time about a possible murder or about the mysterious incident that was keeping me there; I wanted only to know the sequence of events that had brought about that drugged condition.

One of the masked men picked up a glass that had been placed on an upholstered chair beside the chaise longue.

'I don't know,' he said. 'This perhaps?'

The liquid in the glass was clearly opium.

'The man is dead,' I said.

'Dead!' one of them repeated, trembling.

I lifted the corpse's eyelids; the pupils were horribly dilated.

I looked hard at the men one by one and said calmly:

'I don't know why you brought me here. I can be of no use as a doctor, and as a witness I could be dangerous.'

One of the masked men came over to me and said in a grave, insistent tone:

'Tell me, from your experience, do you really think the fellow is dead?'

'Certainly.'

'And what do you believe was the cause of death?'

'Opium, but I imagine that men who go about wearing masks and kidnapping people on the Sintra Road must know that better than I.'

I was annoyed. I wanted to provoke some reaction that would bring this awkward situation to an end.

'Forgive me,' asked another, 'how long do you think he's been dead?'

I did not reply. I put on my hat and began to draw on my gloves. Beside the window, F. was tapping his foot impatiently. There was silence.

The Mystery of the Sintra Road

Everything conspired to give that moment a highly sinister quality, the room heavy with upholstery, the prostrate corpse with its deathly pallor, the masked figures, the lugubrious stillness of the place, the bright lights…

'Gentlemen,' said the tallest of the masked men, the one who had driven the coach, 'you must realise that if we had killed this man we would know perfectly well that a doctor was useless and any witness inopportune! We feared, obviously, that he was under the influence of some narcotic, but wanted confirmation that he was dead. That's why we brought you here. As for the circumstances of his death, we know as little as you. We have a good reason for not handing the case over to the police, for surrounding your visit to this house with such mystery and violence, and for blindfolding you, and that is because we were afraid that the inevitable police investigation might lead to someone whom we are honour-bound to protect from being charged either as a criminal or an accomplice. If this explanation sounds…'

'Your explanation is utterly absurd!' shouted F. 'A crime has been committed here. The man is dead, you masked blackguards! You brought us to this isolated house against our will, and this whole mysterious business simply reeks of crime, and we want no part in it, however involuntary. We have nothing further to do here. Please open that door.'

One of the masked men laughed at F.'s violent response.

'Oh! So you mock me, do you!' roared F.

And lunging furiously at the window, he tried to wrench open the catches. Two of the men hurled themselves upon him, overpowered him, dragged him across to an armchair and let him fall into it, panting and shaking with rage.

I sat through all this quite impassively.

'Gentlemen,' I observed, 'please note that while my friend

reacts with anger, I respond only with apathy.'

And I lit a cigar.

'Damn it, man, do you take us for murderers!' one of them cried angrily. 'Don't you believe in honour, in a man's word? If the rest of you don't take off your masks, then I will! They need to see our faces! I don't wish to be thought a murderer, not even while concealed behind a piece of cardboard! Gentlemen, I give you my word that I do not know who killed this man.'

And he made a furious gesture, at which his mask came unfastened and slipped down. He immediately turned away, instinctively covering his face with his hands. The others surrounded him, glancing quickly over at F., who remained unmoved. One of our captors who had not yet spoken, the one who had sat opposite me in the carriage, kept eyeing my friend with fear and suspicion. There was a long silence. The masked men were talking quietly together in a corner. I, meanwhile, was examining the room.

It was small, its walls hung with pleated silk, and the soft, deep carpet invited one to run about on it barefoot. The furniture was upholstered in red silk with a single diagonal green stripe, as appears on the coats-of-arms of bastard sons. The curtains at the windows hung in wide, loose folds. There were jasper vases, and, pervading everything, the warm, penetrating aroma of verbena and marechala.

The dead man was young and had fine, attractive features and a fair moustache. His tailcoat and waistcoat had been removed too, revealing a ruffled shirt front and gleaming pearl buttons; his light-coloured trousers were narrow and well cut. On one foot he was wearing a patent leather shoe, and his silk socks were patterned with large white and grey squares.

Judging by his physiognomy, his build, the colour and cut of his hair, the man appeared to be English.

At the end of the room was a heavy door curtain, which was kept scrupulously drawn. It was probably the entrance to a bedroom. I noticed, with surprise, that despite the air of extreme luxury, and despite that warm, lingering perfume and the cosy feeling that tends to prevail in any room where people ordinarily sit and talk and live, the room we were in did not seem inhabited. There were no books, no jacket slung over the back of a chair, no discarded gloves, none of the thousand little things that we take as signs of life in all its triviality.

F. had come over to me.

'Did you recognise the fellow whose mask fell off?' I asked.

'No. Did you?'

'No, I didn't either. There's still one man who hasn't spoken yet, the one who's always looking at you out of the corner of his eye. He's scared you might recognise him, a friend of yours perhaps. Don't let him out of your sight.'

One of the masked men approached and asked:

'How long can the body stay there on the chaise longue?'

I did not reply. He looked angrily at me, but said nothing more. Then the tallest masked man, who had previously left the room, returned.

'Right!' he said to the others.

There was a pause. We could hear the ticking of a clock and F.'s footsteps as he paced back and forth, frowning and agitatedly twirling his moustache.

'Gentlemen,' continued the tall man, turning to us, 'we give you our word of honour that we had nothing to do with this man's death. We offer no explanation, but from this moment on, you are to be held here. You are free to believe us to be murderers, forgers or thieves, as you wish. You may choose, if you want, to believe that you are being held under threat of violence, corruption, deceit or summoned by the law itself…

the choice is yours! The fact is that you must stay here until tomorrow. Your room,' he said to me, 'is over there and yours,' he turned to F., 'is through there. I will stay here with you, doctor, on this sofa. One of my colleagues will act as valet to your friend. Tomorrow we will say an amicable farewell and you can either report the matter to the police or write to the newspapers.'

After this calm, collected speech, he fell silent. We did not respond.

The masked men, who appeared rather embarrassed and uneasy, were again standing in a corner next to the bedroom, talking in low voices. I wandered about the room. On one of my circuits I chanced to see something white, perhaps a handkerchief, on the floor near an armchair. I walked past the chair, deliberately dropped my own handkerchief and, as I picked it up, managed to pick up the fallen object too. It was indeed a handkerchief. I put it in my pocket and ran my fingers over it. It was made of fine stuff, edged with lace, a woman's handkerchief. It seemed to be embroidered with a monogram and a crown.

Just then, nine o'clock struck. One of the masked men said to F.: 'I'll show you to your room. And, forgive me, but I must blindfold you again.'

F. haughtily took the handkerchief from the man, blindfolded himself, and they both left the room.

I remained alone with the tall masked man, who had a pleasant, engaging voice.

He asked me whether I felt in need of dinner. I replied in the negative, but he opened out a table and brought over a hamper containing some cold dishes. I drank only a glass of water, while he ate.

Little by little, we began to talk, almost as friend to friend.

Being, by nature, and outgoing fellow, I found the silence hard to bear. He was educated, well-travelled and well-read.

Suddenly, not long after one o'clock in the morning, we heard soft, cautious footsteps on the stairs and, a moment later, there came the sound of someone trying to open the door. When we had first entered the room, the masked man had removed the key and put it in his pocket. We both started to our feet. The corpse was covered over. The masked man blew out the candles.

I was petrified. There was absolute silence; all we could hear was the sound made by the key as whoever it was out there in the darkness fumbled to get it in the lock.

We neither moved nor breathed.

Finally, the door opened, someone came in, closed it, lit a match and peered into the gloom. When he saw us, he cried out and fell to the floor, where he lay, motionless, arms outstretched.

Tomorrow, when I am calmer and my head clearer, I will describe what happened next.

P.S. An incident that may help identify the street and the location of the house. During the night I heard two people come by, one strumming a guitar, the other singing a *fado*. It must have been about midnight. This is what he was singing:

> *I wrote a letter to Cupid*
> *To find out if he knew*
> *If a heart howe'er sore wounded...*

I forget the rest. If those people who passed by, playing and singing, should read this letter, they could prove most helpful in giving the name of the street they were walking along and the house they were standing outside when they sang those words.

V

Today, feeling calmer and more rested, I am able to tell you precisely – through a painstaking reconstruction of the words spoken and the glances exchanged – what ensued following the sudden entry of that person into the room where the body lay.

The man had remained unconscious on the floor. We placed a cold compress on his brow and gave him some *vinaigre de toilette* to sniff. He eventually recovered consciousness and, though still trembling and pale, made an instinctive dash for the window!

The masked man, however, held him locked in his arms and hurled him violently into a chair at the end of the room. He then produced a dagger from inside his jacket and said in a cold, hard voice:

'If you move or scream or try to escape, I'll stab you through the heart.'

'Come on,' I said. 'Quickly! Tell us what you want? What are you doing here?'

The interloper did not respond, but instead clutched his head in his hands and kept repeating, over and over:

'All is lost! All is lost!'

'Answer me,' said the masked man, seizing him roughly by the arm. 'Why did you come here? Why? How did you know where to come?'

He was extremely agitated. His eyes gleamed behind the black satin of his mask. 'Why did you come here?' he asked again, grabbing the fellow's shoulders and shaking him hard.

'Listen,' said the man, speaking in fits and starts. 'I came to find out... I was told... I don't know. It seems the police have already been here... I wanted to find out the truth, to find out who... who had murdered him... I came to look for clues...'

'He knows everything!' exclaimed the masked man in horror, letting his arms fall by his side.

I was astonished. The man knew about the crime, knew there was a body in the room. He alone knew, because those grim events could not possibly be known by anyone else. It followed, therefore, that anyone who knew where the body was, who had a key to the house, who came at dead of night to the scene of the murder, who had fainted on finding himself discovered, must be involved in the crime...

'Who gave you the key?' demanded the masked man.

The intruder said nothing.

'Who told you about this?'

Silence.

'Why did you come to this house, secretly, in the middle of the night?'

Silence.

'But how did you find out about a secret we thought was known only to us...'

Then, turning to warn me with an imperceptible gesture of the course he was about to take, he added:

'...to me and the inspector here.'

The intruder remained silent. The masked man took the intruder's coat from him and went through his pockets. He found a small hammer and a packet of nails.

'What are these for?'

'I happened to have them with me, I was going to fix something at home... a packing case.'

The masked man took the lamp, went over to the chaise longue and brusquely removed the travelling rug covering the

The Mystery of the Sintra Road

body. The light fell on the corpse's livid features.

'Do you know this man?'

The intruder shuddered slightly and looked at the dead man long and hard and intently.

I immediately fixed my eyes implacably on his, gripped his hand and asked softly:

'Why did you kill him?'

'Me?' he shouted. 'You're mad!'

It was a clear, frank, natural, innocent response.

'But why did you come here?' asked the masked man. 'How did you know about the crime? How did you get the key? What was this hammer for? Who are you? Either you tell us now or within the hour, you'll be thrown in jail, kept in solitary confinement, and in a month, you'll find yourself at the oars of a galley. Call the others,' he said to me.

'Wait, gentlemen, wait. I'll confess everything, I'll tell you everything!' exclaimed the intruder.

We waited. Then, controlling his voice and speaking slowly, like someone dictating, he said:

'The truth is this; a stranger approached me this evening and said: "You are so-and-so, aren't you? A brave man. Will you go to a particular house for me?" I was given the key and told the street name and house number.'

I leaned forward, curious and eager for answers. At last I was going to find out where I was!

However, the masked man clapped his hand over the intruder's mouth, squeezing his cheeks and saying in a quiet, terrifying voice:

'If you say where we are, I'll kill you.'

The fellow stared at us. He evidently realised that I, like him, was there for some mysterious reason and had no idea where I was, and that our reasons for being there were equally suspect, and that we were not police officers. He stayed silent for a moment, then said:

'Gentlemen, it was I who killed that man. Are you satisfied now? And what are you two doing here?'

'You're under arrest,' roared the masked man. 'Go and call the others, doctor. He is the murderer.'

'Wait, wait,' protested the intruder. 'I don't understand! Who are you? I thought you were from the police... Perhaps you are... perhaps you have disguised yourselves in order to catch me. I don't know that man. I've never seen him before. Let me go... Oh, this is terrible!'

'The wretch has to explain, he knows the secret!' cried the masked man.

I sat down next to the intruder. I would, I thought, try sympathy and guile. He had calmed down now and was speaking coherently and sensibly. He told me his name – although I will refer to him only by his initials, A.M.C. – and that he was a medical student from the town of Viseu. The masked man was listening, silent and attentive. I placed my hand on A.M.C.'s arm and spoke reassuringly. He called me his 'friend' and begged me to 'save him'. He seemed an excitable young fellow with a fertile imagination, and I found it easy to winkle out the truth about his actions. Adopting a friendly, confiding manner, I asked him questions, which, while apparently sincere and innocuous, were, in reality, treacherous and searching. Being an inexperienced and trusting soul, he gave himself away with every word.

'You know,' I said, 'there is one thing that puzzles me in all this.'

'What's that?'

'That the arsenic left no trace...'

'It was opium,' he said with childlike naïveté.

I leapt to my feet. This man, even if he was not the murderer, knew everything about the crime.

'He knows everything,' I said to the masked man.

'He must have done it, then,' he said.

I took the masked man aside and speaking plainly said:

'Look, my friend, this farce has gone on long enough. Take off your mask, we'll shake hands and go to the police. The person you feared was involved clearly had nothing to do with the affair.'

'No, that much is certain. This man is the murderer!'

And eyes blazing behind his mask, he turned to A.M.C., demanding:

'Why did you kill him?'

'I killed him…' replied the man.

'You killed him,' said the masked man in a slow, terrifying voice, 'to steal the £2,300 in banknotes that he had in his pocket in a wallet bearing his two initials in silver.'

'Me! Steal from him! How dare you? You're lying! I don't even know the man, I've never seen him before. I didn't kill him!'

'Enough of these damned contradictions!' the masked man burst out angrily.

A.M.C. said hesitantly:

'You, the gentleman in the mask… that man was your friend, was he not? You were the only friend he had in Lisbon.'

'How do you know that?' cried the masked man, seizing him by the arm. 'Tell me, speak!'

'For reasons I cannot reveal,' continued A.M.C., 'I happen to know that this man, a foreigner with no connections in Lisbon, and who arrived only a few weeks ago, used to come to this house…'

'That's true,' said the masked man, interrupting him.

The Mystery of the Sintra Road

'And I know that he used to meet someone here…'

'That's also true.'

I looked at them both in astonishment, aware that any clear ideas as to what had happened were being overturned, and that a new factor in the drama had appeared, unexpected, alarming and inexplicable. The intruder went on:

'I also learned that this unfortunate man harboured a great secret.'

'True, true,' said the masked man, absorbed.

'Well, yesterday, a person, who, for reasons I will not go into, was unable to leave the house and so asked me to come here and see if…'

We waited, petrified, for the conclusion to this confession.

'On arriving here, I found him dead. He was holding this in his hand.'

And he took from his pocket a folded sheet of writing paper.

'Read it,' he said to the masked man.

The masked man held the paper to the light, uttered a cry and collapsed onto a chair, his arms hanging loose, his eyes closed.

I picked up the piece of paper and read the following statement in English:

I declare that I have killed myself with opium.

I froze.

The masked man said in a distant, dream-like voice: 'That's impossible. But it's definitely his writing. Ah, mystery upon mystery!'

Day was breaking.

I am weary now of writing. I need to gather my thoughts. Until tomorrow!

VI

I now ask you to pay the closest possible attention to what I am about to recount.

Day dawned. From outside came the sounds of the waking population. From the noise made by the cart wheels, I could tell that the street was unsurfaced. Nor was it a wide street, because the rattle of the carts was loud and, apparently, very close. I could hear the cries of streetsellers too, but no carriages.

The masked man had remained motionless in that pose of utter prostration, his head in his hands.

The man who had given his name as A.M.C. was lying on the sofa, his eyes closed as if he were sleeping.

I opened the shutters. It was daylight. The lace curtains and the blinds were drawn. A gloomy, greenish light filtered in through the window panes, which were frosted like the glass of gas lamps.

'It's morning, my friend,' I said to the masked man. 'Be brave! We need to examine the room, one piece of furniture at a time.'

He rose and drew back the door-curtain at the far end of the room. Behind it I saw a small bedroom containing a bed and a round bedside table covered with a green velvet cloth. The bed had not been slept in and was covered by a red satin eiderdown. It had a single wide, high, soft pillow, of a kind not commonly found in Portugal; on the table was an empty box and a vase of faded flowers. There was also a washstand, with brushes, soap, sponges, folded towels and two slender bottles of Parma violets. A sturdy swordstick was propped against the wall in one corner.

The Mystery of the Sintra Road

There was nothing particularly significant about the way in which the objects in the room had been arranged. In fact, our examination reinforced the idea that the house was rarely inhabited, perhaps only visited now and then as a meeting-place, but not used as someone's home.

The dead man's frock coat and waistcoat were draped over a chair; one of his shoes was on the floor beside the sofa; his hat lay on one corner of the carpet, as if thrown there. His overcoat had been flung down near the bed.

We searched all the pockets of the dead man's clothing and found neither wallet, letters or papers of any kind. In his waistcoat pocket was his plain gold watch and a small gold mesh purse containing a few coins. We did not find a handkerchief. The question of how the opium had been brought into the room remained unanswered; there was no sign of any phial, bottle, packet or box in which it might have been brought in liquid or in powdered form, and that, to my mind, was the first firm indication that this was not a case of suicide.

I asked if there were other connecting rooms that we ought to visit.

'Yes, there are,' replied the masked man. 'This building has two entrances and two staircases. Now, when we arrived, we found that the door communicating with the other rooms was locked from the other side. So the man did not leave this room after coming in from the street and before dying – or being murdered.'

How had he carried the opium, then? Even if it was already in the room, the phial or whatever must be here somewhere. It seemed unlikely that it would have been destroyed. After all, the glass with the dregs of diluted opium was still there. A further fact that seemed to militate against the idea of suicide

The Mystery of the Sintra Road

was that we had not found the dead man's cravat. He would hardly have taken it off, let alone destroyed or discarded it. And it was equally improbable that he would have come into this room, dressed as if for a formal visit, but without a cravat. Someone, then, had been in this house, either shortly before the death or at the same time. And that person, for whatever reason, had taken the dead man's cravat.

The idea that someone else had been there in the room with the alleged suicide put paid to the idea that it had been a suicide at all and led one to presume, instead, that the man had been murdered.

We went over to the window and made a minute examination of the sheet of paper on which the suicide note had been written.

'It's definitely his writing, there's no doubt about it,' mused the masked man, 'and yet there's something not quite right about it!'

He studied the paper meticulously; it was a half sheet of writing paper. I immediately noticed at the top of the page the faint trace of a mark consisting of a signature and a crown, which must have been embossed on the missing half of the sheet. It was clearly paper of a superior quality. The masked man was surprised and startled when I pointed this out. In the room there was neither paper, ink or pens. The suicide note must have been composed and written elsewhere.

'I know the kind of paper he used at home,' said the masked man, 'and this isn't it. There was no mark like that. And he had no other kind to hand.'

The mark was not clear enough for us to be able to identify it. It was, however, becoming increasingly obvious that the note had not been written in his own house, where that particular paper did not exist, nor in this room, where, as I have said, there was no paper, no inkwell, not even a book, an ink blotter, or a pencil.

Could it have been written outside, in the street somewhere? In someone else's house perhaps? This seemed unlikely since he had no close friends in Lisbon and knew no one whose writing paper was likely to be embossed with a crown.

Could it have been written in a stationer's shop? No, the paper sold in shops would never be embossed with a crown.

Could the note have been written on the blank half page torn from an old letter he had received? That, too, seemed improbable because the paper had been folded down the middle and there were no other creases to indicate that it had ever been inside an envelope.

Furthermore, the page bore the same odour of marechala face powder that pervaded the room in which we were sitting.

And when I held the paper up to the light, I was able to make out the print left by a damp or sweaty thumb, besmirching the paper's smooth, satiny whiteness. That thumb-print looked small, slender and female. This was a somewhat vague clue, but the masked man had, at the same time, come up with another far more trustworthy one.

'This man,' he observed, 'always and invariably abbreviated the word "that" to two t's separated by a hyphen. No one else did this, it was entirely personal and original to him. And yet in the note, which, by the way, sounds most un-English, the word "that" is written in full.'

He turned to A.M.C. and asked: 'Why did you not show us this note at once? This statement is a forgery.'

'A forgery!' exclaimed the other, springing up in either alarm or surprise.

'Yes, a forgery,' the masked man repeated, 'intended to cover up a murder. It bears all the hallmarks. But the one

The Mystery of the Sintra Road

overwhelming piece of evidence is this: Where are the £2,300 pounds in notes that the man had in his pocket?'

A.M.C. looked at him, bewildered, like a man waking from a dream. The masked man went on:

'They are nowhere to be found because you stole them. You killed this man in order to steal them and forged this note to cover up the crime.'

'Sir,' observed A.M.C. gravely, 'I give you my word of honour that I have no idea what you are talking about.'

Then, fixing my eyes on the young man, I said very slowly:

'This note is patently false, but I don't see what this other business is all about, this £2,300. What I do see is that this man was poisoned. I don't know if it was you or someone else who killed him, but I do know that the accomplice to the murder was a woman.'

'Impossible, doctor!' cried the masked man. 'What an absurd idea!'

'Absurd? But consider this house, this highly perfumed, silk-lined room, all these fabrics, the subdued lighting filtered through frosted glass, the carpeted staircase, the banister fashioned from a silken rope. Over there, the bearskin rug next to the Voltaire chair seems still to bear the imprint of a man's body. Can't you see the woman in all this? Isn't this clearly a house intended for romantic assignations?'

'Or for some other purpose.'

'And this notepaper,' I went on, 'it's the kind of dainty stuff known as Empress paper that women buy in Paris at the Maison Maquet.'

'Plenty of men use it too!'

'But they don't perfume it with the same aroma that fills this house. This paper belongs to a woman who verified the forgery, saw it being written, took an intense interest in the perfection of the forgery, and whose damp fingertips left a clear mark on the paper!'

The masked man said nothing.

'And what about the bunch of withered flowers in there? It consists of some roses tied with a velvet ribbon. The ribbon is impregnated with the scent of a pomade, and there's a small groove, like a scratch made with a fingernail, with a tiny hole at either end. It's obviously the mark left by a hairpin!'

'The flowers could have been given to him; he himself might have brought them here from somewhere else.'

'And what about the handkerchief I found yesterday under a chair?'

I threw the handkerchief down on the table. The masked man eagerly snatched it up, examined it and put it away.

A.M.C. was staring at me in astonishment, apparently overcome by the harsh logic of my words. The masked man remained silent for a few moments, then in a humble, almost supplicating voice said:

'Doctor, doctor, for the love of God! These findings prove nothing. I'm convinced that this handkerchief, which is, unquestionably, a woman's, is the one the dead man carried in his pocket. It's true. Don't you remember that we couldn't find his handkerchief?'

'And don't you remember, too, that we still haven't found his cravat?'

Defeated, the masked man did not respond.

'When all's said and done, I am neither judge here nor party to the cause!' I exclaimed. 'I vigorously deplore this death, and I speak of it only because of the sorrow and the feeling of horror it inspires. Whether this young fellow killed himself or was killed, whether he died at the hands of a woman or a man, matters little to me. What I must point out, however, is that the corpse cannot remain unburied for much longer. He needs to be buried today. That's all. It's daylight now, and all I want is to leave this place.'

'Yes, of course,' said the masked man, 'in a minute.'

And then, taking A.M.C. by the arm he said to me:

'One moment, I'll be right back!'

And they went out through the door that led into rest of the house, locking it from the other side.

I stayed there alone, pacing restlessly up and down.

The light of day had aroused in my mind a multitude of thoughts, entirely new and different from those that had occupied me during the night. There are thoughts that can live only in silence and shadows, thoughts that the day disperses and erases. There are still others that appear only in the glare of the sun.

My head was filled with a host of confused ideas, which, in the sudden dawn light, had whirled into the air like a flock of pigeons startled by a gunshot.

I wandered, unthinking, into the bedroom, sat down on the bed, and rested one arm on the pillow.

Then, quite how I do not know, on the white pillow case, caught on a mother-of-pearl button, I saw, noticed, fixed upon, a long blonde hair – that of a woman.

I did not dare to touch it immediately. I merely observed it eagerly for some time.

'So it was true! There you are! I've found you at last, poor little hair! I pity the innocent way you lie there, oblivious, careless, idle, languid! You may be cruel, you may be wicked, but you are not crafty or underhand. I have you within my grasp, within my line of sight; don't run away, don't tremble, don't blush; you give yourself, you consent, you offer yourself up, O meek, gentle, trusting hair. And yet, albeit fragile, tiny, almost microscopic, you are a part of the woman whom I had intuited, foreseen, and whom I seek! Is she the author of the crime or completely blameless? Is she merely an accomplice? I don't know, and you cannot tell me.'

Suddenly, as I continued to study the hair, through some inexplicable mental process, I seemed to recognize that blonde thread, to recognise it completely: its colour, its subtle shade, its whole appearance! It reminded me of... and then the woman to whom the hair belonged appeared to me! But when her name sprang unbidden to my lips, I said to myself:

'Oh really! From a single hair? What nonsense!'

And I burst out laughing.

This letter has already gone on far too long. I will continue tomorrow.

VII

Yesterday I told you how I had unexpectedly found a blonde hair at the head of the bed.

My feelings of pained surprise lasted for some time. That radiant strand of hair, languid and almost chaste, was the clue to a murder or, at the very least, to someone's complicity in a murder! Sitting there motionless, gazing at the hair, I immersed myself in long lucubrations.

The person to whom it belonged was clearly blonde, doubtless of fair complexion, petite, *mignonne,* because the strand of hair was fine and extraordinarily pure, and its white root must have been so very tenuously, delicately attached to her scalp.

By nature, the woman would be gentle, humble, devoted and loving, because the hair did not have the coarseness one might find in someone of a violent, overbearing, selfish disposition.

Given its barely perceptible perfume and no sign of its having been curled or capriciously rolled and forced into extravagant styles, the owner of that hair would have simple, elegantly modest tastes.

She had probably received her education in England or Germany because the tip of the hair showed that it had been cut, which is a custom among Northern women, but unknown to Mediterraneans, who allow their locks to grow to their full, abundant, natural length.

These were mere surmises, imaginary deductions that constituted neither scientific truth nor judicial evidence.

How could the woman I was reconstructing from my

examination of a single hair, and who seemed to me gentle, unpretentious, distinguished and well-bred, how could she have been the cunning protagonist of that hidden tragedy? But then how little we know of the secret logic of passions!

I was, however, completely convinced that a woman was involved. That man had not committed suicide. He was certainly not alone when he drank the opium. The narcotic had been given to him in a glass of water, apparently without coercion, but by trickery or deceit. The absence of the handkerchief, the disappearance of the cravat, the way he was dressed, the strand of blonde hair, the hollow recently made in the pillow by the pressure of a head; everything indicated that someone else had been present in that house on the night of the calamity. In short: suicide was impossible, murder very likely.

The handkerchief, the hair, the house itself (clearly intended for intimate trysts), the luxurious living room, the carpet covering the old, worn staircase, the silken rope... all of this indicated the presence and participation of a woman. What was her part in this affair? I do not know. What was the role of A.M.C.? Was he murderer, accomplice or mere concealer of the corpse? Again, I do not know. A.M.C. must have known the woman. He was certainly not an accomplice brought in specifically to commit the crime. There is no need to hire an assassin in order to administer opium in a glass of water. They must have some interest in common. Were they lovers? Man and wife? Were they thieves? I recalled that unexpected reference to the £2,300, which had appeared before me like a second mystery. All these were fleeting notions. But why repeat all the ideas that formed and dissolved in my head like clouds in a sky buffeted by the wind?

There are certainly ambiguities, contradictions and weaknesses in my hypothesis, there are gaps and inconsistencies in the clues I gathered. Doubtless many significant factors eluded me, while many trivial details engraved themselves on my memory, but I was in a morbid state of anxiety, completely disoriented by that affair, which had so unexpectedly installed itself in my life, along with its cortège of terrors and mysteries.

You, sir, who can judge things with a cool mind, and you, the readers, perusing this letter in the comfort of your homes, will be far better able to draw conclusions, make clear deductions, and draw closer to the hidden truth through inference and logic.

I had been alone for an hour when the tall masked man returned, his hat on his head and a pale grey cape over his arm.

'Let's go,' he said.

I picked up my hat in silence.

'A word before we leave,' he said. 'First, promise me on your honour that when you get into the carriage, you will not shout or gesticulate or make any movement that might betray me.'

I gave him my word.

'Good!' he continued. 'There is something else I would like to say. I greatly appreciate your dignity and your discretion. It would be painful to me if, at any time in the future, any scornful or vengeful feelings should arise between us. In this regard I declare to you that I had nothing whatsoever to do with this incident. Later on, I may turn the case over to the police, but for now I am policeman, judge and, possibly, executioner. This house is both courtroom and jail. I know you take away with you the firm conviction that a woman was involved in this crime, but that is simply impossible. Nevertheless, doctor, if, at any point, you name names in relation to this affair, I swear that I will kill you, without remorse, without compunction, as casually as I might pare my nails. Now give me your arm so that I may guide you. Ah, my dear fellow, I was forgetting that your eyes are doomed to wear these cambric spectacles.'

And laughing, he tightened the handkerchief covering my eyes.

We went down the stairs and got into the carriage, which had its blinds drawn. I could not see who was driving the horses for I was only free of my blindfold once inside the carriage. The masked man sat down beside me. I could see a small part of his face lit by the sunlight. He had a fine, pale complexion, and his hair was brown and slightly curled.

Judging by the variations in speed indicating hills and hollows and by the alternations of tarmac and cobbles, the carriage seemed to be following the same route as on the previous evening, at the very start of this adventure. Finally, we rumbled onto the highway.

'Doctor,' said the masked man with some amusement, 'do you know what grieves me? It's that I have to leave you standing alone by the roadside! But there's nothing to be done about that, I'm afraid. Don't worry, though, Cacém is close by and there you will easily find transport into Lisbon.'

He offered me a cigar.

After some time, during which we drove at greater speed, the carriage stopped.

'Here we are,' announced the masked man. 'Goodbye, doctor.'

And he opened the door.

'Thank you,' he added. 'And believe me when I say that I hold you in high regard. Later on, you'll find out who I am. God willing, we shall both enjoy the approval of our consciences, as well as the pleasure that comes with having done one's duty, as is sure to happen when we reach the final conclusion of the scene you have just witnessed. I give you back your freedom.

The Mystery of the Sintra Road

Farewell!'

We shook hands, and I jumped down. He closed the door, raised the blinds a fraction and held out a small card.

'Keep this as a memento,' he said. 'It's my portrait.'

Standing on the road beside the carriage wheels, I eagerly accepted the photograph, but when I looked at it, I saw that the portrait, too, was wearing a mask!

'A bit of fun after a masked ball last year!' he shouted, thrusting his head out of the window as the carriage set off again at a trot.

I watched it disappear down the road. The coachman had his hat pulled down low and a cloak concealed his face.

Shall I tell you the truth? I felt sad to see that carriage moving off, for it carried with it a baffling secret. I would never see that man again. The adventure was melting away before me. It was over.

And the poor dead Englishman was still there, stretched out on the chaise longue that served as his coffin.

I found myself alone by the roadside. The morning was misty, still and melancholy. I could just make out the coach in the distance. A farm labourer appeared, coming from the opposite direction to that taken by the departing carriage.

'Which way is Cacém?' I asked him.

'From where I've just come, sir. Keep on this road for half a quarter of a league.'

So the carriage had headed for Sintra.

I reached Cacém feeling very tired. I despatched a man to F.'s estate in Sintra to find out if the horses had been returned; then I ordered a carriage to Lisbon and sat waiting for it, looking glumly through the window at the trees and fields. I had been there for half an hour when I saw a spirited horse pass by at full gallop. Through the cloud of dust I could only vaguely make out the rider's face. He was wrapped in a pale grey cape and heading for Lisbon.

I asked about the carriage that had taken us along that road the previous evening. There was some disagreement as to the colour of the horses.

The man I had despatched to Sintra returned, reporting that the horses had been returned to F.'s estate by a farmhand, according to whom the gentlemen had met a friend near Cacém, who had then taken them with him to Lisbon by coach. Moments later, my own carriage arrived and carried me back to Lisbon, where I hurried to F.'s house. His servant showed me a pencilled note he had received: *Do not expect me for some days. All is well. If anyone comes looking for me, tell them I have gone to Madrid.*

I scoured Lisbon for him, in vain. I was starting to feel uneasy. F. was obviously being held against his will. I feared for myself too. I recalled the masked man's vague but resolute threats. The next night, as I was returning home, I became aware that I was being followed.

If I went to the police about this affair, vague and incomplete as it was, I would be reporting a chimera. I knew that in response to any initial report I might give him, the Civil Governor of Lisbon would order the administrator of Sintra to deploy all the resources of his police force to solve this crime. Those measures would, inevitably, prove fruitless. The incident described in these letters is, by its very nature, beyond the reach of police enquiries. I did not, therefore, approach the police, preferring to place the case before the public, choosing the most widely read columns of your newspaper for the purpose. Then, fearing that I might become the victim of an ambush, I decided to go into hiding.

The reasons for concealing my identity must be obvious.

Were I to append my name to these letters, I would be exposing rather than hiding myself, as is my wish.

I send you this letter from my impenetrable retreat. It is morning. I can see the light of the rising sun through the shutters. I can hear the cries of the first hawkers, the cowbells, the rattle of carriage wheels, the contented murmur of people getting up after a happy, peaceful night's sleep. I envy those who, not being cursed with secret adventures, are able to walk about, talk and toil in the street, while I—alas!—am imprisoned by a mystery, trapped by a secret!

P.S. I have just received a long letter from F. His letter, written several days ago, has only just reached me. It was sent to me by post, and since I have been absent from the house in which I usually live and have told no one of my whereabouts, this interesting missive reached me only today. Here, sir, copied out by me, is the first part of that letter, the second half of which I will send to you tomorrow. Publish it if you so wish. It does more than merely shed light on this whole obscure business, it provides us with a profound and illuminating piece of prose. F. is a published author, and recognising a man by his literary style is far easier than reconstructing the likeness of a woman from a single hair. My friend is in the gravest danger. And I, feeling too anxious, cautious, hesitant, perplexed and indecisive to reach any kind of resolution through the application of reason, have taken the arbitrary decision to omit, as well as the handwritten original, the two words that comprise the signature on this long letter. I cannot, must not, dare not risk saying more. Spare me the pain of having to make a final statement. Guess it if you can. Farewell!

The Letter from Z.

Note from the Editor, Diário de Notícias:

On the original of the letter that we published yesterday there were some words written in pencil that we only noticed after the newspaper had been printed. These words contained this observation: The photograph of the masked man was taken on the premises of Henrique Nunes, Rua das Chagas, Lisbon. They may have information about the person photographed.

Before we print F.'s long letter, the first part of which was sent to us yesterday by the doctor, it is our duty to make known another extremely important communication, signed only with the initial 'Z.', which we received in the post three days ago. This letter is closely bound up with the events described by the doctor. It reads as follows:

To the Editor,
Diário de Notícias, Lisbon
30 July, 1870.

I write to you in great indignation. In common with a large part of Lisbon's population, I have been reading the letters published in your paper, in which an anonymous doctor recounts the case that your editorial office has chosen to entitle *The Mystery of the Sintra Road*. The story intrigued me, and I followed it with the idle curiosity with which one tends to read such ingeniously devised fables, the kind of tale occasionally used by imaginative French and American writers to bring to the attention of Europe some astonishing phenomenon, such as the Thuggees of India. Unlike most such narratives, however, this story had the particular merit that the events being described were unfolding as one read them, the characters were anonymous, and the plot mechanism so artfully concealed that no reader could possibly test the veracity of this ludicrously fanciful tale, which the author has decided to launch, unheralded, into the midst of our humdrum, monotonous, simple, honest society. I thought that what I had before me was the most perfect, the most accomplished example of the serial novel, until, that is, I read today's instalment, in which I chanced upon the initials of a man's name – A.M.C. – and the additional information that the person to whom the initials belong is a student of medicine and a native of Viseu. Now, I have a very close friend who shares those same initials. And, as it happens, he, too, is a student of medicine and comes from Viseu! This cannot be put down to mere coincidence. It must, therefore, be a cowardly attempt to cast an infamous slur, something that no novelist should be allowed to do.

My first reaction was one of disgust and annoyance. Leaving the house shortly after reading your newspaper, I went to find my friend in order to show him the relevant passage and to place myself at his disposal should he require me to go to the editorial office of the *Diário de Notícias* and demand satisfaction, a satisfaction, which, in the light of such a calumny, no man of education and pride could possibly refuse.

However, I have just returned from my friend's house, where I discovered, to my great confusion and surprise, that he has disappeared and his whereabouts are unknown.

His disappearance and the coincidences I encountered in the doctor's letter lead me reluctantly to conclude that, through some strange twist of fate, my unfortunate friend has unwittingly become involved in this murky affair. The date of his disappearance fits perfectly with the date given in the letter from your correspondent. It is clear, then, that A.M.C. is caught up in some genuine intrigue, a trap perhaps or an act of treachery.

Must I then regretfully accept as true, in whole or in part, the letter printed in your newspaper?

I consider it my duty to state the following:

I have no idea what my friend A.M.C. was up to, going to a stranger's house in the middle of the night, carrying only the key to the front door, a hammer and some nails. Nor do I know why he confessed to having committed a murder only to deny it later on. I do not know the truth behind these contradictions.

What I do know – and to this I and numerous friends and acquaintances can testify – is that on what appears to have been the night of the murder, he was at my house until the early hours, talking, laughing and drinking beer.

He left there at around three o'clock in the morning.

I also declare, and again this can be supported by reliable witnesses, that at nine o'clock that same morning, I went to see him at his lodgings. He was still asleep and awoke with a start at the sound of my voice, then rolled over and went back to sleep as I rummaged through his shelves, looking for a book by Hippolyte Taine.

His landladies told me he had arrived back in the early hours.

'At about half past three,' they said.

Now, the rather long walk from my house – which he left at three – to his house – which he entered at half past three – takes precisely half an hour.

You may well ask, then, when did he commit the crime? His time can all be accounted for. From nine at night until three in the morning he was engaged in jovial and friendly conversation at my house; and from the early morning until

The Mystery of the Sintra Road

nine he was sleeping peacefully in his own bed.

There remains only the half-hour walk between our two houses, for which there are no witnesses. Is it feasible that in the space of half an hour someone could go to another address, prepare some opium, get a man to drink it, forge a suicide note, then go home to sleep the sleep of the just? Does this sound credible?

Moreover, the crime was committed in someone's house, the opium was put into a glass of water and the man duped into drinking it. The body was not fully dressed. All of which indicates that the murderer and the victim must have spoken to each other, chatted, doubtless laughed; the man who later died perhaps felt a little too warm and, making himself at home, took off his jacket; the two people perhaps exchanged anecdotes, and when the man felt thirsty, his murderer gave him the opium in a glass of water. All this in a mere half an hour! *Half an hour!* And that doesn't even allow for the time required to walk from my house to the house where the crime was committed and from there to A.M.C.'s house! Is that possible?

Another point. I know A.M.C. and he is of impeccable character, a simple, compassionate man, who lives an industrious, solitary life utterly devoid of mystery, adventure or drama. He was due to marry soon, quietly and without fuss.

I knew everything he did and everyone he knew. I am quite sure he never met the murdered man, who, in the words of the doctor, looked like a foreigner, had no connections here and had lived but a short time in Portugal.

Could it have been a chance encounter, an unexpected argument? Impossible, given that the man was found lying on a chaise longue, having died from opium poisoning!

Could A.M.C. have been paid to commit this crime? Sheer lunacy! A man of his intelligence, his character and nobility of mind? Anyway, the use of professional assassins, duly remunerated as a public service, no longer exists in Portugal.

Is it conceivable that a man plotting a murder could, right up until the decisive moment, have seemed so relaxed and witty, so unbuttoned in his paradoxes, could sit happily drinking beer? And is it likely that he would return home afterwards to enjoy a peaceful night's sleep, and that a friend visiting him the next morning would find on his bedside table a cup of tea and a history book?

And this is a man who is, by nature, shy and of modest habits, a bookish man of notably forthright opinions, but entirely lacking in aggression!

However, if you were to ask me why A.M.C. would turn up at that house at night with a hammer and nails and declare himself to be a murderer – that, I cannot explain.

I suspect that he may be under someone's influence, someone who with extraordinary promises and unimaginable blandishments has obliged him to present himself as the author of the crime. A.M.C. is clearly sacrificing himself. I have no idea for whom. But he is and, unaware that the police never appreciate such acts of selflessness, he is trying to expiate another's crime. He is ruining himself in order to save someone else.

But as to why and as to what those blandishments were, I have no idea. He, who has always been so indifferent to money, so rigid in his habits and feelings!

Very well. A.M.C. can sacrifice himself, that is his prerogative. But we, his friends, cannot allow it. His body belongs to him alone; he can, if he so chooses, submit it to the foul air of a prison cell or to the weight of fetters. But his character, his honour, his reputation, his very soul, those also belong to his friends, and we must courageously defend the part that belongs to us.

No, A.M.C. was not the murderer. All the evidence says so: the relentless logic of the facts, the unassailable arithmetic of time, our knowledge of his temperament, his coherence of character, as the physiological sciences put it. He is not the murderer. If he says he is, then he is mad, *he is lying*. I will look him straight in the eye and say bluntly: 'If you declare yourself to be the author of this crime, *you are lying*!'

His moral sense has clearly gone astray. If only I could speak to him and, please, for the love of God, clear his mind of these dark clouds of passion and pain! This is all so distressing! Honour, love, family, hope – the man has forgotten everything! If the poor wretch would only remember that he is not alone in the world. If he could only grasp that perhaps by this time, in the depths of the countryside, his mother and his sisters already know that here, in Lisbon, people are saying he is a murderer. If only he could consider the terrible dishonour, his lost future, the solitary hours in prison, the awful shame of public cross-examination, and the prolonged echo that the sinister clank of leg-irons leaves in the human soul.

I will not give my name at the end of this letter because, in this whole confusing agglomeration of events, I can vaguely sense the mysterious and calamitous passage of a crime moving relentlessly towards its target, crushing and shredding any obstacles that stand in its way. I would not want the publication of my name to allow the accomplices to this murder or, perchance, the police, to hamper or confound any spontaneous attempt on my part to unmask the criminals. I have only my own resources to count on, but I need my liberty if I am to make good use of them.

Yours etc.
Z.

From 'F.' to the Doctor

I

21 July, 1 o'clock in the morning.
My dear friend,
I do not know whether or not you are at home – which is where I am sending this letter – or whether, like me, you are still here in this private prison. In either case, these words, whether received now or later, will prove to be, for whichever of us may read them, a useful memorandum of some of the most extraordinary hours of our lives.

I am writing more in order to impose some order on events and fix them in my memory rather than for some other purely hypothetical purpose. I will deliver these few pages of personal reflections to the discretion – or vagaries – of the post, reserving the right to ask you to return them to me in the fullness of time.

I have had no news of you since we were separated last night, shortly after we entered the drawing room where the corpse was lying. The masked man who had been charged with escorting me to the room in which I am now sitting, took me by the arm and whispered into my ear the name of a woman, a street and the number of a house. It was the name of someone you know very well and the address was that of the house where she lives! I believe I inadvertently shuddered, but nonetheless managed to say calmly enough:

'I don't understand.'

This individual was the same one who had remained silent throughout our ride in the carriage, the one who kept such an attentive, suspicious eye on me when we arrived at the house. His build, his manner of speaking, his voice, though barely audible, were not unfamiliar to me.

Speaking even more softly, he responded:

'You won't be able to leave here for another two or three days. So if you need to write a letter or send a message…'

A thought occurred to me: What if he were…?

There was one way of finding out if he was or wasn't a close friend of mine: all I needed was to get hold of his watch; even blindfolded, I could identify its owner simply by running my hand over it. If he was the person I thought he was, his watch case would be as smooth as enamel, apart from a raised coat of arms in the centre.

'I'll write a brief note,' I said. 'Could you bring me a pencil?'

We had reached the room in which I was to stay and I removed my blindfold just as he was leaving the room promising to bring me the necessary writing implements. However, the masked man who came back bearing pen and paper was not the same one who had just left! So I missed my chance to confirm a suspicion or dispel a doubt.

I did, however, write a few lines to my servant reassuring him about my absence.

'Is that all?' the stranger asked, taking the note from me.

'Yes, that's all.'

A sense of delicacy and a shadow of mistrust prevented me from writing directly to the person the previous masked man had referred to.

The man shut the door, and I was left alone.

I found myself in an interior room, quite spacious, but without a window. To one side there was a washstand; stacked in one corner were three steamer trunks in studded Warsaw leather, all of them bearing labels from railways, hotels and steamship companies. The topmost of the three trunks bore, on a strip of paper, the words 'Grand Hotel Paris' in large black letters, and one of the labels was from an English steamship on the India run. On the other side of the room was a bed. The only other furniture in that modestly furnished room was a sofa, upholstered in green morocco, placed in the centre of the room facing a broad table on which my supper was laid out beneath the bright light of a lamp.

May I make a confession? I found the isolation, peace and solitude a great relief after the day's surfeit of excitement.

I stretched out on the sofa and lay there, staring up at the wavering circle of light projected onto the ceiling through the hole in the top of the lampshade, and gradually my frantic heartbeats slowed to be replaced by long yawns accompanied by a lot of nervous stretching, all gently inviting me to sleep. My imagination was still busy, however, with the kind of unconscious work normally carried out by dreams, and it kept extracting from the scene I had just witnessed the most illogical and far-fetched interpretations. Everything that had happened to us between the encounter on the Sintra Road and entering this room was whirling madly about in the air like a vast allegorical enigma, fragments of which were being kicked around by a squad of jeering devils, who laughed and poked their little red-hot tongues out at me.

I sank quietly into a state of languid indifference, my eyelids drooped, and I fell asleep.

On waking after a brief, but peaceful and refreshing nap, I turned my attention to the supper glittering before my eyes.

On the table was a loaf of bread, a tin of sardines from Nantes, a little terrine of *pâté de foie gras*, a partridge, a wedge of cheese and three bottles of Burgundy with green wax seals;

next to these stood four bottles of soda-water. The corkscrew was tucked inside the silver napkin ring. On a metal tray lay a sheaf of plump, glossy, chocolate-brown cigars, bound together at either end by bands of crimson silk. On top of the tin of sardines lay the key required to open it. The glass was of the finest crystal, the fork was silver gilt, the knife-handle mother-of-pearl, and the plates were of white porcelain edged in gold and green. I immediately sprang to my feet. I sat down on the sofa and felt hunger climb onto my back, draw my head down over the supper, wrap its wiry legs around my waist and dig the spurs of greed into my empty stomach.

Meanwhile, on the opposite side of the table, the phantom of fear reared up, fixed me with its eyes and, in a solemn, prohibitive gesture, held out a gaunt, tremulous hand over the delicacies. Puzzled and confused, I listened then to the brief conversation going on inside myself, similar to that which, from time to time, Xavier de Maistre had with his 'beast' during his journey round his room.

I heard a slow, grave voice say:

'Consider what you're doing, O foolhardy one! Open your eyes, you thoughtless mortal! That partridge, whose insidious, perfidious breast glows golden before your eyes, has been seasoned with arsenic. That Chambertin burgundy – which waits for you like a wave on the Stygian Lake, lurking behind that apparently innocent, elegant, inviting label – is, in fact, as dark and deadly as the writing on the wall at Belshazzar's Feast, for this wine, offering you a hypocritical, deceitful kiss, is laced with prussic acid. Those ducks' livers stuffed with lewd, corrupting, licentious truffles have been cooked in lethal sauces concocted in the Borgias' kitchens!'

The other voice, low and wheedling, was singing a soft siren song:

'Come on, fool, eat if you're hungry! Or are you scared of the bogeyman, you nincompoop? Look at that wax seal: aren't the characters stamped on the stopper a sure guarantee of the purity of the liquid within? And that tin of sardines – caught off the coast of France and cooked six months ago in Marseilles – was hermetically sealed and soldered with meticulous care. And that terrine of *foie gras* has been equally religiously sealed and bears Chevet of Paris's impeccable, nay, sacred label. Do you really believe, Mr Self-Important, that half the world has conspired to snatch away your worthless life? Eat, drink and sleep. Chance is offering you these pleasant hours of solitude in the arms of erudition, so make the most of them. Then you can enjoy conversing with yourself as you recline on the warm breast of melancholy, that delicious enchantress who appears only to lovers and the lonely, and who, they say, is the spoiled, more fortunate younger sister of sadness!'

By this time, I had opened the tin of sardines, prised open the *foie gras,* uncorked a bottle of wine and poured it into my glass with a little soda water!

Then I devoted myself to eating, with appetite, courage, delight and a kind of animal sensuality, feeling all the while that somewhere around me fluttered the beneficent spirits that had protected Silvio Pellico as he languished in prison in Venice.

And most remarkable of all: I felt really well!

After supper, I lit a cigar and began pacing the floor, saying to myself:

'Right, let's take a little stroll around the countryside!'

On the wall to the left of the main door to the room was another door. I examined it. It was bolted. The bed stood in the way, so I pushed it to one side and opened the door to reveal a long, deep cupboard built into the wall with, halfway up, a broad, solid shelf.

It occurred to me that at the back of the cupboard there could perhaps be a party wall through which it might be possible for me to hear what was going on in the house next door.

I entered the cupboard, lay down on the shelf and listened. From the other side came a loud, low rumble. It sounded as if a large, cumbersome piece of furniture were being dragged across the floor.

I found that the back of the cupboard was indeed only a thin partition. It may be that it had once been a door. There was even a place where some of the plaster had crumbled away. I could see part of a bare wooden batten that lay diagonally across.

I fetched the corkscrew and painstakingly bored away the remaining plaster until I had made an imperceptible hole that enabled me to see some light and to hear clearly what was being said on the other side.

This is what was going on, at half past eleven at night, in the room next door to my 'prison cell'.

II

Two men were dragging a large wooden bedstead across the room towards the partition wall. I realised that the bed was going to be positioned immediately below the spot where I had just made a hole to serve as both eye and ear.

One of the men was grumbling.

'Say what you like, but I'm not coming here again at midnight to shift furniture.'

'What are you complaining about!' retorted the other. 'I'm paying you a whole *libra* to do this job. Now, isn't that better than being down in the stables, lying by the trough, getting bored to death and not earning a penny, while you wait for the coach to arrive so you can tend to the horses?'

The one who had spoken these words, although he spoke very clearly, had the peculiarities of pronunciation usual in a foreigner speaking Portuguese. From the way he pronounced certain vowels, particularly his a's, he was clearly a German.

The man who had spoken first went on:

'It's good money, I don't deny it, but I'd still rather not come here. I mean you're hardly going to find half a dozen men lounging around outside who'd be willing to come in here at this hour of the night, not even if you paid them their own weight in gold!'

'To move a bed?'

'It's not the bed that's the problem, it's this house!'

'For heaven's sake, what's wrong with the house?'

'Nothing, but it has a reputation, so much so that the owner tried for four whole years to rent it out, and even though he kept lowering the rent and finally even offered it for free, not a living soul would take it! The last people who lived here stayed but two nights, and were so shaken by what they saw and heard, they said it was the Devil himself lives here.'

'Nonsense! Fairy tales!'

'Don't you tell me it's nonsense, sir! I saw the family! I was around when it happened. They fled in the night, fled the second night they slept here, scared to death, they were.'

'So what did they see?' the German asked.

'They saw nothing.'

'Well, there you are, then!'

'They didn't *see* anything, but they heard things.'

'They obviously heard some very remarkable things!'

'Yes, sir, they did. And it wasn't only them either, it happened to all those who've lived here. And they were decent folk, who didn't lie, who had no need to lie, who'd paid their rent and lost it!'

'So what exactly did they hear?'

'You know perfectly well, sir! What do you mean, what did they hear? They heard banging on the doors when no one was knocking or even near them! They heard the flames spitting and the coals crackling, exactly as if someone was fanning the flames, and yet the kitchen was empty and the stove wasn't lit! They felt the beating wings of a bird that started flying through the rooms as soon as the lights were put out; they heard it puffing and panting, coming ever nearer to where they were lying, hovering so close over the bed that they could hear the rustle of its feathers and the hot breath from its beak and, at the same time, the icy chill when it moved its wings.'

'Oh, come on! They'd probably heard the previous tenants talking about it and so imagined they could hear the bird too, and the previous tenants had heard it from the tenants before them, but when it came down to it, no one actually heard

The Mystery of the Sintra Road

anything.'

'So you haven't heard, then, why they ran away, the last tenants who lived here four years ago now?'

'Only vaguely, but no one went into any detail.'

'That's why you don't believe me! Well, this is what happened. The people were poor but honest: husband, wife and a six-year-old daughter. They all slept together in the same room for safety's sake. The little one, who they hadn't warned because they didn't want to frighten her, slept in a cot to one side. They were sleeping with the lamp burning, and since they had worked hard all day, they fell asleep despite the crackling noises coming from the stove and the knocking on the doors. Then came the second night, and they were woken by the child screaming. The lamp had gone out. They immediately lit it again. The door of the room was locked from inside. The windows were bolted. There was no one else in the room but them. And yet the child's bedclothes were lying two or three paces away from the cot where she'd been sleeping, and the little girl, stripped naked now, was frozen with fear, white as a sheet and trembling like a leaf, and when she could finally speak — because she couldn't for a moment — she said that she'd felt something like the feet of a very big hen perched on the bed; that she'd found all the bedclothes had fallen off and she'd heard sighs and sobs and kisses, sounds that frightened her and that she didn't understand, while a feathered chest rubbed itself against her bare breast. The mother dressed the child quickly, wrapped her in a shawl, picked her up and covered her in kisses, warming her with her own breath; then, terrified, she ran like a madwoman out into the street. Her bold, fearless husband rushed about the house, with a lamp and without a lamp, looking in every nook and cranny, grinding his teeth and poking at the walls with the sharp knife he was holding. No one was there! No one could have left! No one could have entered! The next day he took the key back to the landlord, telling him that if he ever had enough money, he would buy the house himself and demolish it with axe and sledgehammer, set fire to whatever would burn, then trample the remaining heap of ashes and pour salt on them.'

'Well, I haven't heard anything like that, and this is the second night I'll be sleeping here,' the German responded.

'Good for you, sir! But aren't you afraid?'

'Not at all.'

'That's why people say what they do about you!'

'And what do people say about me?'

'With all due respect, sir, they say you're a German from the land of the Moors and that you're in league with the Devil.'

'Just a bit further back now. I'll help you!' said the German, changing the subject.

'Far enough?'

'A little more... just a little... so that the bedhead is resting against the door. Fine!'

'Anything else?'

'No, nothing else. Here's your money, and take one of those candles with you in case that big bird should appear on the stairs in the dark and try to carry you off.'

'Don't joke, sir. It's no laughing matter! I can't believe you really like this place.'

'Well, I do!'

'It's your choice, sir! And when you get fed up with the lost souls wandering about here, you can always move next door!'

'Now you're going to tell me that the house next door is...'

'It is. The Devil himself lives there!'

The man who had come to help move the bed, lit his candle and went down the stairs. The German was left alone; he shut the door and began getting undressed for bed.

The dialogue I had just overheard had impressed me greatly and aroused my curiosity.

Without deliberately trying to find out anything, I was, in the strangest way possible, beginning to understand facts, which, however distorted by superstition and ignorance, would help to explain what we had just seen and the presence of the corpse in the room.

Now, my interesting, refined neighbour, it's our turn!

III

As I said, the German's bed had been placed just below the peep-hole I had made. My neighbour lay down and blew out his candle. The room was in darkness and I heard the bed-springs creaking beneath the weight of his body as he settled down to sleep.

'Ah! So you love the murmurings of invisible spirits, do you?' I mused, mentally addressing the philosopher who was lying there on the other side of the wall. 'You enjoy the sonorous undulations of the molecules of animal life that drift around in space in search of the mysterious breath that will condense them and allow them to enter the bloodstreams of living beings? Would you like your spirit to join forces with those formless, capricious links that connect the world of the known to the world of the hidden? Right then, let's see how you employ your talents as a medium.'

And with that thought, I rapped on the wall with my knuckles, three short, sharp knocks, evenly spaced, like one of the secret signs made by freemasons.

I heard him run a hand over the wallpaper as if the noise he had heard might have left some tangible trace.

After a few moments, I began to repeat the signal, knocking on different parts of the partition wall.

I heard him sit up in bed. He struck a match and lit a candle. I stopped tapping. There was a pause, during which I kept still and silent. After some minutes, my neighbour put out his light, and I resumed my gentle, repeated knocking. Having listened in the dark for some time, he again lit his candle and began a careful examination of the section of the wall against which he

The Mystery of the Sintra Road

had positioned the bed.

At the very moment when the flame of his candle passed in front of the peep-hole, I abruptly blew it out.

The German, who must have been kneeling on the bed as he scrutinized the wall, gave a sudden cry, more of surprise than of terror, although it was accompanied by a heavy and readily identifiable noise, the thud of his body as he fell off the bed.

Immediately afterwards, I heard the voice of my neighbour asking firmly and decisively:

'Who's there?'

I replied:

'It is I.'

'Who are you?' he asked.

'And who are you?'

'Friedrich Friedlann, a citizen of Prussia.'

'Oh,' I said.

'I travel throughout Europe on behalf of the largest chemicals factory in Budapest to bring its products to the attention of other large manufacturers.'

'Good for you,' I observed.

Unruffled, he continued:

'A Jewish friend told me about three buildings in Lisbon he knew of, which had remained empty for some time after gaining a reputation for being inhabited by spirits from the other side. I have decided to live in each of the houses in turn and this is the first. I'm compiling a book investigating spiritism. May I know who I am addressing?'

'Of course!' I replied. 'My name can be Tom, Dick or Harry, and I live on the rents from my various properties, sometimes travelling, sometimes living in Lisbon, and occasionally dabbling in politics or literature when I have no more interesting or useful way of shaking off my idleness and boredom. I am not a spiritist.'

'Well, you should be! Spiritism is a complete system and could well become a religion.'

'Piffle!' I exclaimed, laughing.

'What!' Friedlann cried. 'Materialism, driven, on the one hand, by advances in the physical and natural sciences and, on the other, by the simultaneous relaxation of modern-day manners and the continuing and alarming decline in morals, is gradually eating away in the field of philosophy at the rather small space now occupied by faith. New beliefs and new doctrines will appear to take the place of the now dead beliefs and doctrines that previously served to regulate the supernatural. Man – who, in all probability, will never be able to do without the marvellous, so necessary to his imagination – will then naturally go in search of some form of spiritism, duly modified and perfected by the science of the future, some consoling theory about survival beyond death, based on as yet unknown correlations between those beings who exist now and those who preceded them and who will follow after. Of all the contemporary philosophers who refuse to accept the sterile and forlorn dogma of omnipotent matter, today's spiritists will be the only ones capable of making a contribution to the philosophy of the future.'

'May I ask you something?' I asked.

'Please do.'

'Without wishing to insult your judgement.'

'I will take great pleasure in satisfying your curiosity, whatever it may be.'

'Do you believe in any of the things spoken of by the man who helped you move the bed?'

This was a trick question. I wanted to find out if I was

talking to a madman, a visionary, a monomaniac, or simply someone who had a wild, eccentric imagination.

'I neither believe nor disbelieve anything I hear,' he answered. 'My practice is to accept provisionally whatever has yet to be proven and to doubt everything that is presented to me as an absolute fact. It is the only prudent means of never straying far from the truth. If you heard the conversation just now, then you know a little of the history of this house. I denied everything the fellow said because I have made an agreement with the landlord to try and dispel the curse hanging over his property. As a matter of fact, for the last two nights, I've heard a persistent crackling noise similar to that produced when one lights a coal fire, and I have on a table here a bust of Allan Kardec – who, as you may know, was one of the main advocates of spiritism – and somehow the bust always manages to move from the centre, where I place it, to the edge. The dust around the base of the bust, which I have taken the most meticulous care never to wipe off, leaves on the table top a trace of that slow, almost imperceptible, but continuous movement. And two or three times each night, I've heard knocking on the door next to which I've now placed my bed. Very clear and distinct. Each time, I've immediately opened the door (in fact, I moved the bed over here, so that I could reach it as quickly as possible), but why the knocker raises itself up and bangs of its own accord is something I still cannot explain.'

The Prussian said all this with the utmost sincerity and conviction.

'And what have you heard about the house next door, where I am?' I asked. 'What have you been told?'

'Well...'

'The truth, please!'

The Mystery of the Sintra Road

'I, personally, have heard nothing. The previous resident told me that in the silence of the night he had heard the murmur of voices, bursts of laughter and the jingling of money. Some neighbours have seen mysterious figures coming and going, although all those things could be easily explained.'

'So what do you think?'

'It's obviously…'

'What? What?'

'That is, I assume…'

'Come on. Speak frankly, now. No beating about the bush!'

'I assume it is one of two things: either a masonic lodge or a gambling den.'

IV

The German's words had cast a sudden revelatory light on things and I needed to ponder its implications.

What was happening to me, the mystery surrounding me, the corpse I had seen, the tentative assumption that one or more of my friends was embroiled in the affair, all of this was so grave and so extraordinary that I did not dare mention it to the stranger whom chance had given me as my neighbour.

It was now clear to me that I was in Lisbon. Naturally, I was eager to know the street and the number of the house, but I could find no plausible way of getting the German to tell me, other than by questioning him in a roundabout fashion which, given my situation, could have aroused suspicions that might endanger the safety of the other people involved. So I contented myself with saying that I was becoming uncomfortable in the awkward posture I was obliged to adopt and would, therefore, bid him goodnight. My neighbour took his leave by giving three evenly spaced knocks on the wall, just as I had done initially in order to catch his attention. It occurred to me that Friedlann might be a freemason, and would, therefore, in my current circumstances and in the name of reciprocal oaths and mutual obligations, provide me with the protection I was asking him for. So I gave him a single letter, he responded with another, and thus we created a password.

'*Salut, mon frère!*' he exclaimed.

'Remember, not a word to anyone!' I replied in a low voice, responding to his signal by rapping on the wall.

Then I closed the cupboard door, returned the bed to its original position, and lay down fully clothed.

I could not sleep. I began to think and grew sad with thinking.

In this house, under this same roof, I thought, lies a dead man, a young, elegant, handsome man, who entered this house filled perhaps with hope and happiness and plans for the future, only to have his life cut short, poisoned by a mysterious hand, and now, ignored, unknown and alone, far from the beloved woman who may, at this very moment, be waiting for him, far from the family who loved him as a child, far from the place of his birth, from the weeping mother who might have closed his eyes, from the anguished father who, in the name of humanity, might have bestowed on him a final blessing.

Hapless boy! Who knows what mental torments you must have suffered on being torn so violently from the world, leaving to society your inert, impassive body, as mute as an enigma placed anonymously in the middle of a blank page. Who knows what thoughts death stopped in their tracks? Who knows what affections it froze in your heart, through which, not long since, the vital sap of youth flowed so abundantly, a youth now for ever sterile and dead.

Poor lad! Worthy as you are, deserving perhaps to be sadly missed, you sleep your eternal sleep, still dressed for the ball, covered by a travelling rug, stretched out on a sofa, immune for ever to the joys and sorrows of this wretched life; and, in the brief history of your passage through the world, possibly not a single tear will be shed to commemorate this poignant moment, when the dead expect of the living the final, supreme favour that mankind can offer to those they most prize and love – the gift of a grave wherein dwells oblivion.

The eyes of those who love you do not yet weep. They are closed perhaps in sweet tranquil sleep, haunted in dreams by your dear countenance, or else fixed on the usual road along which they expect you to appear, ready to recognise your tardy step, to hear you humming the last waltz you heard as you left the party, to see you arrive home, carefree, smiling and happy.

Poor things! The footsteps of the lad who, possibly only today, said goodbye to you, thinking to greet you once more a few hours later, they will never again take the road to the house where he is expected; his voice will never again answer the voice that calls to him; his eyes will never again gaze enraptured at the eyes that once returned his gaze; his lips will never again brush the lips that once kissed his!

I shed no tears for you because I never knew you, we never met, and I do not even know who you are. But I do not wish to insult the grief that hovers over your death by allowing myself to fall asleep in the same house where you lie unburied, while there is still someone who assumes that you are still alive and in the world.

It was driven by these feelings, my dear friend, that I rose from the bed where I lay and returned to the table where I had eaten my supper to write these long pages, pages we will surely enjoy reading some day, in a frame of mind quite different to that in which we find ourselves tonight.

I had completed a little more than half of this account when the surrounding silence – broken only by the scratching of my pen on paper – was interrupted by the voices of the masked men talking quietly in the room I had walked through in order to reach this one. I had just finished the paragraph previous to this one when I heard the voices again, and this time I felt curious to know what was being said. I went over to the door and, unable to see anything through the keyhole, I pressed my ear to it. Since it was unlikely that our jailers would be sitting in the dark, I surmised that there must be a corridor between this room and the one in which they were talking. I could not make out what they were saying. Only now and then did the odd word reach my ear. I was thinking of returning to my writing or finishing this letter, when one of the men raised his voice and I clearly heard him say:

'But the banknotes, the £2,300! Didn't he have them with him?'

'I'm sure he did,' said another voice.

'Then this is monstrous!'

You can imagine the impression made on me by these words, the only ones I managed to hear!

It proved to me that the house to which we were brought is not the romantic hideaway I had first supposed. We must now accept one of the Prussian's hypotheses: this is either a gaming house or a masonic lodge. The noises heard by people in the adjoining house provide convincing proof. In a lovenest, one does not hear gales of laughter at dead of night or the sound of coins jingling on tables. Given the neighbours' reports of mysterious comings and goings, one cannot help but suspect clandestine meetings. The chink of gold, the laughter, the luxurious appearance of the *boudoir* we were shown into, leaves me in no doubt that this place is a den of gambling and revelry.

The words I heard a short time ago aroused my worst suspicions.

The unfortunate man who lies therein could have been the victim of a premeditated murder, committed in order to rob him of the money he brought with him.

But why then did the masked men go in search of a doctor? The words I overheard may explain this. The criminals who administered the opium to their victim with the intention of robbing him, found their plan frustrated by the absence of the English money they had believed to be in his pocket. At this juncture, they decided to resort to extreme measures and bring in a doctor whom they could easily prevent from reporting the crime; they would show him the opium and trust that this display of solicitous concern and confidence in their own innocence would deflect from them any suggestion of involvement in a crime and shroud the whole affair in mystery. This may not be exactly what happened. What remains indisputable, however, is that the disappearance of the money the victim brought with him does not fit with the idea that this is a house of probity and honesty.

I need hardly tell you what I have made up my mind to do. My Prussian neighbour is a somewhat fanciful man, but he seems sincere and trustworthy. I'm going to close now, address this letter and ask him to post it. I shall easily find a way of passing it to him in his room. Should I succeed in breaking right through the partition at the back of the cupboard, without anyone noticing, I'll go myself instead of sending the letter. Alternatively, as soon as the door to this room is opened, I will hurl myself at the person or persons blocking my path and fight my way past them as would any decent man determined to stand up to a handful of blackguards.

If, like me, you are incarcerated here, I swear to God that we will see each other tomorrow. If you have been freed and you receive this letter, but have no further word from me during the subsequent twenty-four hours, write to 'Friedrich Friedlann, Poste restante, Lisbon'. He will meet you at a place of your choosing and will tell you where I am.

Farewell,

F.

EDITOR'S NOTE: *The following unsigned pages – written in the same hand as the letters from the doctor previously published in this newspaper – were found together with the letter we printed yesterday.*

F. has not appeared. That same day, two days and three nights after receiving the long letter he had addressed to me – the first part of which I immediately sent to your paper, followed later by the second – I tried by every means possible to get word of him. All my efforts were in vain. I wrote to Friedrich Friedlann and received no reply. I sent someone to enquire at the post office and found that the letter I had written to him, suggesting that we meet, had not been collected.

I feel deeply worried, nervous and uneasy.

F. is an impetuous man, easily angered and almost insanely jealous of his honour. Given his temperament and the violence of his reactions, I fear that an outburst on his part might have had fatal consequences for him.

Nevertheless, Sir, I hasten to add that I completely disagree with F.'s views regarding the moral quality of the people who took us to the house where we found the corpse.

The tall masked man with whom I spoke at some length could not possibly be a cowardly murderer. F. spent almost no time with us and had little opportunity to study the other men involved. All his indignation and loathing stem from that one inexplicable and shocking remark, which he happened to overhear.

I dealt with only one of those men – the tallest – but I spent the whole night talking to him. Obviously, I could not study his facial expressions, but I could see his large, bright, intelligent eyes and hear his clear, strong, resonant voice, whose modulated tones followed the ebb and flow of his feelings.

During our discussions and conversations, and throughout our interrogation of A.M.C., I listened with interest, sympathy and sometimes admiration to his sincere and fluent way with words, fresh and vivid without ever being flowery, eloquent but with no pretensions to oratory. His voice was like the limpid mirror of a vigorous, upright, perceptive, sensitive nature. He had bursts of enthusiasm, flashes of righteous indignation and moments of melancholy that doubtless sprang from the fount of tears that all exceptionally good and honest people have at the core of their being. In short, he seemed to me a loyal and honourable soul and, with my wide experience of the world and my knowledge of our all too human capacity for deceit, I am not easily fooled in these matters, especially given the singularly testing situation in which we found ourselves. These, Sir, are the main reasons that, right from the start, prevented me from making public the name of my friend, who is now forcibly detained in a private prison. F. is a public figure, almost a celebrity. Everyone in Lisbon would be sure to recognise his name as that of one of our most acclaimed writers, just as everyone would be familiar with his proud, provocative, immaculately dressed figure, in marked contrast to the depressingly uniform creatures one sees in the streets, in literary salons and in theatres.

If I were to report my friend's disappearance to the police, it is almost certain that they would find a means of locating him, but would that not be tantamount to denouncing, as criminals, the taller of the masked men and his companions, whom I still consider to be innocent?

Indeed, despite the revelation about the missing £2,300, F.'s letter only confirms my impression.

The following passage appears in his letter:

There was one way of finding out if he was or was not a close friend of mine: all I needed was to get hold of his watch; even blindfolded, I could identify its owner simply by running my hand over it. If he was the person I thought he was, his watch case would be as smooth as enamel, apart from the raised coat of arms in the centre.

Now, the watch to which he alludes was, if you remember, the very one I described in the second letter I sent to this newspaper, the one belonging to the masked man sitting opposite me in the carriage, and which I was able to see clearly while it hung, suspended on its chain, from his fob pocket. Therefore, the masked man who escorted F. to the room in which he is being held prisoner is, as he thought, a good friend of his.

Without sowing the seeds of a remorse that will later cast an eternal shadow over my life, how can I report to the police a fact, a name, a particular circumstance, that will not only set them on the trail of this crime, but will also reveal the identities of the people – whether innocent or guilty – who are inevitably caught up in it?

Will the facts I have given to you, the letters I so precipitately began sending to you, and which today, under the cover of anonymity, I feel a moral obligation to conclude and abandon, will they not seem – to the lofty, cold, incorruptible severity of decent men – to be a betrayal of the unwritten laws of friendship, an offence against the inviolability of secrecy, against that private religion based on delicacy, sensitivity and perfection: a religion which, for honest souls, forms part of the supreme principles of the foremost of all religions, that of character?

But should I then do nothing? Remain dumb, inert, neutral in the face of this obscure but dreadful event? Can I really impassively and silently accept responsibility for this vile murder, of which I am the only witness who has the opportunity, freedom and capacity to act?

What would your readers do, if, for a moment, they were to imagine themselves in the same unique and exceptional circumstances?

In the wave of conjectures, plans, resolutions and obstacles overwhelming me, I felt utterly alone in my hiding place, anxious and nervous, and feeling that I had not a moment to lose, I could think of only one clear, practical way forward: to publish an anonymous account of what had happened to me and thus hand my story over to society in the hope that others, the public, might find a solution to a problem I was unable to resolve by myself.

I have received not one word of advice, analysis or criticism!

I feel profoundly sad, exhausted, ill. I need fresh air, freedom, room to move about in. I cannot stay endlessly immobile, like a convict, with the ball and chain of a mystery around my ankle.

Two days after you receive this letter, I will have left for foreign parts. At this time of war with Prussia, the field ambulances of the French army need surgeons. I intend to enlist as a doctor. My country can do without me, and I, like any man in the presence of irremediable misfortune, feel the sweet need to be useful. You know my destiny. One day you will know my name.

In bidding farewell – doubtless for ever – to your readers,

whom I have held captive with my account of this grim affair, may I be permitted a final word?

It is A.M.C., whose name I dare not reveal by writing it in full, A.M.C., whom I neither blamed nor accused, contrary to what his friend Z. alleged when he sprang to his defence in these columns, it is A.M.C. – whatever the reasons that led him to intervene in the circumstances surrounding the crime – who knows the inside story and holds the thread of the plot which I have tried in vain to find.

If these lines should reach the eyes of that young man, I ask one thing only, in the name of his personal honour and dignity and in the name of the honour and dignity of the other people involved in this whole strange business. Go to the post office and collect the letter that I will be sending to you this very day. In it I will tell you who I am and where you will be able either to write to me or come and speak to me in person. Should your age, position in society, concerns about your career, your family's peace of mind, your own lack of authority in this matter, or indeed any other reason, prevent you from seeing this affair through to its ultimate consequences and thus uncovering the secret truth behind this mystery, then address yourself to me. We will work together on this worthy and honourable task. I take full responsibility for any consequences that may arise from it, and I have the means to protect your name, your person and your reputation from any suspicion that may overshadow or sully it.

As for you, my dear, honest F., I do not believe you have been the victim of a treacherous and unworthy ambush! In my view, the only danger you face now is your own prickly nature, your scruples, your courage and, finally, your pride.

They cannot possibly have killed you in cold blood in that clandestine prison which, only a short time ago, you still illuminated with your patience and your wit. On the other hand, it seems entirely possible, even logical, that by now, in order to satisfy your honour, you have felt obliged to gamble your life away in an exchange of sword thrusts or bullets with one of your mysterious fellow residents.

A vague, sad sense of foreboding hangs over me… Poor F.! Are we fated never to meet again? What if the fateful day on which we set out together from Sintra – carefree and joyful, sighing over our happinesses, smiling at our misfortunes – what if that marked the end of our years of sweet friendship?

It is the sorrows and misadventures of others that have dragged us into this terrifying, implacable whirlpool of raw human solidarity!

What can one do?

If this is life, then we must bravely accept it and *avante*! Expect to be unfortunate, since that is the surest way to be happy!

Z.'s Second Letter

Sir,

I have just read in today's edition of the *Diário de Notícias* another letter in which Doctor ***, with malevolent insistence, once again suggests that my poor friend A.M.C. was an accessory to the murder of which the doctor has become the self-appointed historian.

I told you in my previous letter that, with the sole aid of my courage and my wits, I intended to put myself at the service of everyone's curiosity and attempt to penetrate and untangle the grim tale which, for more than a week now, has been appearing daily in the pages of your newspaper and presenting your astonished readers with a mysterious and chilling picture.

Unfortunately, I have learned nothing: all my enquiries, petitions and visits were in vain. The story merely vanishes ever further into the mist surrounding it, and my poor friend A.M.C. is still there, whether in voluntary seclusion or enforced imprisonment I do not know.

Given the impossibility of discovering the truth by tramping the city's streets, I decided to track it down in the doctor's own letters. I analysed them, dissected them, word by word, and now, without describing my processes, I present you with my results.

The *Mystery of the Sintra Road* is an invention, not a literary invention as I had at first thought, but a criminal invention with a specific objective. Here is what I have managed to deduce of the motives behind this invention.

There is no denying that a crime has been committed, that much is clear. One of the accessories to this crime is Doctor

***. Since he has chosen to remain anonymous, I have no hesitation in making this formal accusation. If his name were known, if he had signed his letters, I would only dare to make such a grave affirmation if I had legal proof to back it up.

Yes, Doctor *** is an accessory to a crime. My friend, A.M.C., is an unsuspecting dupe, onto whom the perpetrators are trying to foist any suspicions that may already exist, along with any further evidence that may turn up later. This crime, which has actually been committed, appears before us in the literary clothes of a theatrical mystery. The doctor's letters are a childish fiction, as we shall soon see.

Is it likely that, in a small city like Lisbon where we are all of us neighbours, close friends and relatives, Doctor ***, who appears to be a man known in society, a frequenter of its salons and its theatres, would not know a single one of those four masked men, who clearly all move in the same social circles, sit on the same sofas, listen to the same music in the same salons and in the same theatres?

A black velvet mask is not enough to disguise an acquaintance. His hair, his walk, his build, his face, his voice, his hands, his manner of dress are quite enough to betray his identity. Has Doctor *** really never seen any of these men before? The men were so elegant, so distinguished, such fine horsemen and linguists, so rich, yet the doctor, a medical man, a man with connections, an habitué of the Teatro São Carlos, had, it seems, never seen them before, and this in a country where all of life is concentrated in the few yards of mud that make up the Chiado! And, it turns out, one of the masked men is a close friend of F.'s, but even though they were sitting knee to knee in the carriage, F. failed to recognise him by his hands, his eyes, his build – even by his silence! Pure farce!

And yet at carnival time, when the least well-known, the

least famous of Lisbon youths disguises himself as a Turk, slaps a false beard on his face, covers himself with feathers, dresses up as Mephistopheles, as a *ci-devant* aristocrat or as a melon, no one in the foyer of the Teatro São Carlos would pass him without saying: 'There goes so-and-so!' And that's at night, by lamplight, when we're distracted and conscious that women are looking at us, not while we're being ambushed and kidnapped on a road in broad daylight! That's how well we know each other! What a joke!

And so innocent, so naïve are those masked men, that at a moment of high danger, they go in search of the very man who, given his connections, his profession and his penetrating intelligence, would most easily be able to recognise them. If they feared discovery, why choose him of all people? If they weren't concerned about being recognised, why wear masks?

Why, then, did it have to be a doctor? In order to verify that the man was dead? Or to help? Or to save him? In that case, what kind of men are they, who, instead of heading post-haste for the nearest pharmacy or doctor's house, go calmly to their rooms, put on masks and then, at dusk, drive to a heath two leagues away to re-enact an episode worthy of a play by Frédéric Soulié.

Did they perhaps know that the man was already dead? Why then call for a doctor, a witness? And if they weren't concerned about having a witness, why the masks and the blindfolds? You see, pure theatre!

Consider the doctor's description of examining the corpse; there is not a single scientific word there. Nothing about it rings true, from the serenity of the man's features to the dilation of the pupils.

What kind of men are Doctor *** and his friend F.? There they were in a house in a city street, with their hands unbound, and yet they did not lay a finger on the masked men. How could such proud, generous men put up with such humiliating treatment? If they are the honest, principled fellows they claim to be, how could they, by their acceptance of the situation, allow themselves to be made accomplices?

And then there's A.M.C.! Look how they present him – childish, nervous, timid, imbecilic and meekly obeying orders! – when he is, in fact, a man of great strength of character, courage and sang-froid! How can anyone believe the infantile trick the Doctor used to trip him up?

'The one thing that puzzles me in all this,' the doctor said, 'is that the arsenic left no trace.' To which, according to the doctor, A.M.C. responded: 'It was opium.'

What can be said of the brainless naïveté of a man who resorts to such simplistic drivel?

And although her identity is only hinted at, what kind of woman would be involved in such an affair? Why does the masked man want to protect her? What is all this business about the theft of £2,300? Let's be logical: given that robbery was the main motive for the crime, why, then, would a noble, gentlemanly character like the masked man still feel so protective of a woman who kills in order to steal?

If, on the other hand, he suspects that the motive was passion, how does he explain the robbery?

Besides, if he suspected her of being involved in the death, but was so bound to her that he still wanted to protect her, why didn't he immediately go and see her? Why didn't he question her, instead of ambushing strangers on the highway and bringing them to view a corpse?

How contrived this whole story is, how false and artificial and feeble! Those carriages galloping through the streets of Lisbon. Those masked men smoking cigars in the twilight, those novelettish roads where coaches manage to pass without being stopped at the toll-bars and where horsemen in pale capes gallop through the darkness! It's like a French novel from the days of *le ministère Compte Villèle*. I am not even going to bother with the letters from F., which explain nothing, reveal nothing and mean nothing – unless it is the need for a murderer and a thief to publish his empty prose in the columns of a respectable newspaper.

Conclusion: Doctor *** was an accomplice to a crime. He's aware that someone knows his secret, he senses that everything is about to be revealed, he fears the police may become involved, that someone has been indiscreet; that is why he wants to create this cloud of confusion, to put any investigation off the scent, to mislead, obscure, conceal, obfuscate; and, while he spreads bewilderment among the public, he packs his bags and runs away to be a coward in France, having been a murderer here in Portugal!

What my friend A.M.C. is doing in the midst of all this, I have no idea.

I beg you, sir, please purge the pages of your newspaper of these implausible fabrications.

Z.

The Tall Masked Man's Account

I

Sir,

I am the man who drove the carriage to Lisbon in the so-called Mystery of the Sintra Road that has recently come to public notice through the letters of Doctor ***. With my black satin mask, I am now a familiar figure to all those who may have been following the doctor's extraordinary revelations, in which he describes me as 'the tall masked man'. I am he. I never imagined that I would find myself in the deplorable situation of having to write to your newspaper in order to give my side of the story. However, on reading the trumped-up, illogical and inaccurate accusations levelled at the doctor and at me, I owe it both to myself and to my regard for the doctor's unassailable probity, to clear up all these contradictory hypotheses and unfounded speculations and place before you the whole implacable, indisputable truth. I was initially deterred from doing so by the strongest scruple any proud man can have: I would have to speak of a woman and drag through the pages of a newspaper the thing that is truest and deepest in any woman: the story of her heart. Today, I am no longer under that constraint, for on my desk, beside the sheet of paper on which I am writing, I have this simple, noble note:

*I saw the accusations levelled at you and your friends and at the worthy Doctor ***. Write the truth, print it in the newspapers. Disguise my name by using a false initial. I no longer belong to the world or to its theories and judgements. If you do not do this, I will hand myself over to the police.*

However, despite these fine, sincere words, I have made up my mind not to speak of the crime, but to describe only the events that brought me into contact with that unfortunate young man – now tragically dead – the events that led to his presence in Lisbon and determined what happened in the lonely room of that strange house, by the feeble light of a candle and beside a vase of withered flowers. I leave it to others to tell what took place that night. I will not. I do not wish to hear paperboys shouting out the painful, heartfelt story of someone I esteem.

Three years ago, I spent much of my time in Lisbon at a house where a place was always set for me at table, where I could always find partners for a game of whist and where I could speak gaily of my joys and confide my woes; that house belonged to a nobleman whom I shall refer to as the 'Count of W.' The countess was my cousin.

She was a singularly attractive woman, not pretty, no, worse than that: she had *charm*. She had admirably thick, fair hair, and when it was plaited and curled, it gleamed soft and golden, like a nest of light. If you were to take a single strand and stretch it out like a violin string, it would glow as brightly as if you were holding in your hands a thread taken from the very heart of the sun.

Her eyes were a deep Mediterranean blue and, at once, so imperious they could quell the most rebellious spirit and so tender and mysterious that any man might dream of drowning in them.

She was tall enough to be commanding, but not so tall that she could not rest her head upon the breast of he who loved her. She moved with the same rhythmic, swaying gait with which one imagines mermaids swimming.

And she was, besides, utterly without pretension and full of wit.

It would be an act of foolish pride to say that my eyes never rested amorously on the flawless purity of her brow or on the curve of her breast, for when I first began visiting that house, I did harbour vague feelings of love – a genteel fantasy, an ethereal desire – for that dear creature. Once, I even told her so; she laughed and I laughed too, and we solemnly shook hands. That night we played *écarté*, and afterwards she drew a caricature of me on a sheet of paper. From then on, we were friends, and I never again noticed her beauty, happy to consider her merely as one of the chaps. I told her all about my love affairs, my debts, my sorrows, and she listened sympathetically and always had just the right, consoling words to say. Later, she would confide in me about her nerves, her bouts of melancholy.

'I have a fit of the blue devils today,' she would say, using the English expression.

So we would sit by the fireside, drink tea and talk. She was weary of her husband. He was a cold man, she said, vulgar and dissolute, narrow-minded, cowardly and morally lax. His mistresses were common and uncouth, he was an inveterate pipe-smoker, spat on the floor, and could barely spell. Yet his defects were somehow unexceptional and went almost unremarked. An astonished Lord Grenley once said of him:

'What a strange man! He's an unattractive dolt, who can't ride or spell, has no dress sense at all, and yet he's not an unpleasant fellow.'

The refined and aristocratic countess concealed her aversion for this trivial, boring person. He, on the other hand, held her in high regard. He gave her jewellery and sometimes brought her a bouquet of flowers, but he did all this in the same casual manner with which he drove his dogcart.

The count took a great shine to me, thought me the kindest,

cleverest and bravest of men, attached himself proudly to my arm, quoted me, recounted my bold deeds, and imitated me in my choice of cravats.

The countess began to grow pale and thin. The doctors recommended a voyage to Nice, Cádiz, Naples, or some other Mediterranean city. A family friend who had just returned from India, where he had been Secretary-General, spoke enthusiastically of Malta. The mail boat from India had run into difficulties, and he had been delayed for five days in Malta, where he had enjoyed the streets, the beauty of the bay, the heroic architecture of its palaces, and the brazen, lively Maltese women with their large Moorish eyes.

'How do you fancy going to Malta?' the count asked his wife one night.

'I'll happily go anywhere, but I do, for some reason, feel very drawn to Malta. Yes, let's go to Malta. You could come too, cousin.'

'Of course he'll come!' bellowed the count.

And he vowed that he would not make the trip without me; I was his chess partner, his sole source of happiness, his discoverer of cravats; he would shanghai me and make me his heir.

I gave in. The countess was delighted at the prospect. She hoped there would be a storm; she wanted to go on afterwards to Greece, to Alexandria, to drink the water of the Nile. She declared that we would have to hunt jackals, go to Mecca in disguise and a thousand other such hare-brained schemes that made us all laugh.

In Lisbon we boarded a French steamer for Gibraltar, where we would catch the British mail boat to India.

As we passed Cape St Vincent, a magnificent moon was rising behind it, lending a dark severity to the rugged silhouette of that famous promontory and casting upon the rough sea a vast, luminous net. The countess was sitting in a wicker armchair on the poop deck, her head drooping, her eyes closed, her hands still, a look of contentment on her face and in her posture too.

'Do you know,' she said suddenly in a slow, quiet voice, 'I have such a feeling of happy plenitude, of desires fulfilled…' Then more quietly:

'…and somehow a feeling of love, too. How do you explain that?'

The count was asleep; we were alone on the high seas, in the calm moonlight, beneath which the slowly swelling waves resembled a sighing breast. I could already feel the magnetic heat of Africa. I took her hands in mine and whispered:

'You look very lovely, you know!'

'Oh cousin!' she said, laughing. 'Don't be so silly! We're old friends. But that's what comes from being alone with someone on a moonlit night and mentioning the word "love"! Ah, my friend, you must believe that, inexplicable as it may seem, the love I spoke of was not for you, thank heavens, but for someone I don't even know, whom I haven't yet met, but whom I might perhaps meet. You see? It was like a premonition… that's what it was. Goodness me, how treacherous the moonlight is, and at my age too!'

I was about to respond and make a joke of it all. A light shone in the distance through the night mist. The ship's captain came over to us.

'Do you recognise that light?' he asked.

'I've never travelled on this sea before, captain,' I replied.

'You're Portuguese, aren't you? Well that is the lighthouse at Ceuta.'

It was a humble, melancholy light, and neither of us had

any interest in Ceuta. A few minutes later, we went down to our respective cabins. I was surprised at the countess. She had never opened her heart to me in that way before. She was in that dangerous mood when love can take complete possession of a life.

What would happen if, one night, beneath just such a moon, a noble, strong, handsome man were to kneel before her and swear undying love to her?

The following morning, the Rock of Gibraltar hove into view. We went ashore. In a square at the entrance to the docks, some red-coated English soldiers were marching up and down to Offenbach's 'Air du Général Boum'.

'I loathe the English,' said the countess.

'What!' cried the count indignantly. 'You loathe the English?'

He turned to me, looking profoundly shocked and dismayed.

'Do you hear that, boy, she loathes the English!'

II

In Gibraltar, we stayed at the Club House Hotel. Our rooms looked out over the sea, where, before us, lay a mountain range bathed in light, and on the far side of the strait, obscured by mist, lay Africa.

We set out at once on a sight-seeing tour in one of Gibraltar's famous carts, which consist of two parallel benches, back to back, mounted lengthwise over a pair of huge wheels, and each cart is drawn by a fast, sturdy English horse, which, having lived for some time among Spaniards, has acquired a cantankerous streak!

The finest scenic drive in Gibraltar is a road that encircles the mountainside, halfway up the slope above the city, and which is bordered by cottages whose gardens and orchards are filled with exotic plants from the Orient: aloes, prickly pear, cacti and palm trees; and down below, glimpsed through the foliage, lies the luminous blue stillness of the Mediterranean.

The countess was enchanted; the generous light, the sun-burnished water, the contemplative silence of the clear blue sky, the purple mists on the mountains, the lush vegetation; everything provoked in that poor shrunken soul an unexpected enthusiasm for life. She laughed, and her eyes sparkled; she was full of an irrepressible energy that made her feel like breaking into a run.

We went and sat in the Gibraltar Gardens, where the English had rather overdone the military theme. Instead of fountains, there were statues of generals; a tangle of roses covered the pyramids of cannon balls; and the cannon sat foolish and impassive beneath the magnolia trees. But it was so peaceful there! Such a divine, absorbed silence! Such an air of immortality! It seemed that everything, the plants, the earth, the light, had stopped, plunged deep in meditation, suspended, listening, noiselessly breathing! Below lay the shining sea, as delicate and smooth as satin. In the distance, wrapped in a vaporous blue haze, we could see the craggy outline of the Atlas Mountains. Nothing moved, apart from the occasional dove flying past, ineffably serene. At one point, from a passing regiment of Highlanders, came the sound of bagpipes playing melancholy airs from the mountains of Scotland. And those sweet, ethereal notes seemed to us like the sonorous inhabitants of the air.

The countess had remained seated and silent, soaking up the marvellous serenity, the beauty of the light, the slumbering sea, the keen scents.

'Wouldn't you agree,' she said, 'that it makes one feel like dying, right here, very quietly, alone…'

'Alone?' I asked.

She smiled, her eyes fixed on the lovely backdrop of the bright horizon.

'Alone?' she said: 'No.'

'Be careful, fair cousin, be careful!' I warned. 'You start thinking thoughts like that and along comes an innocent little dream that pitches its tent in your heart and begins to burrow into it, and then, dear cousin, then…'

'Then we have dinner,' announced the count who was suddenly there beside us, all aglow because he had shaken the hand of an English colonel and picked a red cactus flower.

We went down to the hotel. After dinner, we ambled around the Plaza del Martillo. It was time to retire; an English brass band played a melancholy tune. Out at sea, we heard the sound of a gun being fired.

'The mail boat for India has arrived,' our guide explained. And from high up, a cannon replied with a thunderous echo.

'Do the passengers come ashore the day they arrive?' I asked.

'The military almost always do, sir. They have the governor's permission to disembark down below.'

When we returned to the hotel at ten o'clock, having strolled along the esplanades in the moonlight, we heard cheerful voices and corks popping, the unmistakable sounds of a gentlemen's supper party. The countess went up to her room. The count and I went into the dining-room. British officers who had travelled from Southampton en route to the garrison in Malta had disembarked and were having supper.

We had sat down and were drinking beer, when I had occasion to hand a jar of mustard to one of the British officers sitting near me. I dropped the jar, spattering myself with mustard. The officer smiled sympathetically, I laughed at my own clumsiness, we struck up conversation and, by the end of the evening, were walking arm-in-arm together along the esplanade that ran along the sea front past the windows of the hotel. A wash of silent moonlight lent a spiritual quality to the splendid view of the mountains and the vast, motionless sea.

I had taken a liking to that English officer, because of the fine, noble cast of his face, the originality of his thinking, and a certain sad gravity of manner. He was a young artillery officer who had fought in India. The sun of Hindustan had tanned his fresh, pale countenance, deepened the colour of his eyes and given an intense tawny tinge to his fair hair.

We were strolling along, deep in conversation, when a window above us was suddenly flung open, and a woman in a white dressing-gown stepped out and leaned lightly on the balcony to gaze at the luminous horizon and the melancholy sea. It was the countess.

The moonlight wrapped about her, silvering her face and making her body seem somehow slighter, more ethereal, like that of a character out of ancient legend. Her hair tumbled generously about her in large, loose curls.

'What a beautiful woman!' exclaimed the British officer stopping to look, his eyes wide with admiration. 'Who can she be?'

'Actually, she's my cousin,' I said, laughing. 'Married, of course. She's the countess of W. She leaves tomorrow for Malta on the mail boat. I'll introduce her to you on board, my friend, so you can amuse her with tales of India. The unfortunate young countess adores the Romantic. In Portugal, even our romances aren't romantic. Tell me, have you ever hunted tigers, captain?'

'Occasionally. Does your cousin speak English?'

'Like a Portuguese, that is to say, very badly. But she hears with her eyes and always knows what you're thinking.'

We went our separate ways.

'I've arranged a lovely little romance for you, cousin,' I said entering the room where the count was writing letters and smoking his pipe. 'A romance in which we go tiger-hunting with rajahs, where there are temple dancers, forests of palm trees, English wars and elephants...'

'I see. What's his name?'

'His name is Captain Rytmel, an artillery officer, twenty-eight years old, on his way to Malta; he has a fair moustache, a bit of India in his eyes, a lot of England in his eccentricity, and is, in short, a perfect gentleman.'

'A beer-drinker!' said the countess, pulling the petals off the cactus flower.

'A beer-drinker!' roared the count, looking up with comic

indignation. 'My dear, don't say that in my presence, unless you want to turn my hair grey! I have the highest regard for the English and for beer. A beer-drinker indeed! A young fellow of such perfection!' he murmured and continued scratching away with his pen.

At seven o'clock the following morning we went aboard the *Ceylon,* the Royal Mail ship for India. The Rock of Gibraltar, dragged early from its bed, was still wearing its nightcap of mist. There were already travellers and officers on deck. The boards were damp; there was a great confusion of baggage, baskets of fruit and caged birds; the gangway became choked with Gibraltarian hawkers. The countess retired to her cabin to rest for a while. At nine o'clock nearly all the passengers who had joined the ship at Gibraltar and those who had come with her from Southampton were up on deck; the smoke billowed, the small boats departed, the early mist had vanished, the sun lent a rosy tint to the white houses of Algeciras and San Roque, and from on shore came the sound of drum rolls.

The countess, seated on a carved Indian chair, was gazing out at the little Spanish villages strung out along the bay.

Captain Rytmel was some way off, chatting to the count, who was already enthusing over the captain's dignified bearing, his adventures in India and the odd shape of the army hat that he wore with such unusual aplomb. The captain was holding a pencil and sketchbook in his hand.

'Captain,' I said, taking him by the arm, 'I'm going to introduce you to my cousin, the countess. Hide your sketchbook, though, she's a merciless drawer of caricatures.'

The countess held out a small, thin, nervous hand, with nails as smooth as Dieppe ivory.

'My cousin tells me, Captain Rytmel, that you have a whole host of stories about India to regale me with. I must warn you

The Mystery of the Sintra Road

now that I'm not going to let you leave out a single tiger or scrap of countryside. I want to hear everything! I adore India, the India of the Indians, of course, not that of the Englishmen. Have you been to Malta before? Is it nice?'

'Malta, countess, is part Italy and part Levant. That's what makes it so surprising. It has a strange, distinctive charm. Otherwise, it's just a rock.'

'Will you be staying long in Malta?' asked the countess.

'Only a week.'

The countess was nervously twisting her gloves; she looked up at Captain Rytmel, cleared her throat, and said quickly:

'Oh, you must let me see your sketchbook.'

'But, countess, it's empty or almost empty, apart from a few line drawings and topographical notes.'

'I don't believe you. I bet you have some sketches of Indian landscapes, and there's bound to be at least one tiger, if not a temple dancer!'

And with a charmingly triumphant gesture, she snatched the sketchbook from Captain Rytmel's hand.

The captain turned crimson. The countess leafed rapidly through the book, then, suddenly, gave a little cry, blushed, and sat with the book open, her eyes moist and smiling, her lips parted. I looked: on the page was a drawing of a woman in a white dressing-gown, leaning on a balcony and looking out at a horizon of mountains and sea. It was a perfect portrait of the countess. He had seen her in that pose the evening before, in the moonlight, at the hotel window.

The count had joined us.

'Why, it's you, Luísa! But what talent! You really are an admirable fellow, captain. You've caught her to a T!'

'Oh no, not at all!' said the captain. 'Last night at the hotel, I was sitting in my room with my sketchbook open, and the pencil, without my permission, without my intending it, did this drawing of its own accord. It's this disobedient pencil that should be punished!'

'What?' bellowed the count. 'It must be a magic pencil. Captain, I've decided that you will join us for dinner as soon as we arrive in Malta. I won't let you get away, my dear chap. You will be our guide to the island. Yes, caught her to a T!'

And in Portuguese to the countess, he added:

'A beer-drinker, eh?'

At that moment, a bell sounded for lunch.

III

You may be puzzled that I am able to give such a meticulous account of events, capturing the scenery as well as every word or gesture. There is no need for surprise. My memory is not exceptional, nor am I making things up. However, before I retire each night, it is my practice to jot down in a notebook the events, dialogues, ideas and possibilities that I encounter during the day or that my mind creates. It is these notes that I am copying from here.

The passengers were already seated at the luncheon table. Our place was next to the ship's captain. The commander of the *Ceylon* was a thin man, or perhaps 'slender' is the word, with a very red face from which sprang a pair of white mutton-chop sideburns, like rough heather springing aggressively out of the earth.

Seated beside him were two eccentric characters: the Purser and Mr Colney, an employee of the British Post Office. The purser was so fat that he looked as if a group of generously proportioned men had squeezed themselves into a single merchant navy uniform. Mr Colney, on the other hand, was tall and thin, with a sharp, prominent nose, on the end of which perched the golden arc of his bureaucratic spectacles. The purser had one all-abiding obsession – the desire to become fluent in Brazilian Portuguese. He had travelled in Brazil and was full of admiration for Maranhão and Pará and for the great resources of the Brazilian Empire. Every five minutes or so, he would lean over to enquire about some subtlety of Brazilian pronunciation. Mr Colney, for his part, had a stutter and an odd compulsion to sing comical ditties. The other passengers included army officers going to take up their post in India, a few cheerful blonde young English ladies, a clergyman with twelve children, and two elderly philanthropists from the Society for the Education of Young Patagonians.

As soon as Captain Rytmel entered the dining room in the company of the Countess, a man struggling greedily with the carcass on his plate saw him, stood up and announced with loud good humour:

'*¡Viva Dios*! It's Captain Rytmel! Hail, dear friend! A thousand greetings! *Hombre*, you're looking well, you've put on weight!'

He folded Rytmel in a robust embrace and gazed at him fondly with his large dark eyes. After a first brief moment of surprise, during which Captain Rytmel turned very pale, he hastened to shake the hand of the desperately beautiful woman seated next to that greedy, expansive Spaniard, who turned out to be a silk merchant, Don Nicazio Puebla by name.

The lady, whose name was Carmen, was from Cuba and was Don Nicazio's second wife. She was tall and had a magnificent figure; her complexion reminded one of pale marble, her eyes of dark, watered satin, and the luxuriant ringlets of her hair were what Baudelaire would have described as *ténèbres*. She was dressed in black silk and wore a mantilla.

'Were you in Gibraltar?' asked Captain Rytmel.

'No, in Cádiz, my friend,' said Don Nicazio. 'We arrived in Gibraltar yesterday. We're on our way to Malta. Are you returning to India? Ah, Captain Rytmel, I'm sure you remember our time in Calcutta.'

'Captain Rytmel,' said Carmen with a frosty smile, 'is very good at forgetting.'

We all studied Carmen Puebla with interest. The count thought her sublime, as did I, so much so that I whispered to the countess:

'What a beautiful creature!'

'Yes, she has the manners of an ill-bred statue,' she replied drily.

I looked at the countess and laughed.

'Cousin, please! She's so adorable she should be made into a trinket to be attached to one's watch chain. I shall definitely make off with her, here on the high seas, in one of the ship's lifeboats; why, her every move is like distilled music! Oh, cousin, you must agree that she's perfect... I say, old chap,' I called to the count, 'pass me the soda-siphon, will you, I need cooling off!'

Meanwhile, Captain Rytmel had sat down next to Carmen and was talking about India, about old friends in Calcutta, about journeys made together. The countess was not eating, she seemed upset.

'I'm going up on deck,' she announced abruptly. 'Have them send me some tea, will you?'

When he saw her go, Rytmel got to his feet and asked the count:

'Is the countess unwell?'

'A little. She needs some fresh air. Go and keep her company and talk to her about India. I can't possibly leave my curry...'

I wanted to stay where I was, opposite the magnificent Carmen, and therefore applied myself to my food. The captain had promptly picked up his peculiar Indian army headgear.

The Spanish woman turned pale when she saw him follow the Countess. A few moments later, she too rose to her feet, wrapped about her a broad silk cape rather like a burnous and went up on deck, leaning on a long walking cane with an ivory handle.

Luncheon had finished. The talk turned to India, to the

theatre in Malta, to Lord Derby, to the Fenians. Growing bored, I took my leave of the ship's captain and went up on deck to smoke a good cigar in the fresh sea breeze.

The countess was sitting on a bench on the stern deck, with Captain Rytmel beside her on a folding wicker stool.

Carmen was walking briskly up and down the deck. Occasionally, grasping the ropes to steady herself, she would climb onto the step that ran along the inside of the ship's rail and stand looking out to sea, while her mantilla and cape billowed in the wind, giving her a sinuous, flowing silhouette reminiscent of the divinities with which the sculptors of earlier times used to decorate the prows of galleons.

IV

Don Nicazio Puebla, to whom I had already been introduced by the purser, had come to stand beside me at the rail as he smoked his cigar.

'So you were in India, sir?' I asked.

'Yes, I spent two years in Calcutta. That was where I met Captain Rytmel. We spent a lot of time in one another's company. Dined together every night. I went on a tiger hunt with him. Yes, I actually hunted tigers. You should visit Calcutta. Wonderful palaces! Wonderful fabrics!'

'He's a fine officer, Captain Rytmel.'

'Amusing too. What laughs we had! And brave as well. Do you know, he saved my life!'

'When you were out hunting?'

'I'll tell you.'

We had reached the stern by then. I saw Carmen walk purposefully over to where the countess was in conversation with Rytmel and say boldly and proudly:

'Captain, may I have a word with you?'

The countess blanched. Rytmel glanced round angrily, but nonetheless stood up and dutifully followed her.

I went over to the countess.

'Who is that woman? What does she want?' she asked me, her voice trembling.

I reassured her, then went over to Don Nicazio and asked:

'Did you see what your wife did?'

'Yes.'

'It was quite improper. I presume, sir, that you answer for the lady's manners and caprices.'

'I, sir?' shouted the Spaniard. 'I answer for nothing. What do you expect? The woman is a monster! Rid me of her if you can, sir! Would you like her? Well, keep her. She's always creating these scenes and I can say nothing. She's a regular spitfire, and she carries a knife too!'

'That woman,' I told the countess, 'is a creature without manners and, it would seem, without dignity. Do not look at her or listen to her, pretend she doesn't exist. Should there be any further impropriety, I'll take it up with the captain as if she were an insolent cabin boy. It's a shame, though, because she's awfully pretty.'

Meanwhile, standing by the ship's rail, Carmen was haranguing Captain Rytmel, who listened impassively, his eyes downcast.

The count had now appeared, and other ladies were emerging from their cabins and forming into small groups, where they engaged in reading, needlework, card games and so on.

I returned to Don Nicazio's side and, trying to make light of the episode, remarked:

'So your wife makes life dificult for you, does she?'

'She's always like that with Captain Rytmel and has been ever since that tiger hunt. Would you like to hear the tale?'

'Yes, yes, fire away.'

I sat down under the awning that covered the area set aside for smoking, lit a cigar, crossed my legs, leaned my head back and, lulled by the gentle movement of the ship, closed my eyes.

'One day in Calcutta,' began the Spaniard, 'a day of extreme heat…'

But I want you to hear this story from Captain Rytmel himself. Here then is a faithful copy of some of the liveliest pages from his travel diaries.

The Mystery of the Sintra Road

*****

It appears that every trader who goes to India dreams of hunting a tiger.

Don Nicazio Puebla was no exception. His wife, Carmen, decided to accompany him, for she had the courage, impetuosity and taste for danger of some of the early explorers. I liked them as a couple, and so the three of us arranged to go hunting with some officer friends of mine who were in Calcutta at the time. A tiger had been seen two leagues from the city. Only two nights before, it had managed to leap over a bamboo fence surrounding the property of an English doctor, an old colonialist, and killed and eaten the daughter of a servant. It was said to be an enormous animal with a beautifully striped pelt.

We set out on horseback at dawn. Carmen rode in a howdah on the back of an elephant. An ox carried a supply of water in earthenware pots covered in woven raffia. Our party comprised several artillery officers, some sepoys, three bearers and an old experienced hunting guide, a degenerate, debauched Brahman, who lived in Calcutta on the alms given him by nabobs and British officers. Fearless and half-crazy, he sang strange Indian melodies, worshipped the River Ganges and always slept at the top of a palm tree.

We were armed with first-rate rifles, scimitars, short two-edged swords like those used by Roman gladiators, and the ruthless iron tridents that are the best weapons for doing battle with a tiger. A pack of strong, agile dogs was brought along as well, under the control of some natives.

By eleven o'clock we had penetrated into the depths of the forest. The tiger was known to have its lair near a particular

The Mystery of the Sintra Road

clearing. We walked along in silence, beneath the implacable weight of the sun, past palm trees and tamarinds, through dense thickets, breathing in the stifling air filled with pungent aromas. All of nature seemed becalmed by the intense heat; even the birds were silent as they flew lethargically past, their brightly coloured feathers, red, black, purple and gold, resplendent against the dark green foliage. The sky was like beaten copper; the horses drooped their heads as they walked; the dogs were panting; the ox carrying the water lowed mournfully; only the elephant moved with his usual impassive, stately step. To forget their fatigue, the natives intoned Hindu chants in slow monotonous voices.

We were still some distance from the tiger. The horses had not whinnied nor had the elephant yet loosed his gentle, melancholy call. Nevertheless, we were getting closer to the clearing.

I went over to the howdah and called. Carmen drew the curtains open. She was pale from the heat and from the anticipatory pleasure of possible danger. Her eyes were extraordinarily bright. She longed for the struggle, the gunshots, the encounter with the wild beast. She asked me to bring her a cigarette and some cognac and water.

Many times since we first met, I had allowed my eyes to linger on Carmen and had always felt her dark, caressing gaze respond to mine.

Sometimes I brought her flowers, and one night on a terrace in Calcutta, when we were admiring the brilliant constellations of India powdering the sky with light, she had, in a forgetful moment, placed her hands in mine. Her beauty went to my head like strong wine. And there, in that forest, beneath the burning sky, amidst the perfume of the magnolias, her enchanting beauty was full of temptations from which no man would flee.

'Ah, Carmen!' I said. 'Who knows which of us will return alive to Calcutta!'

'You are joking, aren't you, captain?'

'On a tiger hunt one must always remember that the tiger is a cunning beast: he understands the mind of his greatest enemy and the mind of whoever will be most sadly missed.'

'No one would be more sadly missed today than you, captain.'

'Only today?'

'Always, and you know why.'

Suddenly my horse stopped short.

'The tiger! The tiger!' shouted the natives.

The horses in front drew back; the sepoys fell into single file. The dogs barked, the bearers uttered guttural cries, and the elephant silently stretched out its trunk. A sad, solemn silence fell, and a sudden hot gust of wind rustled the undergrowth.

Before us lay a clearing bathed in dazzling sunlight. On the other side was a stand of tamarind trees. This was obviously where the ferocious beast slept. I glanced round at Don Nicazio and saw that he looked pale and ill at ease.

'Don Nicazio! Fire the first round, the alarm signal!'

Don Nicazio spurred his horse and rode over to join me, muttering breathlessly:

'I need to get onto the elephant. Carmen mustn't be left alone, she could be in danger...'

I summoned the bearers, who unfolded the narrow bamboo ladder they used to help visitors onto the elephant's back. The mahout was dozing, sprawled out over the animal's vast neck. Don Nicazio eagerly scaled the ladder, flung himself inside the howdah, and from there, fascinated and fearful, peered out through the crack between the curtains.

But then Carmen decided that she did not wish to stay in the howdah. She begged, she pleaded, she wanted to be on a horse, to be able to smell the wild beast.

'Get me down from here, get me down! I didn't come all this way to sit in a birdcage!'

There was no suitable saddle for a woman nor a reliable enough horse. Carmen could not come down from the howdah. Then I had a strange, dangerous, tempting idea: she could sit behind me on my horse. I told her this.

She was so excited that she nearly missed her footing as she grabbed at the ropes securing the howdah to the elephant's belly; then she ran, placed one foot in my stirrup, threw one arm about my waist and, with a neat bound, seated herself behind me. It was most unwise, the other officers exclaimed. Carmen insisted and held me tight against the curve of her breast, laughing and vowing that not even the claws of the tiger could drag her from that seat.

The bearers took up their tridents and readied the dogs. Because I now had Carmen behind me, I had stationed myself at the rear of the group, motionless and watchful, my feet firm in the stirrups, my eyes fixed on the dense thicket of tamarinds.

But I heard neither growls nor the rustling of vegetation.

Carmen squeezed me excitedly.

'Go on! Go on!' she urged quietly. 'Give the signal to attack!'

I raised my revolver and fired. The noise reverberated around us, and immediately we heard a dull, hoarse, lugubrious roar: the tiger's response. It was close by, among the first line of tamarinds. The dogs started barking.

'Stay together everyone!' called the old Brahman, who had climbed a palm tree, from where he was watching, sniffing the air and issuing orders.

The Mystery of the Sintra Road

Everyone kept their sword or trident at the ready, waiting for the tiger to appear. I had given Carmen a knife. In one hand – the hand holding the reins - I had a heavy calibre revolver and in the other a dagger with a curved blade.

Suddenly, the bushes shook, the tall grass bent, and we became aware of a hot, fetid breath, the smell of blood, and, with a roar, the tiger appeared in front of the hunters and stood stock still in the middle of the clearing.

It had a long body, short thick legs, a bony head, and fierce, tawny eyes that shifted perpetually and convulsively back and forth; its tongue, as red as clotted blood, hung from its mouth.

For a few seconds, the tiger crept very slowly forward, its tail flicking. Then, with a deep-throated yowl, it sprang. But the dogs, racing towards it, took it in mid-air, by the ears, by the thick skin of its neck, by the legs, biting, tearing, snarling as they swarmed over it. Some were quickly torn to pieces.

And at the instant when the beast, having shaken off the dogs, stood alone and magnificent, its head held high, the Brahman gave a signal. Two bullets flew forth. The tiger gave a roar and dropped to the ground, wounded. Almost immediately it got up again and hurled itself at the men. They were all holding their tridents and daggers, and the tiger's belly was pierced by the sharp blades, but not before it had seized one of the bearers in its claws and ripped open his chest. The others, as one, plunged their knives into the animal's body, and yet, even while succumbing to their weight and its wounds, and even though pierced by a bullet, it still struggled ferociously and tore, in its agony, at the body of the poor native.

'Hold your fire!' shouted the Brahman.

I was transfixed. Carmen clung to me, eyes ablaze, body trembling, giving little yelps of excitement. The tiger lay stretched out and bleeding copiously. I could not take my eyes off it, registering the slightest twitch of its muscles. Suddenly, I saw it gather its strength and take a flying leap at Carmen and myself. In what must have been pure reflex action, I fired a bullet into the ear of the horse we were riding. It fell instantly to its knees and we were thrown to the ground. As it leapt, the tiger skimmed our heads and landed some way off, where it lay writhing on the ground. I sprang to my feet, rushed towards the tiger and swiftly drove my dagger between its front legs, straight through its heart. The tiger was dead. I crouched down and with a saw-toothed Indian knife hacked off a paw and presented it to Carmen.

'Hurrah!' everyone cried, and the sound echoed throughout the forest.

Carmen went over to the dead tiger, stroked its velvet pelt and touched the blood flowing from its wounds with the tips of her fingers.

And still the hunters cheered.

Carmen threw herself into my arms and planted an enthusiastic kiss on my forehead, saying loudly:

'He saved my life! I owe him my life!' And then, more quietly she murmured in my ear: 'I love you.'

Evening was coming on, and with aching limbs and a great thirst, we started back to Calcutta, resting briefly at an indigo plantation. And at nightfall, singing and holding aloft burning torches, we set off gaily to Calcutta along a safe road through the forest. In the torchlight the trees took on whimsical shapes; birds woke up and fluttered away; we heard the sound of fleeing jackals. We were like the return of a barbarian hunting party straight out of the ancient legends of India.

Carmen had opened the curtains of the howdah. I was riding alongside her on the dead bearer's horse. She leaned towards me and said softly:

The Mystery of the Sintra Road

'I swear that I love you as only we Cubans can love. I swear that, come what may, I will always put your life before mine, I shall happily face every danger and be your creature, and I ask only one thing of you.'

'And what is that?'

'That from time to time, when you've nothing better to do, you will spare a thought for me.'

The moment, the location, the pungent perfumes and fantastical shadows of the forest, the flickering torches, Carmen's marvellous, fateful beauty, the gunshots, the sound of the elephant trumpeting, the horses neighing, the jackals howling, had so confused and excited me that, losing all sense and logic, I said:

'And I swear that I will love you too and always be faithful to you, and I ask only that on the day you see that I've forgotten you, you will kill me!'

She took my proffered hand and, with a humble show of affection, like a wild animal following a scent, she leaned right out of the howdah and kissed my fingertips.

The night sky, meanwhile, filled up with enormous glittering stars.

V

At lunch on the third day of the voyage on the Ceylon, the day before we sighted Malta, one of the English officers mentioned that it was the twenty-eighth birthday of His Royal Highness, the Prince of Wales. Most of the officers on board had met the Prince and held his character and his Byronic temperament in high regard. They resolved, with the captain's consent, to celebrate the event by waltzing on deck that night, by the light of a vast lantern.

The birthday dinner was a noisy affair; the champagne sparkled like liquid opal in the cut-glass goblets; the pale ale foamed; the sherry fizzed with soda water. The lovely Carmen, in her peculiarly agitated state, was the life and soul of that long, lavish banquet.

There were toasts to Queen Victoria and to the young English princes, to the First Lord of the Admiralty, to the P & O Line, and a well-to-do Englishman made a speech welcoming 'Our foreign guests, the Count and Countess of W.'

'I propose a toast too,' said Carmen suddenly.

Glasses clinked, corks popped.

'Here's to the tiger hunt! To howdahs with white curtains! To hunters who save the lives of the ladies riding pillion on their horses,' she cried.

Most of the diners did not understand, some laughed, but since it was such a novel toast, it was greeted with applause.

'How very shocking!' exclaimed the elderly Irishwoman beside me, who was clearly fascinated by the purser's ample belly.

'Not at all, madam,' I said. 'It's merely her Latin blood.

That vivacity, those flashing eyes, all come from her Latin blood. And if she were now to hurl every bottle in the room at the ceiling and smash them all, that, too, would be her Latin blood.'

The Irishwoman was listening with studious attention.

'If, suddenly, she were to take the ship's wheel and run us onto the rocks, it would be her Latin blood. If she were disrespectfully to snatch your spectacles from your nose, madam...'

'Oh!' the Irishwoman cried.

'That, too, would be her Latin blood!'

'Well, it's all very shocking this Latin blood business!'

The British officers were captivated by Carmen.

In the meantime, the ladies had withdrawn, and a group of serious, committed drinkers had gathered round the count. Cognac and spirits were being served. Carmen had stayed among the men, drinking, laughing and smoking cigarettes.

The countess had gone up on deck on the arm of Captain Rytmel.

As for Don Nicazio, he was munching stolidly through a plate of cheese garnished with mustard, salad, vinegar, salt, horseradish sauce and light ground pepper from Ceylon.

I do not remember how, but the talk turned to women and the female character.

Carmen immediately said: 'I can understand the devout seriousness of Englishwomen; after all, it's the way they're brought up. They were born to be stiff, blonde, cold, and readers of *The Edinburgh Review*. They're true to their character: if they were any less lively they would be porcelain figurines, a little more and they would be "shocking". But what I hate most is the false Germanic innocence, the virginal manner of creatures who, given their country's sunny clime, ought to live more passionately. A young woman from Spain, Italy or Portugal only plays the part of an English "Miss" and puts on fanciful, hypocritical, pious airs in order to conceal a lover – or possibly two.'

These words, I was sure, were intended as a cutting comment on the countess's natural reserve, for she, being blonde, discreet and gentle, was in marked contrast to loud, dark Carmen.

'Forgive me, Señora,' I said in Spanish, 'but these days, seriousness is prized above vivacity. Vivacity may be desirable at the theatre, in a comic opera, in a *corps de ballet*, or in engravings depicting a journey through Spain, but it is quite unseemly in a drawing room.'

Carmen turned slightly pale and fixed me with her gaze.

'*Caballero,*' she asked, '*¿es usted pedante de retórica?*'

I laughed, held out my hand to her in friendship, and it all ended in another toast.

Mr Colney, who had overheard this exchange, found the phrase *pedante de retórica* both picturesque and strange, and, laughing, exclaimed to the other Englishmen:

'Oh, I see, a teacher of rhetoric, most amusing!'

Meanwhile, night was falling and I was feeling weary. I withdrew then to my cabin and dozed for a while. At nine o'clock I went up on deck again. What I found surprised me.

There was neither moon nor stars nor wind. At the far end of the poop deck, an enormous lantern was lit. Its bluish flame flickered and grew tall, creating all manner of strange shadows. The sound of flirtatious laughter emerged from dark corners. A flute and a fiddle could be heard, and already one or two couples were waltzing around the skylight on the deck.

In the lantern light, the ship's rigging became long, blue lines, calling to mind a legendary galleon, the ship of Satan.

The Mystery of the Sintra Road

Some of the ladies were dressed in white, and when they waltzed past the lantern, their dresses were lit with a phosphorescent glow; the white of their gowns took on spectral tones and their shining golden hair a kind of deathly charm; indeed, there was something of the *danse macabre* about the whole affair.

Carmen, possessed by the same excitement as the lantern flame, linked arms with one man, waltzed with another; she poked fun, bandied jokes, fluttered her fan. Don Nicazio sat beside the rail, snoring. From time to time, someone would pour punch down his throat, whereupon he would open a slit of an eye, mutter 'Thank you, gentlemen' and fall asleep again.

'Where's Captain Rytmel?' Carmen asked suddenly. 'Bring him here. I want to dance with him.'

Rytmel was talking quietly with the countess well away from the light.

'Rytmel! Rytmel!' several voices called.

We saw him approach reluctantly, but laughing nonetheless.

'I demand a waltz!' Carmen cried.

The flute began to play. Carmen placed her hand on the captain's shoulder, and they started to dance in wide circles; her skirts billowed, her hair came unpinned; the light of the great lantern trembled; and as they span rapidly, giddily around, caught up in some Byronic Devil's dance, they appeared almost to fly. She leaned back in Rytmel's arms, her head lolling, her eyes closed, her lips parted and moist.

'Bravo! Bravo!' shouted the British passengers encircling them.

The flickering light from the lantern rose up and joined in the waltz. Carmen and Rytmel passed like shadows, borne on a light breeze and lit by the phantasmagorical light of that blue flame. The frenetic notes of the flute pursued them; they

The Mystery of the Sintra Road

seemed about to take flight and disappear up through the rigging and into the night. The Englishmen cheered and waved their hats:

'Hip hip hooray!'

I had noticed, meanwhile, that the countess was strangely tense. She was watching from a distance with feverishly bright eyes, her bosom heaving. Scarcely had the waltz ended than she took Captain Rytmel's arm, and I heard her say to him in a grave, reproachful voice:

'Don't dance any more.'

I was surprised. What was afoot? A secret? Surely not. The countess, so noble, so proper, so timid!

I went over to her.

'Cousin, it's late. Would you like to go to your cabin?'

She looked at me, smiling serenely:

'No. Why?'

And she went off with Captain Rytmel to the far end of the awning where, in the daytime, people went to smoke, but which was now deserted and almost dark.

I followed mechanically behind and arrived unnoticed from the other direction, where, almost unintentionally, I overheard the captain say:

'Why do you doubt me? I despise that woman. Our friendship, yours and mine, remains unaffected, untouched. She was a mere passing fancy, a momentary fling. Now she's barely even a memory...'

They continued speaking in quiet, melancholy tones. I went and leaned against the rail for a few moments. The wind had got up and the steamer was starting to pitch.

As I was heading back to join the rowdier elements, I happened to hear Carmen saying:

'Where on earth has that Captain Rytmel got to? He's

disappeared with the Countess again. Have you seen him? Let's go and find them.'

I spied a plot. Unseen, I quickly made my way to the smoking-tent, entered, sat down on a bench and immediately started speaking loudly to no one in particular. The tent was lit by a single lantern. On seeing me appear so abruptly, the countess turned pale with irritation.

At the same time, some British officers arrived, shouting:

'Rytmel! Rytmel!'

I stepped forward, saying:

'What's up? We're in here. We don't feel like dancing any more.'

The officers moved off. The countess saw that I had saved her from a highly equivocal situation and gave me a look of profound gratitude.

'Go below, countess, go below,' I urged in a whisper.

She turned to Rytmel with a sad smile:

'It's getting cold. Goodnight!'

Rytmel rejoined the other officers.

I felt a desire to take my revenge on Carmen, and it occurred to me to make her once more the centre of all the noise and revelry.

'Señorita!' I called to her, 'Sing us a *seguidilla* or a *habanera*! It would have a special charm out on the high seas. There are Englishmen here who've never heard the music of our countries.'

'Yes, yes!' they all shouted. 'A *seguidilla!*'

Carmen refused at first and made as if to go down to her cabin.

'No, no! Stay, *señorita*. Sing for us!'

The requests became insistent, raucous. In the end, she gave in, and her strong, languid voice rose up in the midst of a silence broken only by the monotonous throb of the engine and the strengthening wind:

A la puerta de mi casa
Hay una piedra muy larga...

'At the door of my house
Is a wide stone step...'

The Englishmen were ecstatic. The applause at the end sounded like fireworks exploding. Glasses were refilled and someone shouted:

'Three cheers for Señorita Carmen! Hip hip hooray!'

The cheering echoed out to sea.

She was deeply embarrassed, aware of how compromising her position was, alone and the object of such male acclamation.

'Well,' I exclaimed with Mephistophelian good cheer, 'it's just a shame the ladies weren't still up to hear you sing, and that it's just us men on the spree.'

Carmen shot me a hate-filled glance; vengeance was mine.

Meanwhile, one of the Englishmen, Mr Reder, continued to raise his glass of punch:

'To Carmen Puebla! Hip hip hooray!' he cried.

'Hooray!' responded the others enthusiastically.

'Hooray!' came the dull echo from the sea.

A bell rang. It was eleven o'clock. The lanterns were doused. Almost everybody went straight to their beds. A strong northwest wind was blowing. The ship was beginning to roll more violently. We were within sight of Africa. With the deck almost deserted, I was more keenly aware of the howling of the wind in the rigging and the slap of the waves against the bows of the ship.

A bell marked the quarter hours, and each time, the melancholy voice of the sailor on watch called out:

'All's well.'

The Mystery of the Sintra Road

It was two o'clock when I went down to my cabin. I soon fell into that vague, confused state that is neither sleep nor wakefulness, but a vague waking dream that takes control of the mind. I saw the countess pass by on a cloud with Rytmel, happily drinking beer; I saw Carmen dressed as a nun and walking the tightrope; and these visions merged with the rolling of the ship and the churning of the propeller.

Suddenly I felt a terrifying thud. The ship shuddered, stopped, and a great shout rang out.

VI

I jumped up and ran to the door of my cabin.

'Steward!' I shouted, 'steward!'

The steward appeared, dishevelled and only half-dressed.

'What's happened?' I asked him. 'Are we going to sink? Have we struck a rock?'

'I don't know. It's probably nothing, the ship's very sturdy.'

Up above, I could hear the sound of sailors running about, as people only do when they are in danger.

'We're done for,' I thought, pulling on my clothes in anguished haste.

At every moment, I was expecting to feel the ship sinking, going under, and huge waves come crashing in, flooding the cabin.

I went up on deck. There were lanterns everywhere. Nearly everyone was up. The white nightshirts and dressing gowns lent the groups a more lugubrious tone. The officers remained impassive.

'What's happened? What's happened?' I asked someone.

'No one seems to know. The engine's broken down. And we're in the middle of a howling gale…'

'Then we're lost!'

'No, the ship's very sturdy,' the man insisted.

Nearby, voices were saying:

'The captain should lower the lifeboats.'

The sky was clear, the stars were shining. The wind blew ever stronger. The ship was rolling from port to starboard in the way large dead fish roll back and forth on the surface of the water. I looked at the stars, the impassive sky, the black water,

The Mystery of the Sintra Road

and felt an immense disdain for life.

All around me I heard conflicting versions of what was happening. Some said we were going to heave to and wait patiently for the storm to come. Others said that the ship was lost. An officer walking by said:

'Please, gentlemen, this is nothing, nothing that can't be fixed. It happened to me twice en route from Aden to Bombay.'

There was no real panic, though; things were as tranquil and normal as if we were sailing down a wide river in broad daylight. At last, the ship's captain appeared.

'Ladies and gentlemen,' he said, 'there's nothing to worry about. We have a major problem with the engine, that's all, and I'm not sure I'll be able to steer the ship at the moment. In calm seas, yes, perhaps, but with the wind that's heading for us now, I can see us being delayed for four or five days.'

In the meantime, the wind had grown stronger. Flakes of sea foam were flying everywhere. We could hear a rumble on the horizon like a thousand marching battalions.

Most of the English passengers, heavy with sleep and wine, had gone back to their cabins, unconcerned about the danger. A few ladies, apprehensive and numb with cold, remained on deck.

Down below, the engineers and mechanics were working ceaselessly.

Captain Rytmel came over to me.

'We're in danger and needlessly so too. That idiot of a captain sailed too far south, and so we're close to the coast of Africa. If the gale catches us now, it'll push us still further towards the coast. But Pernester, the engineer on board, is a man of genius. Where's the countess?'

We went down to the day lounge. The countess was there, seated at a table, serene and pale.

The Mystery of the Sintra Road

'Come up on deck, cousin,' I said. 'At least from there you can see the sky, the water and the coming danger too!'

We went up and leaned against the rail, clinging to the ropes. The plunging waves, fringed with foam, glittered beneath the vague, misty starlight. The wind was terrifying.

'Why don't they lower the boats?' asked the countess. 'At least one could put up a brave fight then. But for the ship to be cast up on the shores of Africa like a dead whale...'

She would have preferred to take a turn about the deck, but the ship was rolling so violently now that she had to hold on to Captain Rytmel's arm. I could barely keep my balance. There was something threatening about the way the waves pounded the sides of the ship. The ship's bell sounded the hours and quarter hours with a disconsolate clang. More lanterns had been hoisted up to the tops of the masts. The frightful moaning of the wind resembled the mournful cries of condemned souls.

I went down to the saloon for a drop of cognac against the biting cold outside. Carmen was sitting quietly on a sofa at the back, staring into space, her hands folded.

'We're going to die, aren't we?' she said.

'Are you scared?' I asked.

'A little, yes, scared of being drowned. Dying from a bullet or a knife wound wouldn't worry me, but here, for no reason, amid the hostile elements, it's too cruel. But at least I won't die alone! Your lovely cousin will die as well.'

'Why do you hate the poor countess?' I asked her, smiling.

'Hate her? I don't hate her in the least. I merely think her a fake. I loathe that sentimental air she affects. She brings shame on the Iberian Peninsula. That's all.'

'Nonsense. It's because you think Captain Rytmel is showing too much interest in her.'

'And of what concern to me is that gentleman?'

The Mystery of the Sintra Road

She gave a short laugh.

By this time, the stifling air in the lounge and the roll of the ship were making me queasy. I went up on deck again. The countess and Rytmel were no longer strolling about. I realised that they had gone to sit inside the smoking-tent. Despite the roar of the wind, I could hear their voices through the canvas.

Even though it went against all my better instincts – for at such moments, human behaviour is not subject to normal criteria – a double impulse: an irresistible desire to know the countess's state of mind and the certainty that we were in real danger persuaded me to eavesdrop on their conversation. Like any good spy, I pressed my ear to the canvas.

Rytmel was saying:

'Are you afraid of dying?'

'Very much and not at all,' replied the countess. 'Very much, because your friendship, which is my main interest in life, will die with me. And not at all, because, frankly, am I really happy?'

'If my friendship is of such importance to you…'

The countess did not respond.

'Oh, I know exactly what you mean,' said Rytmel. 'Do you know why you're not happy, in spite of my friendship? It's because it isn't just my friendship that your heart desires. No, let me speak. It is love, deep, immutable, all-powerful love, a love that will be with you every minute of your life and in your every thought; a love that lives on pleasure and on sacrifice, that will be your only reason for living, your hope, your consolation, your absolute ideal, so ardent that you cannot look away from it, so elevated that it fills your soul…'

'Hush, hush,' said the countess. 'It's madness to talk like that. Let's go for a walk. Let's look at the sea.'

The wind now was terrible. The ocean was flecked with

The Mystery of the Sintra Road

white as far as the eye could see. The *Ceylon* was floundering, helpless and directionless. Meanwhile, they were still working on the engine.

Rytmel continued talking to the countess.

'Hush, hush,' she was saying quietly, wearily.

'No, I must tell you: that word "friendship" is wrong. Two hours' hence we could be dead. When death is nigh, it's only right to speak sincerely. And so I will say it. I love you. No, don't go. The wind will carry away my confession. I love you. If we are guilty for saying those words, the sea will make a good tomb and salt water cleanses everything. I love you.'

'Don't say that. You're mistaken, you're just being kind. Anyway, what would love bring us? Only scorn or suffering.'

I could hardly hear them now. They were speaking very softly. The storm was almost upon us. The ship groaned fearfully. The ropes had snapped in the wind and they now hissed like snakes. The sailors were rushing about on deck. We heard shouts of command, the sound of hammers, the men working on the engine. A wave broke over the bow, flooding the deck.

All of a sudden, I heard a movement beneath the awning: the countess stood up; she spoke in a loud, tremulous voice.

'Captain Rytmel, tell me on your honour, do you think we are going to die?'

'I believe so, countess.'

'Very well, then. I want to tell you that I love you!'

And a moment later:

'Oh, I love you so much,' she repeated in an explosion of passion. 'Now that I know I will die pure, I want to die honest too. I adore you.'

At that point, a strange noise ran through the ship.

I felt a powerful vibration, a resistance to the waves. The

The Mystery of the Sintra Road

vessel was no longer an inert object. She had come back to life. Then I heard the propeller... the propeller! The boat was moving. I watched the bow smashing through the waves. We were on our way! I rushed to the hatch that led down to the engine room.

'What's happening?' I asked an officer who was emerging from below.

'Another of Pernester's miracles!'

Everyone came running. It was an anxious moment.

The skipper climbed rapidly up the polished iron ladder from the engine room to the deck.

He was beaming.

'Can you believe it, Pernester has...'

'Yes, yes,' I interrupted, 'but what now?'

'We're on our way again. So, blow wind, blow! Do your worst. Tomorrow we shall be in Malta.'

'Bravo, Pernester! Well done!' we all shouted.

The great man climbed up from the engine room, breathless, impassive, red-faced, still sporting the white tie he had been wearing at dinner. He mopped his bald head with a handkerchief and said in a matter-of-fact way:

'Right, now what I need is a nice pint of bitter.'

VII

The next night we arrived in Malta beneath a starless sky. The water in the bay was still and black. Valletta rose before us like a mountain, stitched with lights, as grand as a castle. The gondolas plied silently back and forth around the steamer, each with a tall, slender lantern at the stern. There was a great silence, an ineffable peace. Even the gondoliers rowed quietly. Everything was gentle and orderly – a blend of Italian mystery and British policing.

We disembarked, and the count, the countess and I, along with Don Nicazio and Carmen, went to the Clarence Hotel in Royal Street, opposite the famous Church of St John. Captain Rytmel had his lodgings with the other British officers. Our first three days in Malta were spent visiting the many historic places: the Palace of the Grand Masters, the palaces known as 'Inns of Residence', which belonged to the various nationalities of the Order of the Knights of St John, the broad white streets with their tall Renaissance-style houses, as well as Città-Vecchia, Bingemma, Buskett and the Isle of Calypso, so full of charm according to Homer, but, in reality, a large, wave-washed rock full of dark caves. From the first day, Rytmel and a few officers came to dine each evening at the Clarence Hotel. The countess always took her meals in her rooms. The source of all the noise and nuisance at the table was Carmen, who had lost no time in allowing herself to be pursued by Monsieur Perny, a young Frenchman, witty and nimble, blond and passionate, who, as he himself said, 'travelled out of sheer boredom'.

Carmen avoided Rytmel. It was as if they had agreed, by mutual consent, to keep a discreet distance from each other.

Rytmel, on the other hand, invariably joined our excursions into the countryside, to the fortifications and the bay, and he came with us to the theatre every night. The flowing golden tresses of a girl who was always to be seen in the front row of the stalls, had immediately captivated the count. She had a fair complexion and Maltese eyes, the genteel manners of an English 'Miss', the swaying gait of an Andalusian, and was, in fact, the effulgent Mademoiselle Rize, an out-of-work dancer. Otherwise, the count would not be separated from Rytmel.

There in Malta, I was less aware of the countess and Captain Rytmel's comings and goings. Caught up in the company of British officers, with sea excursions, trips to the countryside, suppers and card games, I often did not see the countess for a day or even two. I realised, though, that she was entirely ruled by her passion for him. And Rytmel, it seemed to me, was also hopelessly in love.

I do not intend to explain why I decided to take no closer interest in that situation. I am sure you will understand clearly enough my motives for not knowing, not seeing, not noticing, for opting for the most complete discretion.

Shortly after our arrival in Malta, we had become acquainted with Lord Grenley, who was wintering there in the hope of shaking off his 'blue devils'. He had sailed from England in his magnificent yacht, *The Romantic,* which we would see tacking across the bay each day with the sun glinting on its polished copper fittings and elegant white hull. Lord Grenley kept close company with the count. He was also a good friend of Rytmel's.

The paths of Carmen and the countess rarely crossed, other than at the theatre where Carmen would shoot impertinent glances at the countess, who remained utterly and proudly impervious. Carmen had no contact with 'the ladies' and was thus deprived of opportunities to vent her spleen on the countess – by meaningful looks and bitterly ironic remarks – as she had on the seven metres of the ship's deck, and now had to take her revenge at the dining table of the Clarence Hotel, making all kinds of veiled remarks and caustic comments aimed at Captain Rytmel. Her current tactic was to set Monsieur Perny against the officer, egging him on to oppose all Rytmel's ideas and opinions, although I could not tell whether this was in the perverse hope of provoking a duel or merely for the pleasure of seeing him contradicted at every turn.

One day, the conversation was of India. Rytmel was talking about how England had transformed the country. A roar of laughter interrupted him. It was Perny.

'Did you laugh?' asked Rytmel, colouring slightly.

'Did I laugh?' replied Perny, 'Monsieur, I'm positively splitting my sides, I'm in paroxysms. Just how exactly has England transformed India? By transforming poetry, imagination, sunlight, into something plain, trivial and covered in coal dust? I have been to India, gentlemen. Do you know what those English transformers have done? They have translated the mysterious poem that was India into the mercantile prose of *The Morning Post*. They pile up sacks of peppercorns outside temples; they treat the noble Indian race, the mother of idealism, like Irish dogs; they have steamboats plying the divine Ganges at three shillings a head; they force the temple dancers to drink pale ale and teach them to play cricket; they clear the sacred forest to build gas-lit squares; and, above all, gentlemen, they dethrone ancient, mysterious rulers, who are almost as delicate as ivory, and replace them with side-whiskered old reprobates, riddled with debt, red-faced from drinking too much brown ale, and who, instead of being packed off to Botany Bay in irons, have been appointed governors of India! And who is it who does all this? An island made in equal parts of ice and roast beef, inhabited by beer-bellied pirates in high starched collars!'

Smiling, Captain Rytmel arose, walked over to me and said, 'After supper, will you kindly ask that crackpot comedian to nominate a place, a time and his chosen weapon.'

Then he calmly resumed his seat. As dessert was served, I took Perny to one side and conveyed my friend's words to him.

Perny laughed, said that he had a high regard for the English, that he appreciated their services to India, that Carmen had put him up to contradicting Rytmel, whom he thought a fine gentleman and of whom he begged his most humble pardon. His place was everywhere, he added, his time was always, and his weapon was whatever Captain Rytmel might choose.

'But given that explanation,' I said, 'there's no need for weapons.'

'Ah, I forgot,' said the Frenchman. 'There is still one little thing: I consider Captain Rytmel's hairstyle to be deeply offensive to my character and to the dignity of France. Now that does require reparation.'

The seconds were nominated that night. It was arranged that the duel would not take place in Malta. Rytmel was an officer, and armed duels in military barracks carried the most severe penalties. Since they were on a British island, however, they could not avoid fighting on British soil. It was agreed, therefore, that the duel would take place at sea, a 'cannon-shot' from the coast. Lord Grenley gave them the loan of his yacht, and we set out in the early morning with a stiff breeze and in bright sunshine. It all happened very quickly. We dropped anchor five miles from Malta, the British flag was lowered and the crew furled the sails; since the two adversaries were of equal rank, one was despatched to the stern and the other to the prow. The sun was to starboard. It was seven o'clock in the morning and wisps of white cloud still lingered in the sky. Lord Grenley gave the signal, the two adversaries fired. Perny dropped his pistol and fell to his knees. He had been gravely wounded, with his collarbone broken. He was laid down in a cabin that had been made ready. The British flag was raised once more and we sailed back to Malta, by which time it was late afternoon.

I immediately went to Don Nicazio's rooms. Carmen was there alone.

'Do you know what you've done?' I asked her. 'Perny has been wounded.'

'Nothing that can't be healed. I'll look after him myself. Now what really *is* serious, is what's going on in this hotel. I don't know exactly what, but I have my suspicions. Tell the count to keep an eye on the countess!'

I shrugged my shoulders, smiled, and went straight to the countess's rooms. There I found the count, Rytmel and Lord Grenley. Perny had been declared out of danger. Rytmel was relieved.

We talked blithely. We arranged to visit the island of Gozo, eight kilometres from Malta. Lord Grenley had suggested making the excursion the following day and was again offering his yacht for the purpose. The count was shilly-shallying, saying that, in his current nervous state, the sea would only upset him.

'It's that confounded Rize woman!' he told me in a low voice. 'I've promised her an outing to Bingemma tomorrow.'

'So?'

'You go with the countess. Grenley is going and Rytmel too. You really must do me this favour. Mademoiselle Rize is very demanding, but then, poor thing, she has Maltese blood!'

Later, when I was returning to my room, a figure approached me in the corridor and took me by the hand.

'Listen,' a voice breathed.

It was Carmen.

'If you are a man of honour, take care tomorrow on the trip to Gozo.'

And she vanished.

VIII

The following morning at six o'clock, I went to Rytmel's lodgings. The countess had been in an acute state of nerves all night and had barely slept, but she did not wish to miss the chance of a trip to Gozo. I found Lord Grenley taking tea with Rytmel.

It appeared, from their weary faces, that they had not slept either. Lord Grenley certainly hadn't because he was wearing the same jacket as on the previous evening, and still had in his buttonhole a now faded sprig of cape jasmine.

'Nice morning!' said Rytmel.

They had opened the window to let in the fresh air. Birds were singing in the trees in the garden.

'Yes, lovely!' I said. 'The countess was ill all night, but is determined to go on the excursion. By the way, Rytmel, do you have a revolver?'

'Whatever for?'

'They tell me there's great fun to be had shooting at the birds that hide in the caves on Gozo. It creates a bizarre echo apparently. We definitely need a gun.'

'Take this,' Rytmel said, handing me a small revolver with an inlaid handle. 'I have my pockets full enough already with sketch books and pens. Oh, you do know, don't you, that Lord Grenley isn't coming?'

'But why, sir?'

'I have to attend some awful official lunch with the Governor,' replied Lord Grenley 'Damned shame.'

At seven o'clock we went to find the Countess. Her husband accompanied us to the quay at Marsa-Muscheto.

The Mystery of the Sintra Road

I noticed on boarding the yacht that there was a larger crew than usual and that the helmsman was an Arab.

We set sail in a brisk wind at eight o'clock in the morning; the gulls flew around the sails; the white houses of Valletta had a rosy blush to them; we could hear military music; the sky was delightfully clear and blue.

The countess, a little over-excited, gazed out with eager anticipation at the vast glittering azure sea, free and boundless.

'How unpredictable women can be!' I thought to myself. 'This proud, discreet lady is delighted to find herself the sole woman on a yacht at sea, surrounded by young men. For her that's almost an adventure in itself!'

I admit I felt somewhat awkward. There I was, the prim representative of husband, family and duty acting as chaperone to that pair of charming young lovers, yes, God preserve us, an ardent, passionate, twenty-four-year-old charged with playing policeman to their delightful romance! I told myself, however, that the sea is wide, the sky infinite, and honour still exists! In two hours we would be on Gozo, where we would explore, laugh, dine, and at nightfall, when the Almighty had scattered his flock of stars across the sky, we would sail back in the breeze and the phosphorescent dark, silently listening to the Arab helmsman singing sweet melodies from Syria, and to the languid murmur of the waves.

Rytmel had gone below to give instructions for our lunch. The countess remained standing at the prow of the yacht. She was wearing a chequered dress and ankle boots, and was wrapped in an ample Scottish cloak. I had never seen her look so lovely.

We sailed along the coast of Malta in a westerly wind.

We were approaching the island of Comino when Rytmel

came to tell us lunch was served, and that in half an hour's time we would be disembarking at the Calle Maggiara in Gozo. We would visit the island's many attractions first, then we would board the yacht again to sail round Gozo to see the terrifying caves where the sea plunges down into an abyss, and at nightfall we would arrive back at the quay in Valletta.

Lunch was a cheerful affair. There was champagne, a splendid Rhine wine, a Moorish stew, and even a piano in the dining room. After lunch, Captain Rytmel, who appeared oddly preoccupied, sat at the piano playing endless improvisations. And on we sailed. When I happened to take out my watch, I got a terrible fright. It was two and a half hours since we had gone below decks. Yet, when lunch had started, we had been only half an hour from going ashore at Maggiara! Why then were we continuing to sail? I hurried up on deck. The Arab helmsman was at the wheel. There was almost no land in sight; we were on the open sea, running before the wind at an extraordinary speed.

'Where's Gozo?' I shouted to the helmsman first in English, then in French and finally in Italian.

He did not even deign to look at me. A moment later, Rytmel and the countess came up from below.

'Where's Gozo?' I asked Rytmel.

'Perhaps there's too much mist,' he replied vaguely and looked away.

The horizon, however, was utterly clear and cloudless for as far as one could see. In the distance there was a hazy smudge of land, but we were racing away from it!

I ran to look at the compass. We were sailing westwards.

'We're sailing in the wrong direction, Captain Rytmel! Away from Malta! What's going on? Where are we heading?'

For several long seconds Rytmel looked at the countess,

then he turned to me and said:

'We're going to Alexandria.'

In a flash, I understood everything. Rytmel was eloping with the countess!

I stared at Rytmel and, trembling, said to him:

'This is scandalous!'

He turned terribly pale, but the countess intervened and in a tremulous voice cried:

'No! It is I! I am the one who is going to Alexandria.'

'In that case, cousin, I am the one who is disgraced.'

There was a silence. The countess's eyes brimmed with tears. She ran to me, grasped one of my hands and said, sobbing:

'What do you mean? It's no one's fault. I love this man, and I'm eloping with him.'

Rytmel had taken my other hand.

'It's too late,' he said. 'We cannot turn back. We've taken an irretrievable step.'

I gave up: this entirely unforeseen situation had left me reasonless, voiceless, will-less.

I, the count's friend, was an accomplice in this elopement! And as if that were not enough, standing there between that love-struck pair, each of whom was pleading with me and clasping one of my hands, I felt utterly ridiculous – and that only added to my despair. The countess, meanwhile, went on:

'Cousin,' she said, 'what does it matter? I know very well that I'm dishonoured. But what do you expect? Should I stay at my husband's side, knowing that I love another man, and living a perpetual lie, happily installed in ignominy? No, never! That would be truly disgraceful. At least this is honest. I'm breaking with the world, I've become an adventuress. I shall henceforth always be a fallen woman, but I'm keeping myself for one man alone and staying true to him.'

'Captain Rytmel,' I said, 'give the order for a boat to be lowered into the water.'

'What are you going to do?' shouted the countess.

'I'm going to strike out for land. Don't you see how shameless it was of you to bring me on board this boat?'

'You're mad,' said Rytmel. 'There's only one longboat on board. The wind's getting up, the sea's growing rougher. That longboat won't last ten minutes.'

'All the better! Give the order!' I shouted.

'Don't move, anyone!' bellowed Rytmel.

Then, turning to the countess:

'Tell him it would be certain death! He's not an accomplice in this! He was forced, tricked into it. He has nothing to answer for.'

'Give the order!' I shouted.

Suddenly, Rytmel seized an axe, ran to where the longboat was hanging and cut through the ropes securing it. The boat fell into the water with a dull splash and remained there, half-capsized, bobbing about like a corpse.

I stamped my foot in impotent rage.

'This is disgraceful, Captain Rytmel! Disgraceful!'

And for some absurd reason, wishing to vent my feelings by committing some violent act, I shouted to a group of sailors standing at the prow:

'Is there any Englishman here who values his flag?'

They all turned, astonished, but uncomprehending.

'Well then,' I cried, 'I declare that this flag is covering up a vile act, a dishonourable act, and I now spit on the face of England by spitting on the British flag.'

And, running to the stern, I spat, or made as if I were spitting, on the British flag hanging there. At that, one of the seamen obviously did understand my meaning, because he made a threatening move towards me.

'Stay where you are, everyone!' Rytmel shouted. 'I'm the one he's trying to offend. My friend,' he said, his voice breaking, 'you're right; when I deserted Malta I ceased to be a British officer. Now I'm an adventurer. This flag should not be here!'

He took a step forward and hauled down the flag.

And with a dramatic gesture as senseless as mine, he hurled the flag into the sea. The waves enveloped it, and, strangely, it unfolded itself upon the waves and for some moments lay spread out on the surface, serene and motionless, until it finally went under.

Then, in a romantic, passionate impulse, Rytmel snatched the countess's handkerchief from her, tied it to the halyard and rapidly hoist it up the flagpole, shouting:

'From now on *this* is our flag!'

In the midst of this madness, I felt as if I were caught up in some incoherent nightmare.

I moved and felt the revolver in my pocket. I don't know what deranged ideas of honour were in my mind, but I took it out, cocked it, and turned it on myself, crying:

'Bon voyage!'

'No!' screamed the countess.

IX

Rytmel hurled himself at me and grabbed the revolver.

I merely muttered:

'Fine! I'll do it at the first port we come to.'

The Countess stepped forward, looking white as a ghost, and said (I never will forget the tone of her voice):

'Rytmel, we must go back to Malta.'

'Back to Malta? Back to Malta? Why, for God's sake?'

I interrupted, babbling all kinds of nonsense:

'Rytmel, give me the revolver, let's be men about this. Our actions ought to be the equal of our characters. Nothing could be simpler. Passion cannot draw back nor honour yield. Death is the only solution. I will shoot myself, and then you two can flee as far away as you wish.'

But the countess, who was the only one of us who still seemed blessed with a glimmer of common sense, doggedly repeated the same words, in which I could hear her inner pain:

'Rytmel, we must go back to Malta.'

He looked at her for a moment, then a full awareness of the whole ghastly situation seemed to overwhelm and subdue him. His bowed his head and obeyed. He went to say a few words to the helmsman.

A moment later, we were once again heading for Malta.

A great silence fell, a weariness following that battle of the emotions. Rytmel was pacing briskly up and down the deck, and despite his unruffled countenance, I could sense the torment within.

'So here we are!' he exclaimed suddenly, stopping his pacing and folding his arms, with a strange fire in his eyes. 'It's all over. We're going back to Malta. What more do you want? What's left for us now? To say goodbye forever? Forever! We were going to Alexandria. We were safe, alone together, young, happy! And now? Happiness, love, passion, hope, joy, all gone. Ha! Poor me! They talk to me of honour, but what kind of honour is it that's going to kill me every day, uproot me from my paradise, make me the most wretched man on earth? Honour, you say! What's left for me to do? A bullet through the head in India. To die there, alone, like a dog.'

The countess kept her eyes fixed on the sea and said nothing.

Rytmel came and seized my arm in a desperate gesture:

'Don't you see? I was prepared to risk everything for her: dishonour, disgrace, scorn. I was prepared to leave the world behind, to betray my uniform, embrace poverty, ridicule, and all for her. A woman says to a man "I love you" and agrees to elope with him. She's there on the boat, and all of a sudden, only half an hour away from happiness, from paradise, when we're already out of sight of land, up pops a scruple, a pang of guilt, a nostalgia for her husband perhaps, the memory of a ball she once attended or of a flower that particularly suited her – and it's goodbye forever. And she wants to go back; and the man, miserable wretch, is left to suffer, cry, tear out his hair and die like a dog somewhere. My friend, I have no voice or strength; let the helmsman know that her ladyship the countess is in a hurry to reach land!'

'William! William!' cried the countess, rushing to him and clasping his hands. 'Don't you understand anything? In Malta, as in Alexandria, I'm yours, yours alone. Yours before God, yours before men.'

Shortly afterwards, we heard the distant sound of bells, the bells of Valetta. We could see land ahead.

It was the sweetest of hours; the air was indescribably clear.

The Mystery of the Sintra Road

We could already make out the whitewashed villages and Valletta's proud profile. The sun was just going down. Its last oblique rays set the city's balconies glittering. There were the flower-sellers on the quayside. Two gondolas came out to meet us. There was a great rustling of sails and much piping as the crew manoeuvred us into position, then we dropped anchor. We had arrived. The bells of Malta continued to ring out.

X

As soon as we had disembarked, I ran to the hotel. The count had not yet returned from his excursion to Bingemma with Mademoiselle Rize. Rytmel had shut himself up in his lodgings in a terrible state of rage and passion.

Carmen immediately came to my room, looking for me. She entered quickly, saying:

'Why have you come back?'

'So you knew?' I responded, astonished.

'Everything. Purely by chance. I knew that they wanted to elope. Rytmel was busy the whole night organising things. They had agreed to run away three days ago. Lord Grenley knew. And now?'

'Now,' I said, 'it's all over. Naturally, the countess will leave on the first steamer.'

'I doubt it. But if they don't leave, there'll be the most enormous scandal. It's terrible, I know, but what can I do? I love that man, I love Rytmel. More than that, I have an obligation towards him: he saved my life. But above all, it's this stupid passion that keeps gnawing away at me, that's killing me, although not as fast as I would like. I do everything I can to hasten my death. I wake up at night sweating, then go to stand on the terrace in the cold air. What is the point of living? My love for him is all I live for. It has grown even stronger since seeing him again. Who could help but adore him? Sometimes I even consider killing him!'

We talked for some time. A feverish light burned in the poor creature's marble-pale face. I tried to calm her. I was beginning to feel sorry for her.

The Mystery of the Sintra Road

The countess did not leave her room for two days. I told the count that she'd had a terrible fright on Gozo, during our visit to the sea caves, an area fraught with danger for any boat. I spent nearly all my time with Rytmel. Slowly, hope was being reborn in him. He was, with some distaste, adapting himself to a more rational, albeit less pure, situation. He was a recovering lover. And, at the end of five days (human nature is full of such compromises!), the countess was once again seen at the theatre, relaxed and radiant, and beside her white shoulders glinted Captain Rytmel's golden epaulettes!

We entered calmer waters then, with no romance and no conflict. Everyone's heart was beating more quietly and more gently. The count made visits to the countryside with Mademoiselle Rize; Lord Grenley, plagued with boredom, smoked his opium pipe; I enjoyed a few fencing bouts with the British officers; Don Nicazio did some business deals; Rytmel walked about with a mysterious, happy look on his face; the countess received visitors, drove her pony-trap, and every night at the theatre, her splendid golden hair and her lovely pale pearls gleamed under the gaslights. Such peace!

The weather was perfect. Malta glowed, the bay glittered in the sunlight, the gardens bloomed, the eyes of the Maltese ladies sighed. It was orange-blossom time. Only Carmen grew ever thinner and lived shut up in her room.

Monsieur Perny was almost fully recovered. He spent his time lying on a sofa, by day composing a comic opera, by night playing cards with the officers and puncturing the serious-minded British with his Bonapartist double entendres.

One night, on leaving Perny's rooms, having lost a few dozen English pounds at the card table, I was returning to the Clarence Hotel feeling slightly irritated with myself and taking a perverse pleasure in singing *fado* songs in the streets of Valletta, a thousand leagues from Lisbon's Bairro Alto. The wing we inhabited at the Clarence Hotel gave onto a garden, dark with trees and thickets of flowering shrubs.

Usually, the count and I entered the hotel through the garden. We had a little key that opened a green door in the moss-covered wall, all overhung with the branches of oriental bushes. That night, as I opened the door, singing, I caught a glimpse of someone disappearing rapidly into the dense foliage. The air was still, I lit a match, and by its flickering light I plunged into the shadows to see who it might have been. But the person, aware they were being followed, and realising the impossibility of making a quick escape, turned and walked nonchalantly towards me – an entirely artificial nonchalance – and spoke my name. It was Carmen.

'What are you doing here?' I asked.

'I'm killing myself. Didn't I tell you that whenever I wake in the night sweating, I get up and walk about in the night-time dew?'

But she was dressed entirely in black silk, and was even wearing a large hooded Moorish-style cape!

'Ah, my dear,' I said, 'you are killing yourself, but with love. At this hour, in that outfit, here in this garden, with its perfume of orange-blossom! What's all this nonsense about dew and night sweats?'

'I'm telling the truth. Do you think I wouldn't much rather meet someone among the shadows?'

'What about Don Nicazio? Ask *him* to woo you, to serenade you, to climb up a rope ladder to your window or seduce you here in the garden.'

As I was speaking, the bells of St John's were striking the hour, and Carmen was showing signs of unease. Every few seconds she glanced over at the garden door, nervously playing with the glove she had taken off.

I realised that she was expecting someone, the 'someone' being *el querido*, *el precioso, el saleroso, el niño* that any true Andalusian woman would be waiting for. I stole away discreetly, like a fellow conspirator, and just as I was walking along the sandy path that led to my room, I heard the tender, plangent creak of the garden door opening.

'That must be him,' I thought. 'Carmen's *querido*, her sweetheart. Poor Carmen! She suffers and stands out in the dew because of Rytmel, but as soon as night comes, she can't resist waiting under the orange trees for some French hairdresser with a tenor voice or perhaps for a Maltese tenor with a hairdresser's moustache.'

I went up to my room, but sleep eluded me; the night was sweet and languid, and I felt a rather base curiosity too. So, as crafty as a Neapolitan burglar, I crept downstairs, along by the garden wall, and when I leaned over, I saw Carmen. To my great surprise, she was alone!

'Where's your *querido*?' I called to her, laughing.

She spun round, startled, and said with some bemusement:

'What *querido*?'

'The fellow who just came in.'

'No one came in.'

'I saw him.'

'Did you recognise him?'

'No. Where is he?'

'He opened his wings and flew away!' said Carmen, laughing, and walked off toward her rooms.

'Well, I'll be damned!' I said to myself. 'This is a new twist on Dumas' *Tour de Nesle*. She welcomes them in, chops them into little pieces and buries them in the sand!'

Nevertheless, the brief event had pricked my curiosity.

The Mystery of the Sintra Road

Someone had entered the garden by stealth, and using a false key too, because only the count and I had keys to the little green door in the garden wall. But what had become of that someone? Had he entered and immediately left again? In that case, it was no lovers' tryst! But, if it wasn't a secret romance, why all the mystery, the late hour, the silence, the stolen key?

Was there someone still hidden in the garden? I searched it thoroughly, bush by bush, jasmine by jasmine. It was deserted.

With that adventure revolving in my head, I went back to bed. At lunch the next day, a waiter announced loudly that a small dagger had been found in the garden, and that the guest to whom it belonged could reclaim it downstairs, at the office. It was a curved dagger of the kind used in Hindustan. It had been found in a box hedge in a position that suggested it had been deliberately thrown there, rather than simply lost. No one claimed it.

All this was making me most inquisitive.

'Well!' I said to myself. 'There may be English police here, but we're on Italian soil and it's probable that, in spite of the large quantity of beer in Malta, there might still be some of the Borgias' deadly *acqua toffana* about. I must be careful.'

The following night, about one o'clock, I was seated at my desk, writing to a friend in Portugal, when I heard hurried steps in the corridor, and my door was thrown violently open.

I stifled a cry of horror. Standing in the doorway, deathly pale, her hair all dishevelled, and her white dressing gown covered in blood, was the countess.

'What's happened?' I cried.

She slumped onto a sofa, dumb-struck, her half-crazed eyes staring, her teeth chattering.

I sprinkled her with water, clasped her hands, spoke softly to her, and, terrified, questioned her, calling her by the kindest

The Mystery of the Sintra Road

names so as to soothe her:

'What's happened, my dear, what is it?'

I looked at her bloodstained clothes.

'Are you hurt?'

She shook her head.

'What then?' I asked.

The poor woman tried to speak; she rose, gasping, struggling and in terrible distress.

Suddenly, she threw herself into my arms and burst into tears.

'Speak,' I urged her.

'They've killed him,' she said.

'Killed who?'

'Rytmel!'

'How? Where?'

'In the garden. Go and see!'

XI

I ran down to the garden, my steps instinctively hurrying me towards the small green door in the wall.

It stood open. Beside it, close to a clump of vanilla bushes, I saw Rytmel stretched out on the ground, leaning on one elbow.

'How are you?' I gasped, kneeling anxiously beside him.

'I'm only wounded.'

'How? Where?'

He did not reply, his eyes closed, and he fell back onto the grass.

I ran to the pond to wet my handkerchief, with which I moistened his face and hands. The wound was on the upper part of his chest, on the right side, below the collarbone. I could see that it wasn't fatal.

I was at a loss what to do. Where could I take the fellow?

The most sensible thing would be to get him to a room in the hotel, but that would bring with it a clamour of publicity and the attention of the police, perhaps even dragging the countess's name into the British courts. Then, suddenly, I saw everything very clearly. I knew who, on the previous evening, had slipped quietly through the green door using a forged key. I knew who owned the Indian dagger found in the box hedge. I understood Carmen's agitation when I had come upon her waiting there in the garden, wearing that Moorish cloak. And, unfortunately, I also knew to whose room Rytmel was going, when he hurried through the Clarence Hotel garden.

It was, therefore, essential to cover up the whole affair. And Rytmel, even as he regained consciousness and with his mind still fogged with pain, had evidently thought about this too, for he said to me in a faint voice:

'Hide me somewhere!'

I left the garden and spotted one of those light, one-horse carriages that ply the steep streets of Valletta with great quietness and exceptional speed. The coachman was an Italian. I made vague mention of a duel, gave him a handful of shillings, threatened him with the police and swore him to secrecy.

With the coachman's help, I lifted Rytmel into the carriage. We made him warm and comfortable in a sort of nest of cloaks, and the horse trotted swiftly along the Via San Marco to Captain Rytmel's lodgings. The British officers there were greatly concerned. I told some rambling tale involving a fencing bout and the lost tip of an epée. The story was patent nonsense, but they soon grasped that behind it lay some personal secret, and that was enough for those reserved English gentlemen to ask no further questions.

After his wound had been dressed, Rytmel relaxed and dozed off.

Everything had been done in silence, unnoticed. I went back to the hotel to reassure the countess. It was three o'clock in the morning. A gale was blowing, and I could hear the sea breaking on the rocks in the bay. In the Clarence Hotel, not a soul was awake.

'Now for the next call!' I said to myself. And I made my way to Carmen's room.

A light was on. I opened the door, drew the curtain aside and went in. At first, although I could see no one, I could hear sobbing. At last, I saw Carmen lying curled up on a sofa, her face hidden, hair unpinned; she was covered in blood and clasping a crucifix. On a table beside her stood a bottle of cognac and a small blue cut-glass bottle. When she heard my footsteps on the carpet, Carmen raised herself up a little on the sofa. At that moment, she looked astoundingly beautiful.

Her hair hung loose, her eyes gleamed like black steel, and her dressing gown, the top buttons of which had come unfastened, revealed the splendid beauty of her breast.

When confronted by that woman so terribly possessed by passion, I admit that my first thoughts were not of vengeance or punishment. Tragic heroines came to mind, Lady Macbeth and Clytemnestra, and such beauty, such magnificence, filled my mind with amorous, vaguely pagan thoughts.

She sat up and asked bluntly: 'What do you want?'

Words failed me.

'I know what it is. You've come looking for me. I killed him. The police are outside aren't they? I'm ready. I'll just put on a shawl.'

'No one knows anything about it,' I said quietly, and without knowing why, I felt rather moved.

'What does that matter to me? I'm not hiding anything. I killed my lover. It was me. But... so what? We women give our life, our passion, our soul, we surrender our whole being, we pour into that love our entire existence, our honour, our salvation in the next world; and then along comes a woman whose hair is fairer or whose waist is smaller, and it's goodbye for ever! "Sorry, my dear, I despise you now. You were just a moment's folly, a caprice, nothing!" In that case, let him die. What more do you need to know? Go and fetch the police.'

I said quietly:

'I found him bathed in blood.'

Carmen gave me a brief, wild look, then prostrating herself on the sofa, she embraced the crucifix, and with tears streaming down her face, she said between sobs. 'Oh, dear God, forgive me! Forgive me, Lord Jesus! Forgive me! I killed him! I must be mad. Poor Rytmel! Rytmel my love! I will never again see him, never again speak to him! It is all over forever! Oh, my poor head... In Calcutta he adored me, that man. He knelt at my feet, I would have been willing to die for him. Listen: tell me, have they buried him? Is he badly wounded? I didn't cut his face, did I? No, not that! Go quickly. Go and fetch the police! Why haven't they arrested me? Oh my poor Rytmel! I'm dying, I'm dying! In a moment the bells will start to toll!'

She got up, gesturing madly, went over to the mirror, frantically tidied her hair, before once again passionately embracing the black crucifix.

'Listen,' I said, 'Rytmel isn't dead.'

'Not dead?' she cried.

She suddenly flung herself into my arms, took my face between her hands, and fixing me with a look of terrible anguish, said:

'Tell me again: he isn't dead, you say? Will he survive?'

'Yes,' I said.

'You swear it?'

'I swear.'

'Then I want to see him, I want to see him now,' she cried. 'My shawl, my shawl! Find my shawl for me. I bet they haven't dressed his wound properly... I'm sure they haven't! I must go to him! What did he say? Was he crying? The poor thing! Is he asleep? Where is the wound? What a wretch I am, what a cursèd wretch!'

In a kind of delirium she began rummaging through drawers, overturning furniture, hurling clothes around, talking, gesticulating, and sometimes singing.

'My goodness, it's late! Now what was I looking for? What time is it exactly? Did he say my name?'

She came and took my arm:

'Let's go.'

'Where?'

'To see him. I want to see him. I must! Don't tell me I can't. I want to beg his forgiveness, to love him, to serve him, to be his maid, his nurse...'

She stopped and, letting go of my arm, said:

'And that other woman. I don't want to find her with Rytmel! Is she there? I don't want her to look after him. I'll kill her if I see her. No, not that woman! Don't let her near him, I beg you. No, don't let her near him. I alone am enough.'

All of a sudden, she closed her eyes, shuddered, gave a great sigh, and fell motionless to the floor.

I lifted her onto the sofa, sprinkled some water on her face; and she said in a faint voice:

'I'm dying! I'm dying... Call a priest. I didn't tell you... I took poison.'

'You took poison?' I cried in horror.

'In that bottle – there!'

XII

The doctor – whom I immediately summoned – assured me that Carmen was in no danger. She had taken only a minute and greatly diluted dose of the poison. He was, however, concerned that her extreme nervous susceptibility, her heightened emotions, might bring on a brain fever. By daybreak, however, she had fallen asleep, succumbing at last to utter exhaustion, and the only signs of life she gave were the occasional sobbing sighs that racked her body.

I then went to see the countess. She had not slept at all. She was sitting at the end of the bed, wrapped in a shawl, in an attitude of grief and inertia that filled me with pity. It was dawn by then, but the shutters were still closed, and the lamps filled the room with a melancholy light. The vases were full of flowers. On a small table stood two blue china cups. The hot chocolate in them had gone cold, and the flowers were drooping.

How is he?' she said on seeing me.

'His wound has been dressed and he'll be better in a month. You must leave Malta in the next two weeks, countess.'

'I want at least to say goodbye to him... to spend a moment, even an instant by his side! You can't deny me that. You won't stop me, will you?'

'On the contrary, I myself will arrange for you to see him.'

'And what about *her*?'

'*Her*, cousin? Well, I went to her room with the intention of marching her off to the first policeman who came along, but left there vowing that, come what may, she will find me at her side to defend her and, if she so wishes, to love her.'

'Perhaps you're right; she is a strong, passionate woman.'

'She's more than that, cousin. If ever passion in its divine form was made flesh, she is that woman. She's the goddess of passion; besides which, she has one great quality: logic.'

I had conceived a boundless admiration for Carmen! I, who had never addressed a single gallant remark to her in the days when she was happy and her beauty at its most radiant, was now, in her hours of grief and sickness, her *cavaliere servente*. Don Nicazio had gone to Sicily, so I, alone, watched over her recovery. I helped her take her first steps around the room; she was wretchedly thin, her eyes sunken, her face morbidly pale and her mind troubled.

She spent long hours praying and reading pious literature. Her intention was to enter a convent in Spain and there punish her body through pain and penance. She now spent whole days in churches. Her habits and her manners were entirely changed. Her very beauty took on an ascetic quality. She had literally detached herself from the world. Sometimes she would look at me and, thinking of her future in the convent, she would say suddenly:

'How sad! And at only twenty-eight years of age!'

But religious fervour soon reclaimed her, and she would lose herself in hopes, in ideas of redemption through prayer, fasting and contemplation. While she was in that passionate frame of mind, shaken by exalted emotions, the sombre Catholicism of Spain entered her being and, finding the place empty of all other world views, happily pitched camp there.

One day she asked if she could see Rytmel before leaving for Spain.

'In my new role as Sister of Charity, of course!'

I took her to Rytmel's house one night. The room was lit by the flickering light of tallow candles. Rytmel's pale face against his equally white pillow was painful to see. Carmen went in, fell to her knees beside his bed, clasped one of his hands and stayed there, sobbing, for a long time. Rytmel wept too.

I had leaned against the wall, filled with a sadness as deep and unfathomable as the night itself. A neighbour, whose window opened onto the same narrow courtyard as Rytmel's, was playing a plangent melody on his violin; it was the waltz from Verdi's *Un ballo in maschera,* whose sweet, plaintive tones aroused all kinds of conflicting feelings: celebration and death, love and the life of the cloisters.

Rytmel wanted Carmen to get to her feet so that he could talk to her. But she remained prostrate with grief, her face buried in the bed clothes, sobbing and occasionally saying:

'Forgive me, forgive me!'

In the end, Rytmel, with great tenderness, helped her up and took her in his arms. He spoke graciously and gently to her and then, lovingly and with infinite charm, kissed her eyelids.

The poor creature blushed, and I felt tears well up in my eyes again. Poor dear Rytmel! How perfect was his tenderness at that moment and how divine his forgiveness!

With a simplicity in which one could already sense the great inner strength given her by her faith, Carmen spoke to Rytmel about God, about her preferred Order, the convent she wished to enter, and she did so with such naturalness, in such touching terms, that both Rytmel and I were filled with sadness for her. Finally, she kissed her lover's hand.

'Goodbye,' she said, 'for ever. I will pray for you.'

Still overcome with emotion, she slowly made her way to the door, where she stopped, turned and gazed at Rytmel for a long moment, her eyes lit up with a sombre, passionate light. Her breast heaved, she turned deathly pale and, with arms outstretched, her lips pregnant with kisses, she ran towards him, with all the impetuousness of her old self, all the frenzy of her old passion, intending to throw herself into his arms. But when she reached the bed, she dropped to her knees again and, in reverent silence, chastely kissed his fingertips! Then she took my arm and we left.

The next day Carmen called her maids together and distributed among them all her dresses, gowns and lace. She gave her jewels to an English priest to distribute among the poor. Vials, trinkets, perfumes, she gave them all away. She made her confession, spent hours on her knees in St John's Cathedral, and prepared herself for her journey. Everyone who knew her wept.

In the evening, while packing her one small trunk, she sent for me, closed the door of her room and handed me the will she had written and which I was to leave there in Malta to await Don Nicazio's return from Sicily. She had left everything to him.

Afterwards, she went silently over to the mirror and removed the net from her hair, leaving her mass of splendid, thick, poetically sensual curls to tumble almost to the floor.

She then took a pair of scissors and feverishly attacked those marvellous tresses, which would once, in ancient Greece, have been considered a national treasure.

I was captivated by her beauty and wounded by such carnage. To me it seemed as if the walls of the convent had already closed around her.

Carmen gathered up her fallen hair, wrapped it in a sheet and, handing it to me, said:

'Keep this as a remembrance of the real Carmen, the Carmen I'm leaving behind me. Now I have one last request. Prepare your luggage and travel with me to Cádiz. Tomorrow... is that possible?'

'Not tomorrow, no, but I promise you that within a week, we'll be in sight of the mountains of Valencia.'

In the meantime, she quickly ran her hands through her hair, shaping it into a more masculine style. And she looked enchanting. Her beauty took on an extraordinary sweetness and innocence. She smiled at the mirror, and as I watched her, it seemed to me that her image, caught between the two lamps, was wrapped in a luminous blue mist. Slowly, abstractedly, she had taken up a comb and was arranging her hair. I stood behind her, smiling. Carmen, caught in the spell of the mirror and surprised to find how lovely she looked with short hair, was smiling too. It seemed to me that her cheeks took on the colour of life again and that her bosom once more swelled with passion. I was about to speak tenderly to her and entice her back to the world, when she flung down the comb and, bowing her head, went to kneel silently beside her bed, before the large cross on which Christ was dying, His head drooping, His lacerated forehead dripping blood, His arms outstretched, His side pierced.

XIII

Twelve days later, the countess and the count sailed once more for Gibraltar on the mail-boat from India. The count did so reluctantly, for he was leaving Mademoiselle Rize behind and going back to the Chiado and society life! Furthermore, he disliked being alone with the countess: her melancholy moods, her inexplicable tears, her desperate pallor, her contradictory nature – all of which he, the hardened libertine, attributed to nerves and hysteria – bored and wearied him, or as the count put it: he was sick to death of romanticism. The countess herself was resigned to her departure. Rytmel, once he had recovered, would be going to Italy to regain his health in the Neapolitan sunshine, travelling later to Paris and then to Lisbon, where they would have a few months in which, as the poets of old used to say, they could weave together gold and silk and kisses.

It was with great regret that I watched them embark. I was staying on to perform the melancholy duty of travelling to Cádiz with the unhappy Carmen, who had, until only recently, been such a radiant beauty, and was now overwhelmed by bitter feelings of contrition.

Lord Grenley, who was intending to leave for Cádiz in four days' time, had placed his yacht at the disposal of Carmen and myself. I had accepted with pleasure. It was a spacious, private mode of transport, and I would be glad of Lord Grenley's company, because I hated the idea of having to watch Carmen grow ever weaker and more languid during the long sea voyage. And so, one afternoon, we set sail.

It was growing dark, the sky was cloudy, rain was in the

air. Carmen was extremely ill. Thin, pale almost to the point of transparency, lacking even the strength to walk without help, unable to sleep, existing almost solely on tea, her life seemed at any moment about to step out beyond human bounds. She hardly raised her eyes from her prayer books. Disappointed by life on Earth, that passionate spirit was feverishly searching out every possible road to Heaven.

It was with great sadness that I watched Malta vanish into the night mists. Never again would I see that white city. Not that I had been particularly happy there, but we always love those places where, for whatever reason, for whatever emotion, our hearts beat more strongly. I myself had left some tears there too.

On the first full day of the voyage, Carmen was close to death. There was a heavy swell. The sea was rough, and we feared we might meet foul weather when we approached the currents of the Gulf of Lions.

Carmen chose to spend most of her time on deck, in the air and the sunlight, gazing out at the sea. A bed had been made up for her, and there she stayed, looking, thinking, grieving, and conversing with Lord Grenley's chaplain, a kind old fellow who had a singularly charming way of speaking of heavenly matters. It was a sad scene, particularly at sunset, when the sun was going down and a great darkness covered the sea; Carmen would be talking quietly, and we, around her, either listened or kept silent, watching the waves or the dying of the light. A Scottish sailor would sometimes come and sing traditional airs from the Highlands, sad, tender songs, as broad and expansive as the view over a loch.

On the third day of the voyage, Carmen unexpectedly went down with a fierce bout of fever and wanted to make her confession. The ship's doctor told us she would never see the mountains of Spain. What painful hours those were! You have no idea, sir, how much more intense human suffering seems on the boundless expanse of the ocean! It becomes mingled with that sense of vastness and a terrible feeling that there is nothing one can do about anything.

Carmen's confession took a long time. When she had finished, she asked to speak to me.

'Goodbye,' she said, 'I'm going to die.'

I told her she was mistaken, tried to offer her some brief hope.

'No, no,' she replied, 'there's no mistake. But I have courage enough. Who isn't brave enough to be happy? Call Lord Grenley.'

She began to speak to us of her life. She told us of her youth, her romantic follies, her excesses, and she spoke eloquently, too, of her relationship with Rytmel, almost as if they had been man and wife. She had no complaints, no regrets, no scorn for anyone. Her final words were very dignified. Afterwards, she produced a rosary from her breast.

'It came from Jerusalem,' she told me. 'Give it to *her*.'

My eyes were wet with tears. Carmen, meanwhile, had grown terribly pale.

'Take me up on deck, I want to see the sea, I want to see the light.'

It was a dull, cloudy morning. The sea was quite calm. We made Carmen comfortable with cushions and shawls, facing back towards Malta where she had left her life. She remained quiet for a long time, with her hands folded in her lap.

'What land is that?' she asked, pointing with a tremulous hand to a dark line on the horizon.

'Africa,' Lord Grenley replied.

She continued to stare vaguely in that direction.

'I went to Tangiers once,' she said slowly. 'I was young then. I was happy! It was a lovely day... in May.'

She stopped. And turning to me she said:

'It's months now since we passed this point, do you remember? And do you remember that party on board the *Ceylon*, when I sang a *seguidilla*! I used to sing then... How wonderful it is to be happy! But that's all over. Never again! Never again!'

And as if talking to herself, she went on:

'Such passion, such turmoil! And here I am about to die alone, at sea. Poor me! And yet if I had met him when I was single. I asked for so little in those days, only a loyal heart. I always had simple tastes. The madness came later. That sailor who sings Scottish songs, where is he? Call him, will you? No, don't, he'll make me cry.'

We listened to her; and her soul spoke much as a bird sings at its death. The clouds dispersed, the sky cleared, the sun was about to appear.

'Just think,' she went on. 'When I was young, men used to tell me how pretty I was and how much they loved me. And now here I am dying, and who gives me a thought? Where are the people who knew me then? Some dead, all forgotten. They're happy now, they love someone else, they go to the theatre. And here I am dying. And what about *him*? Does *he* remember me? No. It makes me weep to think that I will never see him again, that he's not here, that I'm dying and he doesn't give me a thought!'

And she buried her face in the pillow and sobbed.

'Rytmel is a noble soul. He thinks the world of you, believe me...'

'No, he's forgotten me,' she said sighing and wiping her eyes. 'Besides, everyone's forgotten me. I'm not the kind of woman people make a fuss of, asking: "Are you well? Are you contented? All right, then, I love you." Now it's: "Are you dying? Well, go and get yourself buried somewhere else!" What a sad place this world is!'

Lord Grenley, his eyes brimming with tears, was anxiously chewing the stem of his pipe.

'You'll take good care of my hair, won't you?' she said to me. 'People used to admire it. If by chance I don't die, we must all go to Seville. It's so lovely there. In the evenings, in the Jardines de las Delicias, all the ladies carry posies of flowers.'

Suddenly, Carmen opened her eyes very wide as if she had seen some ghastly sight. She raised her hands to her face and cried:

'Father, Father, I'm frightened. Has the punishment already begun? And what if I fall into Hell?'

'Hell is only a symbol, my poor girl!' said the chaplain. 'God's punishments are not made of fire.'

'Yes, you're right. I can feel that I'm dying. Come closer everyone. Remember me, won't you?'

Some of the sailors did move closer. The chaplain knelt. Everyone doffed their hats and prayed quietly. Lord Grenley remained standing, bareheaded and motionless. Heavy, dark clouds were once again chasing each other across the sky. The wind began to whistle.

'Goodbye,' she said to me. 'Let me hold your hand. There, that's better. I was a good girl really… a little wild perhaps. Thank you, Lord Grenley. How awful to have someone die on your yacht! What's that in the distance? Land? No, just clouds. Ah, Rytmel my darling! Oh, my love, hear me, wherever you are!'

Two great tears trickled down her face, and she just had

strength enough to wipe them away. Then, smiling, she said:

'Listen, don't think of me with sadness. But, sometimes when you're together, and he's there with you too, remember this girl who died at sea, and say: "Poor Carmen! Now, there was a woman who knew how to love!"'

And saying this, she shuddered, spoke incoherently of Malta, Seville and Rytmel, and then, with a deep sigh, died.

The ship's bell began to toll slowly. Lord Grenley bent over, kissed her brow and closed her eyes. I was weeping.

An old sailor approached and spread the British flag over the body that had once been Carmen.

XIV

You can well imagine, sir, the sad spirits in which we found ourselves. Lord Grenley retreated to his cabin, while I and the chaplain kept vigil over the body. Evening was coming on. A thick mist covered the sea. A mournful wind was blowing. We were, all of us, deeply moved. Even old sailors who had suffered shipwreck in the Indian Ocean and rounded Cape Horn, even they had tears in their eyes.

'Poor child,' they said.

For those rough and simple natures, that pale, beautiful woman dressed in white was a young lady, a virgin, a child! One of them fashioned a wreath from dry seaweed and reverently placed it on her bosom – a bouquet of sea flowers.

I considered travelling on with Carmen's body to Spain, but the captain said that with four or five more days sailing ahead of us we could not expect the body to remain uncorrupted for that length of time. We resolved, therefore, to give her a sea burial later that night. And so the chaplain and I stayed with the body throughout the evening, recalling her beauty and her great misfortune.

Night fell, and darkness concealed the waters. The chaplain went below. I remained alone. A lamp suspended from a rope lit up the body. I uncovered Carmen's face and stroked her cropped hair. Her beauty was set in angelic immobility as if death had restored her virtue. The lovely curve of her breast was still visible beneath the flag that covered her. Never had the life force produced such grace! I gazed at her for a long time, absorbed in contemplation. Tears fell from my eyes. In the solitude of my thoughts, I said to myself:

The Mystery of the Sintra Road

'Poor creature! You are going to the very deepest of graves, to the shifting vault of the sea. A fever of love consumed you in life, an eternal storm will trouble you in death! Like the sea, you were beautiful, proud, boisterous. Like the sea, you had your troubles, your hidden calms, your caves, your nameless monsters, your religious heights, your grubby foam. Your mind was filled with tender ideas as pure and bright as the fishermen's sails filling the sea; with burdensome, modern ambitions, as fast and incisive as the paddlewheels of a boat; with the brute exigencies of temperament, as dumb and triumphant as a battleship. You were wrecked on the reef of a love grown cold, just as the sea breaks on the dark, unfeeling rocks. Your passion was your tyrant, just as the wind is the sea's tyrant. Go, poor girl, and rest in peace amidst the dark green seaweed! Yours is a sorry fate. Who ever felt, loved, trembled, blushed, desired as much as you, who ever conquered as many hearts? How many tears you provoked! How many pulses you set racing! How many desires flocked to you like pigeons! How many now forgotten voices called to you! How many promises did you break! How much puffed-up pride did you puncture! And now, after that life of action and wilfulness, after being such a focus of energy, you will be thrown into the sea once a cabin boy has attached a couple of weights to your feet and head! And then there will be nothing but the roar of the wind and the foaming waves.

'What use was your existence, what use the blood, will, nerves and thoughts dredged up from the very essence of your being! What ideas, what memories, what feelings of pity did you leave behind you? Were you ever more than just a beautiful body, desired and photographed? During your lifetime, you were one of those impassive natural beauties that man uses and discards, like a camellia or a peacock's feather. You were an adornment, not a person. Just as you never had a fixed place in life, so, in death, you will have no fixed tomb. Farewell, then, for ever, O sweet ephemeral one. It is your fate to be dispersed among the waters!

'That is why you are here alone! Where are those who loved you? Where are those you loved? Here you are, in your white dressing gown and chequered shawl, lying on the deck of a boat, a lone woman among men – as in life! There are no flowers here to place on your breast, no lace with which to frame your dead face. You die among sails and rigging, in the company of illiterate sailors who have just drunk their ration of rum. There is not even a Catholic priest to speak to you of the angels, those sweet companions of your youth. No kinsman to draw the winding sheet over your face! No responses will be chanted around your coffin. You will not cause brides to ponder as they see your funeral cortège go by, for the tarry hands of old sailors will hurl you into the sea!

'Does it really matter, my friend? Your life has reached its logical conclusion. You lived a rebel and die one too. You lived outside narrow human conventions, and you die in the freedom of nature.

'You will not find your bed surrounded by grasping relatives, uncaring servants, priests who yawn as they administer the last rites in a dark, stuffy room reeking of medicines. You die beneath the sublime sky, rocked by the waves, surrounded by the salt sea, exposed to the elements, and mourned by old Lascar sailors!

'You will not be clothed in old silks or wear an ancient funeral wreath, your body will not be adorned with fake gold braid; you will depart this life in your white gown, like a joyful bride dressed for your nuptials!

'They will not nail you into a narrow coffin, nor bind you

The Mystery of the Sintra Road

up like a bale; you will be in contact with living things; the tears of the sea will run through your hair; you will be able to touch the seaweed. The sun's rays, like an old lover, will be able to seek you out, and the lid of your casket will be the infinite blue sky.

'At your funeral, you will hear no chants in bad Latin, no clanging bells, no shrill choirboy voices, nor the inane comments of mourners or the grating sound as the sexton shovels the earth into your grave. No, wearing the British flag as a shroud, you will be launched out into your watery grave in a military silence, to the ceaseless plain chant of wind and water.

'You will not be forever crushed beneath six feet of earth, feeling the mouths of roots grazing on your breast and a host of worms invading your body as if it were a vanquished citadel. No, your death will be a perpetual journey. You will live in transparent grottos, you will guard mysterious treasures, visit glowing coral cities, fall in love with the charmed body of some fair prince, once a Norman pirate! You will be dispersed into the elements, an eternal ghost, soul of the sea!

'No townspeople will come and sit on your tomb, sacristans will not cross themselves as they pass by nor chickens cluck and peck above you; instead, over your blue tomb the wind will wander like a melancholy old man visiting his dead.

'Your epitaph will not be composed by a hired poet skilled in elegies and approved by the City Council. Your epitaph will be the ineffable light from the stars that will intersect to form the letters of your name on your grave...'

A sailor tapped me on the shoulder.

'Sir, it's eleven o'clock,' he said.

I sprang to my feet, and recalling the vain chimera, the sad thoughts, that had formed inside my head, I said to myself:

'Oh, dear, I forgot about the sharks.'

It was eleven o'clock at night. There were no stars. Everyone had gathered on deck. Lamps had been attached to the rigging and torches had been lit.

Two seamen lifted up Carmen's body. The chaplain blessed it. The British flag was tied about the body with a rope. The cabin boys brought two heavy weights. They bound one to her feet and attached the other to her neck. Her small black silk boots protruded touchingly from beneath the hem of her gown and the flag in which she was wrapped. The flames of the torches cast vague, flickering reflections on the waves. In the silence, I could hear the crackling of the resin as they burned.

Finally, the ship's bell began to toll as the seamen raised the body to the height of the ship's rail.

A grave, melancholy, infinitely sad chant began. The chaplain was praying with his hands resting on the corpse. Then, taking a step back, he said:

'In aeternum sit!'

To which everyone responded: 'Amen!'

The wind was moaning around the ship. Lord Grenley stepped forward and in a clear voice said:

'This day, on board the British vessel *The Romantic*, the death occurred of Carmen Puebla, a Spanish citizen. For the eternal protection of her mortal remains, since she is being buried on British territory, her shroud was the British flag. *In pace.*'

'Amen,' came the response.

'In the name of the Father, the Son and the Holy Ghost,' said the chaplain, 'blessèd be the tomb in which she lies and may these waters be as holy ground for her.'

'Amen.'

'Into the sea!' commanded Lord Grenley.

The two crewmen held the corpse over the water; we all moved closer and formed a semicircle with our torches. When the corpse was thrown into the water, it made a single lugubrious splash and vanished, covered by the foaming waves.

The torches were sadly, silently extinguished, and the yacht moved off. Leaning on the rail, I kept my eyes fixed on the vague spot where the body had disappeared. There lay Carmen's dead body. A feeling of profound regret filled my heart. I remembered her dancing on the deck of the *Ceylon* and laughing over dinner in the Clarence Hotel. That was all over. Never more! Never more!

The wind grew colder.

'East wind,' called the sailor on night-watch.

'It's coming from Malta,' I thought to myself.

And my last tears fell into the sea.

XV

I have reached the end of my account.

When I disembarked in Lisbon, the countess had left for Sintra. I saw her in Cascais at the end of the summer. She appeared to be happy, which was, perhaps, a way of being sad! Cascais was idiotically merry: people were even dancing to the *fado*. The following Winter the countess met Rytmel in London and in Paris. She returned from that trip sadder and paler. Gradually, it seemed to me that she was no longer confiding in me as once she had, and so I withdrew into a tactful silence. In our brief conversations, which were always held now in public places, she never again mentioned the trip to Malta.

In the meantime, I continued to receive frank and personal letters from Rytmel. Our friendship, born of excitement and shared passions, had now settled into a quiet communion of feelings and ideas. In one of his letters, Rytmel mentioned a Miss Shorn, an Irish girl.

'She is descended from the poets, a ghost of Ossian, the soul of green Erin!' he wrote.

In early Spring I received a note from Rytmel that contained these few words:

'*I am on my way. Need an empty, private room in your house; good cigars; a vacant house in some far-flung poor neighbourhood; a dark carriage with good blinds; discretion and friendship. Fraternally, Rytmel.*'

I carried out his instructions to the letter.

Rytmel arrived by steamer from Southampton some two months later. He seemed sadder and more preoccupied.

He clearly harboured some secret, some anxiety, some concern. I expected that he would open his heart to me as we sat in the garden discussing human nature. However, he never once confided in me; the name of Miss Shorn – who, according to him, was merely a new friend of his sister's – occasionally cropped up in our conversations, but that was all.

He kept very much to himself during his time as my guest and seemed more like a political refugee than someone's lover. He had no other friends or acquaintances in Lisbon. On some mornings he would disappear in the carriage that he kept permanently stationed at the door, its blinds tightly drawn.

In the evening, at eight o'clock, he would go out again, and I would not see him until the following day, over lunch, during which he always seemed slightly annoyed by the letters that arrived for him from London and Paris. I noticed, too, certain mystical tendencies in him, he who had hitherto been such a straightforward positivist. Once I even caught him reading *The Imitation of Christ*.

In a character as cool and logical as Rytmel's, that state of mind was clearly a sign that all was not well romantically.

He sometimes spoke about Carmen, sadly and nostalgically. He enjoyed discussing religious matters and the stories people told about Heaven. He talked about the Trappists, the eternal quiet of the cloisters, and life's illusions. I found this odd.

Through some lofty sentiment of reserve and pride, I had not visited the home of the countess since Rytmel had been in Lisbon. At the time, she was utterly free. The count was in Brussels, where Mademoiselle Rize held him captive with the clever, agile tips of her toes, which, at the time, were composing minor poems each night on the stage of the Théâtre Royale.

Then, one day, out of the blue, I received a note from the

countess saying:

'Dear cousin, if ice cream taken on the terrace with an old friend does not unduly over-excite your nerves, I expect you this evening at… (and she gave the address of a country house on the outskirts of Lisbon where she occasionally stayed in summer). Bring your friend, Captain Rytmel.'

I showed the note to Rytmel, and by six o'clock that evening we were trotting up the drive of that estate in a carriage with its blinds drawn.

The countess had already dined. The three of us strolled along the shady paths of the estate, we picked flowers, and recovered the spirit of the lively, carefree hours we used to spend together. The countess was radiant.

About eleven o'clock, we went to take tea on the terrace under a splendid moon. Below the terrace was a large pond full of water lilies and broad-leafed aquatic plants, and which was just large enough to row a boat on. We could hear the water gently lapping. It was a truly blissful moment. The rounded clumps of shrubs in the garden, the groves of trees, loomed out of the darkness like large, heavy, mysterious shadows. In the distance, fields and meadows melted into a pale, slightly luminous mist. A silence hung in the air. Everything around us seemed to be thinking and dreaming.

A table was set with a Japanese teapot and three tiny Sèvres porcelain cups, one of which, the countess's, was particularly attractive. We had drunk our tea, and I was studying the unusual shape, the delicate design, the absolute perfection of the marvellous little cup that the countess always referred to as 'my cup'.

'King Arthur would only drink from his own tin mug,' said Rytmel, smiling.

'And I can only drink tea from this cup,' said the countess. 'I don't know why, but to me it represents peace and contentment. If I drink from it when I'm in low spirits, it seems to drive away the clouds. If I want to preserve a cut flower, I put it in this cup, and it doesn't wither. Even the tea tastes different. Why don't you try it, Captain Rytmel?'

The glorification of that cup had ended in allowing Rytmel, in my presence, to drink discreetly from the countess's cup – a charming and romantic superstition that has long been part of the traditions of love!

Rytmel thanked her and poured a little tea into the tiny golden cup. I, meanwhile, was looking at the countess.

She was exceptionally lovely. Her dress was modestly décolleté and, lit as she was from behind by the moonlight, she was surrounded by the poetic glow that all mysterious sources of light – be they dead planets or guttering candles – lend to the fair of complexion.

There was a piano on the terrace; the countess sat down before it, and for a moment, the ivory keys beneath her fingers spoke sadly. The silence, the moonlight, the contemplative atmosphere, the murmuring of the water in the marble fountains, had lulled us, all unsuspecting, into a state of vague romanticism.

Suddenly, the countess began to sing. It was the 'Ballad of the King of Thule'.

Someone had translated the ballad into Portuguese, and it was those words that the countess chose to sing rather than the usual banal Italian lyrics:

> *There once lived a King of Thule*
> *Whose true love, when dying she lay,*
> *Gave him as a fond remembrance*
> *A cup of the finest gold made.*

I was standing beside the piano as I smoked my cigar. Rytmel, meanwhile, still holding the countess's cup, was leaning on the balustrade, caught up in the plangent charm of the song as he stared down into the waters of the pond and at the moon's shimmering reflection.

The countess's fingers were still running nimbly over the ivory keys, and her voice continued, as melancholy as the ballad itself.

> *In that cup the king always encountered*
> *The taste of sorrows old,*
> *And his eyes would fill with tears*
> *When he drank from that cup of gold.*

'Don't sing any more,' said Rytmel suddenly, turning round. In the moonlight, I could see that his eyes were bathed in tears like those of the king in the song, and in his hand the golden cup trembled.

The countess gave Rytmel a long, sad look, before continuing her song, her voice, in the silence, sounding an ever more mournful note.

> *From Normandy in his great castle*
> *Lashed by the cold, cold sea,*
> *He summoned old comrades of battle*
> *At his round oaken table to meet.*

She stopped, her hands resting on the keyboard. 'It was perhaps on just such a night,' she said. 'What more could we want to complete the legend: the terrace lapped by water, the moon, old friends reunited, the keepsake from his doomed lover, who is slowly fading from his memory, the presentiment of death…

What a perfect night for the king to throw his cup into the sea!'
And she sang the final verses of the ballad:

> *The king, with steps slow and unsteady*
> *Walked out on the castle wall*
> *And with the last strength of his ancient hands*
> *Threw the golden cup in the swell.*
>
> *Gathered around his royal body*
> *In vigil sad the courtiers stand,*
> *While the golden cup goes voyaging*
> *Through the waters that circle his land.*

Suddenly, Rytmel gave a faint cry. Either through thoughtlessness, a careless movement or perhaps an irrepressible impulse on the part of the all-revealing heart, Rytmel had dropped the little cup into the pond among the water-lilies.

The countess stood up, ashen-faced, pressing her hands to her heart, her eyes swimming with tears, and she said to Rytmel:

'At least the King of Thule waited for her to die.'

He apologised perfunctorily, as if the loss of that fragile treasure from Sèvres was of no great importance. The countess gave me her slightly tremulous arm, and we went into the drawing room.

A few days later, the tragedy occurred. I leave that for others to describe. I now set down my pen in the knowledge that it has been as honest as my intentions were sincere.

The Revelations of A.M.C.

I

Dear Sir,

In sending these lines to you, I am submitting myself to the verdict of a court of honour convened to judge the matter brought to public attention by the letters of Doctor ***, previously printed in these pages. As a player in this painful drama, I feel obliged to explain my part in what happened, which is precisely what I intend to do here. I only hope that these confidences, written with an eye to scrupulous accuracy, will contain the lesson that lies at the bottom of any truth: that the innermost existence of each of us is an integral part of the history of our times and of humanity! There is no heart which, in revealing its actions, does not offer either an endorsement of, or a challenge to, the principles that rule the moral world. The novel today is still only in embryonic form, but when it reaches full maturity as an expression of truth, the Balzacs and the Dickenses of the day will be able to build a complete character out of a single emotion and, through that character, the psychology of a whole era, just as the Cuviers of our day can already reconstruct an unknown animal from just one bone.

*****

As you know from the doctor's letters, I was born in Viseu. I was brought up in a village wedged between two mountains in Beira-Alta; thrashed on occasion by my father for tearing off branches from some precious tree belonging to the estate manager; blessed by my mother as the hope of her old age; and showered with prophecies of a glorious future by the rector, who saw me as the parish's young San Marcello and with whom, when I was ten years old, after assisting him at Mass, I would sometimes sit in the vestry and discuss the declensions of Latin nouns. This young marvel had as witnesses the sacristan and the church treasurer, who would stand with their hats under their arms, scratching their heads and gazing at me, wide-eyed with wonderment. In one corner, her eyes brimming with fond tears, my mother would smile at me from the depths of the cave formed round her face by the large, imposing black silk shawl covering her head.

Later, I attended school in Viseu and then came to Lisbon to study medicine.

I live sparingly, humbly and obscurely, my existence constrained by a small monthly allowance and confined to the friendship of a few fellow students and the ministrations of a pair of impoverished, elderly ladies – the sisters of a retired sea-captain who once shared a billet with my father – and in whose guesthouse I lodge for a very modest rent.

The only light piercing the darkness of my dreary life of exile and work came from my memories of Teresinha.

Teresinha! The sweet, dear, gentle companion to whom I principally dedicate these pages, which recount the sole chapter in my life of which she knows nothing – the honest confession and complete account of the one error of which I can accuse myself before her innocence, her kindness and her love!

Teresinha! Beloved flower, hidden among the rock-roses of our mountains, unknown, unseen, ignored, yet who, nevertheless, fills my youth and my life with the sacred perfume of a chaste love, as pure and calm and imperturbable as the light from the stars.

I pray, my innocent friend, that you will understand my words!

If you see fit to forgive the brief and inexplicable lapse, the story of which I place trustingly in your hands, I ask not for a balm to heal a wound, but for a benevolent smile of forgiveness for the strange melancholy that once assailed the convalescent kneeling here at your feet!

Whatever the outcome, my beloved, I believe in my heart that I am discharging a sacred duty in telling you absolutely everything that happened to me, omitting nothing and holding nothing back. The truth is that I love you. I love you now and have always loved you! Another image, irresistible and vaporous, hung over me for a while, but vanished like the shadow cast by an unhealthy dream, pierced by your candid, all-seeing gaze fixed always on mine.

One night, two months ago, at about nine o'clock, I was walking back to my house, which is well away from the centre of Lisbon, when I came upon a hired cab whose coachman was arguing rudely with a lady standing beside the cab. She was all dressed in black, her head and shoulders covered with a long lace veil. After exchanging a few words with her much older companion, she spoke again to the coachman in a fine, tremulous, delicate, musical voice, the like of which I had never heard before.

'Where may I send payment? I haven't any more money with me.'

'Too bad, lady,' replied the coachman. 'If you've got no money, you walk. I told you how much the fare'd be. If you don't pay the rest, I'll call the police. If you haven't got any more money on you, give me something as security.'

She stamped her foot impatiently, threw back part of the veil covering her face and angrily began to peel off a glove. I imagined she was about to remove a ring from her finger. The coachman quickly passed the reins through the grille of the driver's seat and climbed down. Meanwhile, I had approached the group, and as he took his first step forward, I dealt him a blow across the face with the back of my hand, a blow that sent him staggering backwards against the horses.

And then, giving him a gold coin I had in my pocket, I said:

'Here, this is for the blow across the face. Otherwise, be satisfied with what these ladies paid you for the ride.'

It was as if someone behind me had suggested these gallant words to me, indeed, even today, I'm amazed that I, all unaided, came up with a solution of such oratorical impact.

The coachman held up the coin, studied it in the light of the lantern, climbed up again to his seat, and departed, calling out to me:

'Good night, sir!'

Confused and disconcerted, I automatically doffed my hat to the lady and stammered a few barely intelligible words, not knowing how to take my leave.

It was the first time I had been so close to one of those handsome society ladies; she was more exquisite, refined and delicate than anyone I had ever seen. She had a milky, velvety complexion, like the petal of a camellia – a marvel of refinement comparable only to a woman who once passed me in the foyer of the Teatro São Carlos on the arm of another man and who wore a very grand cape, white with pink stripes.

I suppose that those who know these magnificent creatures, who see and talk to them every day, are unimpressed by their appearance, but for those who encounter them for the first time, there is nothing more unsettling. Men accustomed to confronting the most violent of disturbances, undaunted by danger, misfortune or glory, tremble before this simplest of things: their first contact with an elegant woman! Thence comes the magnetic power wielded by queens over pages and chatelaines over minstrels. It's a unique sensation. A human being struck dumb and transformed momentarily into a vegetable that can see.

I stood there, motionless and tongue-tied.

The lady looked me rapidly up and down, then, with a tremulous 'Thank you,' held out a gloveless hand from beneath the black cloud of her lace veil.

I surrendered my coarse hand to her cold, delicate, trembling one, and that brief handshake – which set her thick chain bracelet jingling – sent a kind of electric shock through my nerves.

Obliged to say something, I leapt without thinking to the hideous words of a phrase common enough in Viseu, but which I am sure had never, until that night, been heard by such a person, and which doubtless sounded to her like the howl of a wild beast heard for the first time in some dense unexplored jungle.

To my eternal shame, the words, which, alas, I had retained in my provincial ear and which my equally provincial mouth unleashed, were these:

'At your service, ma'am!'

Horrified at the sound of my own voice, I turned on my heel and strode away as fast as I could. I was angry, ashamed, crestfallen, as if I had uttered a sacrilegious obscenity. It made me want to melt into the walls or be swallowed up by the earth! I dared not look back, and I felt as if I were surrounded by fantastical, but silent gales of laughter. I fancied that everything was mocking me, lamp posts, stray dogs, cobblestones, the numbers on house doors, the posters on street corners, the water-carriers who passed, groaning under their barrels, and the grocers weighing out rice on the counter in the back of their little shops.

I rushed into my house, climbed the stairs, locked myself in my room and began pacing back and forth in the darkness.

As if lit by a satanic flash of lightning, I could see the two hands that had just clasped each other for the first time in the street below – mine and hers – one weather-beaten, rough and hot, the other white, nervous, icy cold. Then I began to reconstruct the appearance of those two people.

She, pale as ivory, had the melancholy profile of a Madonna whose infant child had been snatched from her arms, and in her laces and satins she moved with all the fluid grace of a mermaid. I, stiff and awkward in her presence, not knowing quite how to manage both hat and cane, offered a flagrant display of my personal defects and my undistinguished, petty bourgeois poverty.

Alongside that ideal, transcendant, ethereal presence, I became painfully aware of how base and wretched I must have looked: a ready-made jacket bought on the cheap; clodhopper boots with misshapen soles caked in mud; trousers bagging so badly at the knees that they made me look as if I were sitting down even when I was standing up; frayed shirt-cuffs, and the tip of the middle finger on my right hand stained with ink!

We truly were polar opposites, placed together on the same latitude by foolish chance and immediately separated for ever by those dreadful words that kept buzzing in my ears like the early symptoms of a stroke:

'At your service, ma'am.'

I do not know what strange attraction fixed the image of that woman in my mind. It wasn't just a vague feeling of compassion nor was it hidden desire or even the first stirrings of love. I felt intensely drawn to her and yet the only emotion I could find in my heart – and I say this sincerely – was that of hatred. Yes, hatred, inexplicable, monstrous hatred, the kind I imagine a complete outsider might feel for the society into which he was born!

I found that noble creature's aristocratic distinction, her effortless, native elegance, humiliating and infuriating; it aroused in me the ferment of demagogical revolt that every commoner carries with him, concealed in the depths of his consciousness like an illegal weapon.

The woman undoubtedly had a mind less cultivated than mine, inferior reasoning powers, a weaker will and a narrower life. However, to compensate for these shortcomings she enjoyed the repugnant, inadmissible superiority that comes with breeding. A fine cradle, a delicate constitution, a feather bed, a cosseted childhood spent among upholstered furniture, carpets and the sound of a piano, that was enough for any man brought up in the bright light of day – with the harsh mountainside for a carpet and, for music, the wind roaring in the oak trees and whistling through the pines – to seem ridiculous, wretched and despicable by comparison!

Between me and her there would always be a barrier.

She would always be beautiful, superior, naturally seductive, instinctively charming, vivacious and beloved within her own little world of aromas, velvet, crystal and candles!

With a plaster figurine adorning my pinewood shelf and a cotton bedcover on my iron bedstead, I will always be glum and useless – miserable when I try to be slightly less ridiculous and laughable whenever I have a fancy to be slightly less miserable!

I lit the two wicks of my brass lamp and tried to study.

Impossible. I ran my eyes over the letters of the book before me, but after three or four pages, I had not understood a single word. I abandoned my reading and sat for a while, inert, stupid, dead, my gaze fixed on the empty eye-sockets of a skull I had on my table, and which was laughing at me with the open-mouthed sarcasm that exhumed skeletons bring with them from the grave. I hated life. I snuffed out the light, undressed and went to bed.

My bed had been made that day with a pair of sheets with starched borders that my mother had generously provided for my student trunk. They had the rough texture of new sheets and the characteristic smell of bed linen from the provinces.

'My poor dear mother!' I thought, as I lay breathing in that faint, distant, olfactory memory of my family home. 'Poor thing. In your own simple way you thought that by edging my sheets with the lace that you yourself had so tirelessly made, you would be lavishing upon me a luxury that would turn Lisbon on its head! If you only knew. This labour of love that took you two years of patient effort has been admired by no one, seen by no one, noticed by no one, except for this morning when, with sacrilegious peals of laughter, a housemaid asked if the priests in my part of the country wore sheets like mine on days when there was a sung mass! What does it matter, though, if others do not appreciate it? They are bad, corrupt, perverse creatures! I thank you, my unsung mother, my old friend. In the arabesques of the lace you made for me, and which I can feel beneath my fingers, I imagine I can trace the many tears you shed on winter nights when the wind was buffeting the trees, the hail was clattering against the windows, while you stayed awake, resignedly kneeling beside the cot of your fretful little boy. When I feel the rough touch on my cheek of the prickly lace trimmings, I kiss them reverently as if a guardian angel had touched me with the tip of its pure white wings.'

But along with the smell of homespun cloth that wrapped about me like a caress from afar, there was, in my bed, another markedly different fragrance, that which had perfumed the skin of the unknown woman and which lingered on the hand she had grasped. I breathed it in with an irritating eagerness that pierced and tormented me. I was lost! I pressed my lips to the palm of my hand and began to drink in the mysterious scent of a strange, remote paradise.

The whirlwind of ideas stirred up in my head by that warm, penetrating, alien aroma was monstrous, infernal.

I felt the flames, the palpitations, the hallucinations of a fever.

When I got up in the morning, having slept not a wink all night, my pillow was soaked with tears.

Forgive me Teresinha, forgive me! Those bitter tears were not shed for you, my perfect angel!

II

A few days later, I learned that the lady I had met was the Countess of W. Her face had become moulded into my memory much as a death mask fixes the face of a corpse in plaster. I was in the Rossio when a friend, on seeing her pass by in an open carriage, told me her name.

She was sitting, no, almost reclining, in the corner of an open cabriolet and looking languid, abstracted, indifferent, as if an invisible aura set her apart from the sights and sounds of the street, which were far too vulgar to touch her. She was wildly beautiful. Dressed for summer with tasteful simplicity and freshness, she had a grace that one divined rather than saw, that one did not so much need to see as to breathe in. On her breast she wore a pale yellow rose, and a single lock of fine, golden hair had escaped and strayed onto her forehead.

I fixed my eyes on her and raised my hat. She saw my greeting and looked at me as if for the first time, showing as little interest as if she were staring into an empty shop window or at a blank sign, and she went on her way like an idle image of perfection, snatched from its pedestal by a liveried coachman and a pair of trotting horses.

I continued to amble along with my colleague, making caustic remarks about politics in order to conceal, as best I could, the turmoil I was feeling.

Moments later, a black brougham passed, travelling in the same direction as the countess's carriage. It bore neither name nor coat of arms, and its curtains were tightly drawn. This perfectly common occurrence filled me with indignation and rancour. It seemed to me that the second carriage was following that of the countess, and, through what impulse of heart or mind I know not, there arose in me a desire to wrench open the door of that carriage and humiliate the doubtless male occupant.

'You're shaking!' my friend said.

'It's nothing... just nerves.'

'You're terribly pale, your lips are white and your ears are red.'

'It was a dizzy spell. I have them sometimes.'

'There you are! That's what late nights and too much tobacco do to the workings of the heart.'

'Don't forget weakness from hunger,' I exclaimed, smiling and scarcely able to stand. 'I'm off to find some supper!'

I got into the first cab that came along, as my companion was saying:

'Now you're all flushed and red as sealing wax – take some iron and bromide.'

When I arrived home I had a fever, and I could see the pounding of my heart through the thickness of my coat.

I did not meet the countess again until the night of the catastrophe.

My absurd, mysterious romance ended there and then, giving way to the tragic events in which the two of us became embroiled.

III

At two o'clock on the morning of 20th July last, I was returning from Z.'s house. I was almost home, when I heard footsteps behind me. I stopped. Two women passed me, hurrying down the road. I caught a glimpse of them in the lamplight. One was tall, thin, upright and elderly; the other – need I describe her? – for it was she. The briefest of glances sufficed for me to recognise her.

She was distressed, breathless, sobbing. I was so greatly moved by the unexpected sight of such anguish, by the awful suffering of that beautiful woman – who only a few days before had seemed so contented, radiant, inviolate – that I would have given my life not to see her laid low in the mud of a dark, deserted street by that most violent, most wilful, most hostile and most inexorably human of events: misfortune. She, the living image of delicacy and charm, the supreme expression of beauty, dignity, earthly omnipotence, was suddenly caught in the coils of the very serpent whom I had imagined would have been trampled beneath her feet, as she stood on a crescent moon!

For a moment, I was utterly perplexed. Finally, though, I hastened after her, caught her up and managed to blurt out:

'Countess, I see you are upset. I can tell that something extraordinary and terrible has happened. You seem so alone and unprotected in this neighbourhood. Only in the most exceptional circumstances would I take the liberty of speaking to you. Use me, madam, as you would use a friend or a slave, whether it be for life and for death.'

She was clearly greatly distracted, listening without fully

understanding me. Then she repeated my final words in a near hysterical voice:

'For death! Who told you? How did you know?'

And leaning on the lady who accompanied her, whose arm she had grasped in terror, she looked up and stared at me, tremulous and pleading, her wild eyes filled with tears.

'What do you want? Tell me!' she said. 'Are you going to arrest me? Here I am. Take me away.'

And then she turned this way and that, looking up and down the street with an expression of confusion, shame and fear on her face. She was anguish personified. My heart was filled with compassion and pity.

'Forgive me,' I said, 'and, please, don't be upset! I know nothing. I haven't come to arrest you or question you. I'm not a judge or a spy or an executioner. This is only the third time in my life that I've seen you. The first was on this very street about a month ago, when a coachman was demanding payment from you. The second was in the Rossio, a fortnight ago, when you happened to pass by. I am an unknown friend, obscure and anonymous. I imagined you were the very apogee of fortune and happiness, and I felt nothing for you but envy and hatred. Now I find you, it seems, on the edge of an abyss, and there is nothing in my poor, bruised heart except sympathy and devotion! Poor lady. So you are as unfortunate as the rest of us. Poor soul.'

My sadness for her was deep and sincere, my compassion unlimited.

'I'm sorry,' the countess replied, 'I'm so distraught that I cannot properly understand your words; I'm so distressed that I barely recognise you or only half remember… but you seem generous and sympathetic. Oh, I can barely stand!'

I offered her my arm, which she took, remaining for a

moment, motionless, leaning on me and on her companion, her head back and her mouth open, drinking in long draughts of air.

'We must go!' she said after a pause. 'I cannot stay, I cannot die here. I have a letter I need to write. I must get home as soon as possible.'

And supported by her two companions, she managed to walk on, with slow, tottering steps, desperate, breathless, stopping every few seconds to fill her lungs with the air she lacked.

I was utterly at a loss what to do in the face of such grief. I occasionally thought of something to say, but dared not speak, for fear she might imagine that I, with gross impudence, was trying to fathom the cause of her distress.

The street was under repair, and so we had no choice but to walk over the sharp angles and edges of the loose crushed stones covering it. We were nearly at the corner of the street, when she turned to the woman accompanying her, a servant I now realised, and said:

'Betty, can you put my shoe back on. It's come off.'

The servant knelt down and exclaimed:

'Countess, the satin's all torn! Your foot is bleeding!'

The countess, however, seemed not to hear and pressed on resolutely.

I was amazed and touched by the brave spirit inhabiting that feeble form and felt an urge simply to pick that perfect, courageous body up and carry it in my arms. Luckily, a vacant cab appeared out of a nearby side street. I hailed the driver, and the countess, who was clearly in a great hurry to reach her house, got in along with her maid. I closed the door and, handing her my card, I said to the countess, almost whispering in her ear:

'Whatever the cause, whatever the consequences of the strange event that has befallen you, you may be absolutely sure that not a soul in the world will know of our meeting. If you never have need of my help, I will continue to be what I am today, a complete stranger, who henceforth will consider his relationship with you to be exactly as it was before he saw you for the first time.'

Greatly moved, she replied:

'Thank you for those kind words, which may well be the last I hear in this world. When you find out, as you inevitably will, what, after this horrific night, I will be deemed to be in the eyes of the courts and of society, tell your mother, your sister, your lover, if you have one, tell them all not to hate me! Tell them that I am far less guilty than I may appear and that I made this confession to you as I said goodbye, somewhere halfway between life and death. Goodbye! I will not shake your hand. I am unworthy of the friendship of decent people. The most I can ask for myself is pity. Have pity on me. Goodbye.'

The carriage had travelled no more than a few feet, when it stopped again at a gesture from the countess. She herself opened the door, stepped down and came towards me. I went to meet her.

'I should like to talk further with you,' she said.

After a short pause, during which she appeared to be organising her thoughts, she continued.

'It was perhaps providential that we should meet here, at this time, in this street... You may be the one person God has appointed to protect me, to come to my aid. I have a relative to whom I will write immediately, entrusting him with my secret. I fear, however, that he may not be in Lisbon at present. If he is not, I don't know who else I can confide in. If you have mercy and kindness enough in your heart to help me, come to my house at eleven o'clock tomorrow morning.'

And, giving me her address in Lisbon, she climbed into the carriage again and departed.

What an extraordinary mixture of emotions she aroused in me, that woman who, according to her own lights, had committed some crime. I felt inclined to kneel at her lacerated feet and worship her!

IV

The following day, at the appointed hour, I presented myself at the countess's house.

It was a modest, whitewashed two-storey building, with all the shutters closed. The front door was opened by a servant dressed in a blue jacket with white buttons, a crimson waistcoat and breeches. He was an old man with white hair, as polished and plump as an ambassador, as serious as a statue, and coiffed like an English gentleman. He greeted me in French and ushered me in.

The stairs were painted in white lacquer and gleamed like a starched shirt-front. The velvet carpet runner was fixed in place by sparkling copper stair rods. Projecting from the landing wall was an alabaster seashell filled with long-leafed plants, into which dripped the water from a miniature fountain. In the room at the top of the stairs, the furniture was also white and the green-papered walls were liberally hung with gold-framed paintings in oils. A clear, lofty light poured in through the opaque glass panes. The house exuded the calm air and perfumed silence of an elegant, contented tranquillity. It seemed to me neither a nobleman's palace nor a bourgeois mansion, but rather the comfortable retreat of a poet or an artist.

The servant drew back a curtain, and I entered a room lined with leather and furnished with sofas, studded Morocco leather armchairs, large porcelain vases and a few bronze sculptures, including a signed and dated bust of the countess herself, from Milan. One of the heavy curtains covering a door leading into what had clearly once been another salon was drawn back to reveal a large ebony piano with the name Erard displayed on its side in silver lettering. Beside it, leaning against an armchair, was a cello and, before it, an ivory music stand. On the marble mantle-piece there stood a few more books and a couple of flower vases. The various pieces of furniture were so arranged as to make them appear to be conversing quietly together about delicate, personal matters. All that happy comfort gave one a sense that this was home to an intelligent, contented existence. The air and the objects gave off the perfume, harmony and warmth emanating from whoever had happened to be talking, reading and making music there. Suddenly, I looked up from a book I had found lying on the table in the middle of the room and saw before me, frozen in the depths of a large mirror, a grim, spectral figure. I spun round, unable to suppress a cry of shock and horror. It was the countess.

What a terrible transformation! During the few hours that had passed since the last time I saw her, the Countess of W. had aged ten years. Her sunken eyes were fixed and dull, her flesh grey and opaque; her tense face was now furrowed and haggard; her hair, caught back in a tight bun, made her nose look sharper and her ears somehow more prominent, stiff and cadaverous.

She beckoned me to follow her, and I did so like someone entering the cold domain of death. We crossed another sitting room and entered one of her own private rooms. She gestured towards a sofa and sat down beside me, looking at me impassively.

She remained like that for a long moment, mute with indescribable grief – the terrible pause in which the soul clambers out of an abyss of tears and flails about before it can find a voice. Her lips were half-open as if she were about to cry out, and her jaw was trembling like that of a terrified child just before he or she bursts into tears. Finally, she spoke, uttering each slow, heavy, resolute word as if she were cutting her heart into little pieces and handing them to me one at a time.

'Please do not condemn me for what I am about to say.'

And after a short silence, she added in a low voice:

'I killed a man.'

'What?' I cried. 'You're mad! You've gone mad!'

'No, I am not mad,' she replied gravely and calmly. 'I have not yet gone mad, which surprises me. The hours have ticked by, minute by minute, second by second, but my reason has not succumbed to that ultimate misfortune, without cure, without end, without remission! I killed a man. Unintentionally, it's true, but I killed him nonetheless. I want to hand myself over to the law courts, I am ready, I have made up my mind. I look into the future and see only one hope, only one solace, that of dying in torment, for which I will give thanks as Heaven's greatest blessing, dying of hunger, scorn, misery, prostrated in the depths of a dungeon or the hold of a ship; or marooned on some African beach to be burned by the sun, gnawed by cancer, ravaged by thirst and fever... For myself, I fear only two things: the madness that would fleetingly allow me the horrible joy of believing that I am still loved and happy; or the sudden death that would snatch from me the one consolation that God concedes to the very worst culprits: the freedom to suffer. But what about him... his name revealed, his body profaned, his secret betrayed!'

She continued to speak abstractedly, as if in a dream:

'Poor unfortunate man! What disastrous fate led him to me, hurling him into my heart, wherein lay his death? Why did he not love other women, who deserved him more than I? Why did he not let himself be loved by Carmen Puebla, who adored him and died for him? How blind, how misguided, how unlucky he was!'

And hiding her face in her hands, she burst into uncontrollable sobs, in which life itself seemed to be tearing at her breast and spilling forth tears.

'Come now,' I said when the crisis had abated, 'calm down for a moment while we think about what needs to be done. Firstly, are you positive that the count is dead?'

'The count!' she exclaimed, standing up abruptly and wiping her eyes. 'Oh, of course, I still haven't told you everything. The man I killed was not my husband.'

Standing before me, wild-eyed, she added in a very different voice:

'He was my lover.'

Then she stood perfectly still, awaiting my response, like a criminal in the dock about to hear the judge's sentence.

My first reaction on hearing her terse and unexpected confession was surprise, followed by instinctive revulsion. I sprang to my feet and took a few steps about the room. The countess stayed where she was, in a state of utter impassivity that could as easily have been the shame of remorse as the indifference of guilt. I was appalled. I was filled with horror at the thought of that pure, exquisite statue – to whom I had almost built an altar in my heart – suddenly tumbling into the mire. I could bear the knowledge that she was a criminal, but not the fact that she had prostituted herself, no, that was too much. I looked at her, my eyes full of the scorn she aroused in me at that moment, and after a painful silence, I exclaimed:

'That's too horrible!'

She trembled, feebly closed her eyes and steadied herself on the back of a chair.

'You perhaps find my reaction odd,' I said. 'That's only natural. I've heard that Lisbon society takes a very lenient view of this sort of thing, seeing such misdemeanours as trivial, a part of everyone's domestic life. However, as a mere savage, brought up to believe that faithfulness in a woman is as sacred a duty as honour is in a man, I reject that interpretation of free love, in the name of the only women whom my inexperience of the world has allowed me to know – she who bore me and she whom I love. I cannot comprehend how a virtuous person could fall into such error. Adultery is quite simply filthy and indecent. Killing a man in those circumstances not only breaks every law regarding the inviolability of human life, it shows an equal lack of respect for the dead. It's tantamount to throwing a corpse into the gutter. It's tragic... worse than that... it's utterly sordid.'

She heard me in silence, utterly still, as if hypnotised by my instinctive but rough and cruel response.

Suddenly, without an exclamation, without a cry, without warning, she collapsed onto the floor, stricken and unmoving, as if she were dead.

I wanted to call for help and was about to ring the servants' bell when it occurred to me how inopportune it would be for anyone else to be a witness to that scene. I went over to where she lay on the carpet and knelt beside her. I lifted her head. I could feel no pulse. Then I picked her up in my arms. Her pale forehead rested on my shoulder, close to my lips.

I carried her over toward a sofa. Then, out of superstitious respect, I thought better of it and placed her in an armchair, before running off to investigate the adjoining rooms. Next door was a dressing room. There, on a washstand, I found a bottle of eau-de-cologne, and I dabbed a few drops on her temples and wrists and made her breathe in some of the fumes by holding the uncorked bottle under her nose. I listened to her chest. Her heart was beginning to beat again. A pulse reappeared.

I had knelt beside the armchair in which she was reclining and was sadly contemplating her unconscious face.

From that angle, her closed eyes, her half-open mouth affording a glimpse of small, pearly teeth, her head resting on the back of the chair, all combined to give her the look of an angel rising up out of a tomb. Beneath the hem of her dress, in sepulchral stillness, I could see her dainty feet in their silk stockings and black satin shoes. One hand lay in her lap; beneath the pale skin I could see the tenuous blue network of veins; on her ring finger she wore a band of large diamonds and rubies; and emanating from her black lace gown was the same perfume that had lingered on my hand the first time I met her.

I remembered her face glimpsed by gaslight in the street and, later, in broad daylight as she passed through the Rossio in an open carriage. And yet those two occasions, however vivid in my memory, seemed to me to have happened years ago.

How she had aged!

Her hair, dry and dull as if dead, had turned white at the temples and at the crown.

In her terrible grief, the violent contraction of all the muscles in her face had transformed and disfigured her features overnight. The corners of her mouth had sagged under the weight of her tears as if under the weight of the years; two deep furrows marked her now flaccid cheeks, and her forehead was covered with fine lines.

In the few hours that had passed since I saw her, what frightful, dark, immeasurable anguish must have passed through that unhappy body – and to such devastating effect!

In the street, a short distance away, a barrel organ was

playing arias from various operas, and to the sound of that idiotic, mechanical, hammering music, I seemed to see, parading past between the poor countess and me, a stampede, a tragicomic evocation of all the great symbols of the sentimental life, a living litany of elegant passions, caught up, beneath the ever-turning handle, in a funereal whirl, a dance of the dead, encircling the feeble body of the countess, just like the visions of the past that hover above the deathbeds of dying nuns in old paintings.

It was as if – as I listened to that music, as automatic as the steps of a sleepwalker – I saw passing before me the whole cavalcade of temptations that had carried that creature to her fateful end; the pale Manricos and the febrile Manfredos, concealing beneath the cloak of poetic adventures the chivalry and valour of El Cid or Roland the paladin, the melancholy of Hamlet, the overwrought emotions of Werther, the rebellion of Faust, the satiety of Don Juan, the world-weariness of Childe Harold; and the whole dramatic legion of beautiful and beloved women: Francesca da Rimini, Marguerite, Juliet, Ophelia, Virginia and Manon.

And, garlanded with dry kisses, with the wooden kisses that came clattering forth from that barrel organ in the street, all those figures from romantic legend seemed to be dancing mysteriously to the sound of *La Traviata*, *Lucia di Lammermoor*, *Un Ballo in Maschera*...

'Love! love! love!' was doubtless the unchanging theme of the aria that had been sung to her throughout her existence as a beautiful, elegant, cultured, wealthy woman.

This was the moral universe inhabited by the countess's imagination, and in which she acquired the distinctly limited world-view of the lovely, desirable, idle woman.

In the midst of an existence as intricately artificial as hers, how could she have any sense of the honest serenity of simple lives?

Apart from elegance, fashion and possibly art, what would she know of the important, serious things in life, beyond religion and love? She had a prayer book and a husband, but that is very little to keep a soul on an even keel, particularly once the prayers cease to convince and the husband ceases to love.

The women who have a salon, a carriage, a box at the opera, a casket of jewels, a room full of dresses, cannot be like the homely women who, in the words of Shakespeare's Iago, suckle fools and chronicle small beer; nor, to quote Sancho Panza, can they return to the simple fate of spinning, weeping and bearing children. The countess had no minor accounts to keep and had never learned to spin. All that remained for her was to weep.

Who knows, perhaps in her gilded existence, the bitterness of today's tears had more than made up for a bitterness she had never previously known!

I was filled with genuine compassion for her and deep remorse for the cruel words I had spoken.

What could I do to save her? I had no idea, but of one thing I was sure, I would do anything, even sacrifice my life to help her.

I must also say that seeing her and listening to her, I did not for a moment imagine that the murder of which she accused herself could be what one could truly call a crime, the result of an infamous or wicked intention. A criminal, a coward, a murderer, does not weep like that or speak like that, does not accuse or blame himself, nor confide, as she did, in a virtual stranger. She had told me her story without the least concern for herself, as if shouting it from a window. I even wondered fleetingly whether this was merely some strange neurosis, perhaps a hallucination or some kind of rational delirium. But delirium does not cause such suffering. I've seen many insane people in the hospital. However pained their expression, they had never plumbed such depths of grief. To suffer as she suffered, one needed to be in possession of all one's emotional faculties. Among the truly insane there is a certain possibly nameless quality, but which could be described as 'the isolation of the mind'.

When the countess came round, she seemed a little calmer. So as not to cause her any further agitation by eliciting some long account of events I thought best left alone, I asked her, partly in the role of medical student, but principally as a man of honour:

'Does anyone else know about this?'

'My maid knows, the woman who was with me yesterday when we met, and quite soon my cousin 'H' – to whom I wrote today – will know too. My cousin, however, is in Cascais. The dead man is a foreigner. My cousin is the only person in Lisbon who knows him. Nobody else is even aware he is here. What I most want to avoid is having to hand his body over to the police, thus revealing his name, nationality and family connections. If those things can be avoided, I will then hand myself over to the law courts, commit suicide, flee abroad, bury myself alive... whatever people think best!'

'Does your cousin know how the gentleman died?'

'No. He will know only that he is dead.'

'Can you count on the silence of your maid, for a few days at least?'

'Yes. For as long as she lives.'

'If you can, make sure that your letter does not reach your cousin today. And... *he*, where is he now?'

'In the same street where we met yesterday, at number ...'
'How does one get into the house?
'I have a key,' she replied.
And having pondered a little, she continued:
'Yesterday, when I asked you to come to my house today, I was mad with despair and horror. It seemed to me that everything I touched brought only punishment and retribution, and that everything drifting away from me was making off with my last hopes, with the only help I might have been able to call upon in this world! It was in that state of delirium that I begged you, a complete stranger, to come and see me. Why? Even I didn't know why. So that I could tell this story to someone, I suppose, come to some decision, find a solution, hasten some kind of conclusion, or escape from myself. Going to the police would mean subjecting that poor man to the most dreadful of profanations. But how could I possibly go to one of the ladies of my acquaintance or knock at the door of a respectable family who would receive me in their dining room when supper was over, who would shake my hand and bring in their children for me to kiss, how could I then say: "I had a lover and I killed him. I've come to invite you to this festival of shame and ignominy!" No, better to choose the unknown, surrender myself to chance. When I spoke to you on that dreadful night, those were my thoughts, if you can call such disconnected fragments thoughts. I'm no more clear-headed today than I was yesterday. I still don't know what to do. I feel only that I am lost, that I need someone to guide me. You seem to me to be a generous man, loyal, compassionate and kind. You know what happened, you know where *he* is. I've told you which house it was. Now here is the key.'

She drew out a chain she was wearing around her neck – its links were sharp and angular like those of a chain worn as a penance – removed a small key and handed it to me.

She slumped into an armchair and leaned her head back, prostrate, silent, exhausted, overcome by the profound weariness that follows any great crisis of nerves.

Without knowing exactly what I would do, but certain nonetheless that, sooner or later, I would find some practical solution to this entirely unforeseen and extraordinary situation, I put the key away. I felt, above all, that I needed to leave that place, to breathe some fresh air, to be alone in order to reflect and consider.

'Madam,' I said, 'if, by noon tomorrow, I have not sent back this key, that will be a sign I have been arrested, that all is lost. If you hear no more from me, I mean, if the key has not been returned, then flee, go into hiding, do whatever you think best. If questioned, deny everything. For me, I would far rather accept responsibility for that man's death than implicate you, and there is no way in the world that I will ever mention your name. In the meantime, if you would like the advice of a doctor: in order to collect your thoughts, calm your mind and not surrender to madness, force yourself to get up, open a window, then sit down again, with a notebook this time, and write an exact account of what happened. Then burn what you wrote. The only way of mastering and understanding a situation such as yours is to analyse it. There was a philosopher once, who left this advice for unhappy people: *If sorrow afflicts you, turn it into a poem.* So write it down. It can be your memoirs or your will, but write. And then burn it. Now, I'll say goodbye. Goodbye until tomorrow, or if not tomorrow, goodbye for ever.'

The countess had remained in exactly the same position in her chair. Her mouth was slightly open, her lower lip quivered in the touchingly childish fashion that desolation brings to a woman's face, and large, silent tears trickled down her cheeks and dripped slowly onto the lace edging of her dress. She made as if to get up, to say a word of thanks. Deeply moved, I took a step back, bowed respectfully, and left.

V

Having closed the door of the room in which she remained sitting, I walked through the room where I had waited on my arrival, and an idea came into my head. On one of the tables lay two large scrapbooks. I leafed rapidly through them. One contained only a series of travel notes written in Portuguese and, judging by the uniformity of the writing, this was clearly the work of one person. Specimens of plants and flowers were stuck or pinned between the notes and there were numerous architectural studies as well. It appeared to be a sketch book. The other contained a motley collection of observations, maxims, poems, drawings and watercolours, all bearing different signatures. I studied every page.

I had not dared to ask the countess the name of her lover – aware that her lips would never again utter that name – but I needed to know it and to see his handwriting. That unknown name was sure to be in the album I was looking through. But how could I find it when I had no time or leisure or peace of mind to interpret every phrase I read? I would have to abandon that plan, and yet the album I held in my hands was perhaps the only means at my disposal to find out what I wanted. After a moment's hesitation, I put the book under my arm and left the house.

Out in the street, I hailed a cab to take me to my house, made myself comfortable in one corner of the cab and set about reading each and every passage of poetry or prose in the scrapbook.

The Countess had told me that her lover was a foreigner, but such scant information wasn't enough for me to be able to pick him out in that Tower of Babel. Page after page surprised me with a new language. There was French, Italian, German, English, Spanish... The name Ernest Renan appeared above two Chaldean words; Garcin de Tassy, an orientalist at the Sorbonne, had signed a quotation in Hindi; Abd al-Qadir had merely left his name in Arabic; Princess Dora d'Istria from Turin had contributed a few lines in Albanian. There were only two Portuguese names.

I was no further forward than if I had made only the most cursory inspection of the various names and languages.

When I reached home, I realised that the house the countess had indicated to me was a rather shabby two-storey building, almost opposite where I was living, near the corner, beside a far more prepossessing house, and with its door set back slightly so that it was hidden from most of the street. On the other side, stretching as far as the corner in the other direction, were various unused warehouses. In front was an old stone wall, over the top of which I could see the dry fronds of bamboo plants. The position of the house where the dead man lay meant that I could enter and leave without being seen.

Inside I would perhaps find a document, a letter, a note that might reveal the name I was seeking.

I turned the key in the lock and went in. At the top of the stairs, next to a closed door lay a glove and two pieces of paper. One was a half sheet of smooth, blank paper. The other was a piece torn off an envelope; the top bore the Lisbon post office stamp with the previous day's date, and in one corner was an uncancelled French postage stamp; the addressee was Mr W. Rytmel.

I had seen that name in the countess's album below two lines of verse in English.

The glove I picked up from the floor was a man's glove,

made of white kid with black lacing. Inside was the name, in blue lettering, of a glove-maker in London. It was evident that I had found what I was looking for. The dead man's name was Rytmel.

I then opened the door in front of me and a shudder of horror ran through me. Stretched out on a sofa lay the corpse. The expression on his face suggested a quiet contentment; in fact, he looked as if he were sleeping. I touched him, and he was as cold as marble. Near him was a glass containing a small amount of liquid. It was opium.

I glanced around the room. On the black satin lining of a hat that had fallen to the floor, I saw embroidered in red a baronet's coronet and two large letters – a W and an R.

There was no time to waste. I returned home, settled myself at my desk and opened the album at the page where I had found the poems signed by W. Rytmel.

I should tell you that I have the same skill that Alexandre Dumas deemed degrading and insulting to the intelligence, for as you will have seen from this letter, I have excellent handwriting. I scrupulously copied, letter by letter, the two lines of poetry before me, repeating the process thirty or forty times. Then I began to construct different words using the letters I had practised. Finally, after careful study and many attempts, I took the half page of paper I had found in the house where the tragedy had occurred and in English - in a hand that no one in the world would ever dream could have been written by anyone else but the person who had written those lines of verse in the album and signed them with the name of Rytmel - I wrote a note confessing to suicide by means of opium. In this way, regardless of whether or not I found a convenient way of burying the body, any suspicion of homicide would vanish.

The countess was safe as long as I entered the house before

anyone else and placed the note I had written beside the body.

But I was still a forger. I repeated that sinister word to myself and felt a tremor of disgust. I had to think of an alternative, but what? Meanwhile, time was slipping away. Darkness fell. Remembering that the countess's cousin, forewarned by her, would be coming from Cascais, I decided to take with me a hammer and nails, so that as I left I could nail the door shut and thus delay the cousin's entry to the house where the dead man lay. A thousand fanciful ideas occurred to me, each more absurd than the last. I walked for hours, brooding, anxious, nervous, feverish, weary, conscious that I had in my pocket the terrible note with which I could remove the responsibility from a criminal's head, while taking upon myself an equal part in her remorse.

Finally, at around midnight, without really knowing why or to what purpose, but in obedience to a combination of fateful fascination and inspiration, I crept along by the wall, opened the door and went into the house. It was then that I unexpectedly encountered the doctor and the person known as the Tall Masked Man.

Deeply concerned by the disappearance of his friend Rytmel, who had been staying at his house in Lisbon, living the life of a fugitive, the countess's cousin, accompanied by two close friends, had arrived from Cascais at noon and gone directly to the mysterious house, to which he had the key and to which he knew Rytmel to be a frequent visitor. There they found the corpse. Aware of Rytmel's relationship with the countess and conscious of the need for the utmost secrecy, yet at the same time judging it vital to have a doctor certify that the man was indeed dead – for he might only appear to be so – the cousin planned and carried out the ambush of Doctor ***, whom he happened to know would be travelling along

The Mystery of the Sintra Road

the Sintra Road that evening.
 You know what happened on that night.

VI

The following day at eleven o'clock in the morning, those of us still remaining in that fateful house were gathered, with no masks now, around the corpse.

The Doctor had already been escorted back to the place on the Sintra Road where he had been kidnapped on the previous evening.

F., locked up for the night in an interior room of the house, had managed to make contact with a German living in the adjacent building and, in the morning, had passed a letter through a hole made in the communicating wall, the letter to the doctor that was subsequently published in the *Diário de Notícias*. He then broke down the door of the room that served as his prison and, during a violent struggle, tore off the mask worn by the countess's cousin. The other two masked men, seeing their companion exposed, took off their masks as well. One of them was a close friend of F.'s.

'What is going on here?' F. shouted angrily.

And then, pointing at the corpse, he went on:

'That man is dead, and he was robbed. Come on, explain yourselves! What happened?'

'Gentlemen,' exclaimed the Tall Masked Man, 'the secret that it has been my duty to keep safe within the walls of this house, and which I hope may remain buried here forever, belongs to a lady. Part of this secret, the part that most interests us and also explains the presence of this body lying here before us, is known to this gentleman.'

And turning to me, he added, 'In the name of our dignity, I appeal to you, on your honour, to tell us what you know.'

The Mystery of the Sintra Road

'I swore not to divulge it,' I replied. 'And I never will. When I entered this room, aware of a danger which I judged to present an immediate threat to the people most closely caught up in this mystery, I suddenly lost consciousness and fainted like a girl. In the face of danger I lack the physical energy that is the visible face of valour. Don't imagine, however, that I also lack the moral strength required to keep a secret, even at the cost perhaps of my own life! When questioned by masked individuals, whose identity was unknown to me, it was permissible for me to lie, to put a mask on my reply. Before decent people, who question me, invoking their dignity and my honour, my duty is to remain silent. I warn you that any attempt to compel me to do otherwise will be entirely in vain.'

'Not a very hard duty to fulfil!' the Tall Masked Man remarked ironically. 'The body of this poor fellow cannot stay here much longer. It's imperative that we make a decision and meet the responsibility weighing on us, in such a way that our consciences can rest easy with whatever steps we decide to take. Seeing that this gentleman refuses to begin, I shall do so myself.'

And he penned the following lines on a sheet of paper, reading them aloud as he wrote them.

'Dear Cousin:
The following men are currently gathered around a corpse at number... Rua de... (here followed our names). We form a supreme court, convened by chance, and which, in its first and final sitting, is about to pass judgement on the crime that Fate has set before us. If you have any evidence to give to this court, I ask you to do so.'

'Forgive me,' I said, 'could you, please, add these words: *A.M.C. refuses to give up the key.*'

He did as I asked, signed the letter, folded it up and said to one of his friends:
'Go now and deliver this document to the Countess of W.'

Half an hour later, a carriage came galloping down the street and stopped at the door of the house. We trundled the sofa on which the body lay into the bedroom and drew the curtain shut. The door opened and the countess entered.

She had followed my advice. She had used the twenty-four hours that had elapsed between my leaving her and her return to that house to write, with passionate and feverish eloquence, her unhappy tale. The notebook I am sending you contains a copy of the long letter she addressed to her cousin. I now relinquish the place I have been occupying in the columns of your newspaper to this document, which should really be called *Post-Mortem of an Adultery*.

After that, I will explain how we dealt with the body, and what became of the countess.

Her Confession

I

It sometimes seems to me that all this occurred in a distant life, like a novel that provokes sad longings or an old secret someone once told me and that only my heart remembers. But, all too soon, cruel reality descends on me, and then I suffer all the more, guiltily aware that I should never have stopped suffering. I am glad that I decided to make this confession. To describe a grief is to console it. Since making the decision to write down my personal story, I have felt a sense of relief and a stirring as of dreadful sorrows preparing to leave their hiding places.

My misfortunes began in Paris. That is where I began to die. I remember the day, the hour, the colour of the grass, the colour of the dress I wore. It was at the end of the winter before last, in May. He too, was in Paris, and we were constantly together. Sometimes we used to drive out of the city and spend the day in the countryside at Fontainebleau, Vincennes, or Bougival. It was a warm, serene Spring. The lilacs were already in bloom. We used to take along a little raffia basket containing fruit on a bed of lettuce leaves. We laughed like young newly-weds.

We had been in Paris for three months. The count – as I think I mentioned – was fox-hunting with Lord Grenley on the Duke of Beaufort's estate in Scotland.

Then there was a ball at the Hôtel de Ville, one of those official balls at which a motley crowd jostle each other beneath the chandeliers. I had just danced a waltz with an Austrian colonel, when the Viscountess of L., who was living in Paris at the time, came over to me, smiling gaily.

'Do you know someone by the name of Miss Shorn?' she asked.

'No, I don't. Is she an American?'

'No, she's Irish. An absolute gem. The mayor has danced with her, Countess Walevska planted a kiss on her forehead, and Gustave Doré promised he would make a drawing of her. She's going to be presented at the Tuileries. But do you know what I think? I find her a rather insignificant creature, although she does have lovely hair. In fact, people talk of little else! But you must know her.'

'Why?'

'She's danced with Captain Rytmel, and they seem very close. Are you laughing?'

'Laughing?'

'Yes... you laughed!'

'I never laugh, my dear, except when I feel like crying!'

'Come now!' she murmured, looking at me very hard.

And she moved away. My poor heart was pounding. Sometimes, deep inside us, an alarm bell rings and sleeping doubts awaken, take up their weapons and fire upon us.

Captain Rytmel had returned to my side.

'You look positively radiant,' I said to him. 'Tell me, who is Miss Shorn?'

He replied gravely: 'A close friend of my sister.'

We danced a quadrille, but that dance, usually so lively, reminded me, rather, of the ceremonies of some religious cult. My bouquet ended up scattered on the floor. At that instant, without knowing why, I hated Paris, the noise, the empire. I longed for the shaded walks of Sintra, the quiet, melancholy corners of Belas filled with the murmur of water.

I suggested we leave. In one of the last rooms, an extremely thin, distinguished old man was helping a tall blonde woman put on her cape.

Captain Rytmel, who had given me his arm, bowed slightly as he passed her and said softly to me:

'That's Miss Shorn.'

She really was very pretty, with her mass of thick, blonde, lustrous hair, her large, intelligent, serious eyes, her perfect figure.

That night I cried. In my bedroom, the lights and the fire were lit. When I entered, I went straight to the mirror. I let my cape fall from my shoulders. Then I looked fearfully at my own reflection, which gazed back at me as if wrapped in a kind of luminous mist. I thought myself ugly. I looked again. My arms were bare, my brightly lit head held high. Slowly, it dawned on me that I *was* still lovely, and that thought filled me with happiness. It's so good to be pretty!

Two days later, there was a military parade at Longchamp Racecourse. Captain Rytmel accompanied me. I had a seat in the Jockey Stand. There was an enormous crowd. The empress, the royal court, the foreign diplomats were all there – the stand was resplendent with uniforms, jewellery, feathers and shimmering silks. The regiments had begun their march past. The military bands, the bugles, the proud beating of the drums, the dull tramp of the marching battalions, the glittering bayonets, the shouts of command, the galloping horses, the gleaming helmets, the magnificent sky like a vast blue pavilion, set everything pulsating and provoked strange thoughts of war and glory. One's whole body trembled when those mighty ranks of men marched past shouting:

'Long live the emperor!'

Yes, it made even a mere woman like me tremble!

The infantry had passed. Rytmel had gone to speak to Miss

Shorn, who was accompanied by Lady Lyons. Baron Werther, the ambassador for Prussia, was seated next to her.

The artillery and cavalry were about to march past. The emperor, along with his general staff, had positioned himself in front of the stand reserved for members of the Jockey Club. We all craned our necks to see the generals surrounding him: Montauban, who had taken Peking; Canrobert with his long white hair; the solid figure of Bazaine; the haughty, high-complexioned profile of Mac-Mahon, back from Algeria…

Miss Shorn was also much studied in the Jockey Stand. The word was that the empress had smiled at her, and that Madame de Talhouet had sent her a posy of violets without even having met her!

But all eyes began to turn to the far end of the field, whence the cavalry would set off, and a wave of enthusiasm spread through the crowd at the sight of that great military presence. That morning there had been talk of certain differences of opinion between the Cabinet in Berlin and the Tuileries. Memories of Sadowa had surfaced, and a thousand other things of which I know nothing, and Baron Werther, smiling his pompous Prussian smile, was the object of many curious glances.

In the meantime, the cavalry had formed up in a line. The bugles sounded, flags were unfurled and, suddenly, that huge mass charged in close order from the end of the course to the Jockey Stand.

Helmets, breastplates, sabres, all glittered in the sun. The ground shook to the sound of galloping hooves. We could already hear the jingle of metal. We could make out the colonels – slim, much-decorated young men. We could hear the panting of the horses. The emperor had uncovered his head, and everyone in the stand was on their feet. Suddenly, as one, that huge column stopped, vibrant, motionless, gleaming, brandishing their sabres and shouting:

'Long live the emperor! Hurrah!'

'Hurrah!' responded the occupants of the stand.

Then, at the sight of such a splendid cavalry, such a mighty force, such imperial glory, and gripped by an irrepressible pride in their traditions or else possessed by military fervour, officers in the other divisions stepped forward and, raising their swords, shouted:

'To Berlin! To Berlin!'

Throughout the racecourse one could hear belligerent cries of:

'To Berlin! To Berlin!'

And in the stand some voices could be heard shouting:

'Yes, yes, to Berlin!'

The emperor stood up in his stirrups and raised his hand, as if demanding silence or saying: 'Wait!'

At those unexpected cries of 'To Berlin!', all the general staff had closed ranks around the emperor, and I, from my seat in the first few rows of the stand, saw Marshal Mac-Mahon abruptly rein in his horse, turn in his saddle, and with one hand resting on the gold-bordered scarlet cloth covering the animal's rump, look with faint amusement at the part of the stand where the Prussian ambassador was sitting. I followed his gaze and also saw...ah, I can hardly bear to say it. I saw Rytmel. I saw him standing beside Miss Shorn, bent towards her, talking, smiling, utterly engrossed, gazing into her bright eyes. She, intent and serious, returned his look with one that was equally deep and persuasive and in which I saw the end of my life.

II

Ten days later, the count returned and we left for Portugal. During what remained of my time in Paris with Rytmel, I said nothing of my doubts, and he seemed unconcerned about anything but our love for each other.

I returned to Lisbon and received regular letters from him. I used to study them, picking the sentences apart word by word to find the emotion concealed behind them. Alas, I always ended up discovering a gradual cooling in his feelings for me. Rytmel wrote very cheerfully and logically, trying to put his heart into what he wrote. His love was clearly changing from passion to reason. He spoke critically of love: proof that he was not dominated by it. He had even begun to use clever literary words. He waxed rhetorical! At the same time, his handwriting became firmer; he no longer wrote with the crooked, jerky, impetuous, pulsating hand that had so enchanted me. Now he wrote in a vile English cursive script, prudent and correct. He no longer wrote to me on whatever scrap of paper he could find, on pages torn from notebooks, on the backs of old letters, as the passion took him. He wrote instead on perfumed paper bought at Maison Maquet! The poor darling, what his heart may have lacked in love, his paper more than made up for in perfume!

And I? Perhaps the time has come for me to speak of my feelings. I hesitated to do so. I did not wish to place my heart on this page as if on a dissecting table. But I have thought better of it. I am no longer *someone*. I do not exist. I have no individuality. I am not a living woman, with nerves, defects, modesty. I am a case study, an example, a sort of specimen. I do not live by breathing nor by the circulation of my blood: I live abstractly, through the opinions and comments of those who read the *Diário de Notícias*, through the discussions that my griefs provoke. I am not a woman, I am a *novel*.

III

Do not think that I say this out of bitterness. The greatest happiness I could possibly have would be the annihilation of my individual self.

Therefore, I have no scruples. The wretchedly unhappy are like little children: they should be seen naked.

More than anything, I suppose these pages could prove to be a useful lesson for those caught up in the illusions of passion. So listen carefully!

It is eleven o'clock at night. At this hour, who knows how many women are suffering, hoping, lying, in the grip of a feeling that gives them little more than the joy of being wretched! You, my poor friend J., a woman who suffers discreetly and whose eyes I have so often seen brimming with tears! And Th..., you who have spent your life trembling, fearful, humiliated, watchful, always ready for flight... And you who find yourselves plunged into the cruel element of passion, barely alive, doing battle with human truth: listen to me – all of you!

The moment I fell in love, my life was in a state of permanent imbalance. I did not yield voluntarily to the attraction, but proudly and reluctantly. A thousand things were weeping inside me, but what suffered most of all was my pride. It refused to be reconciled. It resisted constantly and still protests. It seems subdued, resigned, but suddenly it rises up within me and strikes at my heart.

How I suffered! How I blushed! I blushed in front of poor Joana, my old nursemaid, an aged angel who knows as much about loving as she does about forgiving! I blushed in front of the servants. I felt happy when they smiled at me and trembled when they frowned. I gave them dresses, taught them how to style their hair. Sometimes they would go out in the afternoon and not come back until late at night; I blushed in my heart, but smiled at them.

I could not bear men to look at me: their eyes seemed laden with insults. I imagined that my affair was public knowledge, that people judged me to be a creature of easy virtue, which gave everyone the right to make me blush. How often I must have left the theatre in tears. I analysed every gesture, every stare, every unheard comment. So-and-so looked at me with contempt! That woman over there laughed insolently as I passed. Someone else pretended not to see me. If I were choosing a dress at a dressmaker's and the assistants said: 'This is a nice bright colour!' I would think to myself: 'I know what they're thinking, they're advising me to wear brash, lurid colours, scandalous colours, the kind that actresses wear!' And so I would leave, draw the blinds on my carriage and sob.

I didn't dare to kiss a child; I would look at her with infinite tenderness and go to take her in my arms, but at the last moment say to myself: 'Let the poor little angel be. You are not pure enough to touch her!'

There is worse. I blushed when my coachman looked at me! I smiled at him with the greatest affection, constantly fearing a sharp response, an impudent remark, an accusing word. When I got into the carriage and he stood respectfully to attention, I was so pleased that I felt like hugging him!

You find this distasteful, don't you?

One terrible example defines my condition: when my husband tenderly clasped my hand, it upset me as much as if I'd seen my lover betray me!

Poor me! How many times I tried to soothe my pride by

thinking of the theatrical glories of pain and suffering! How often I compared myself to those lyrical figures of passion, who stand before the footlights to recount their tales of anguish accompanied by the thunderous roar of an orchestra; characters such as Violetta, Lucia, Elvira, Amelia, Marguerite, Juliet, Desdemona! But alas, where were my castles, my pageboys, my cavalcades? A woman who lives the society life of the Chiado, who wears creations by Aline... what can possibly be glorious about her love?

And then, I know it's cruel but I have to confess it, there is always a point at which a woman wonders if it is really her lover's great moral qualities that keep her in thrall to him. Because if so, there would be some justification. And we feel deeply humiliated when we finally realise that when we love a man, what sways us is not only the nobility of his ideas and his idealism, but a certain something else, the colour of his hair, for instance, or the way he knots his tie. Let us be frank. Why do we continue to deny the narrow pettiness of our affections? Why do we have to paint in idealistic colours the very ordinary object of our desire? I am not saying that moral elevation may not be a powerful aid to our instinctive feelings of attraction, but in reality, what moves us is a man's external appearance. Let all those women reading these painful confessions look into their heart and ask what exactly made them love that man: his character or his physiognomy? And those who answer honestly will admit that, for them, the colour of a tailcoat had far more influence than an elevated mind.

Yes, I say this openly from my little corner of the world where everything has the hollow sound of a coffin lid banging shut. There is almost no way to explain or excuse women's romantic follies.

I was young and, like all women, my idle hours were

often filled with daydreams. I had my own private romances that were born, languished and died in the time it took me to embroider two flowers. I created adventures, passionate dramas and thrilling elopements while safely ensconced in my armchair by the fire.

Later, I read about other female characters and their loves and disappointments. I even experienced the shock of passion myself, yet I never saw, never understood, that these imaginings and attractions sprang from some natural reality, from the logic of circumstances, from the irresistible workings of the heart. I always thought they came from the ephemeral little world, romantic, literary and entirely fictitious, that exists in every woman's head.

I can see you smiling, cousin. Don't be surprised to hear me speak like this. Do you remember those intimate, serious conversations we used to have in Rua de...? Do you remember the terrace of the Clarence Hotel in Malta when the silent moonlight covered the sea? Surely you remember the ideas and imaginings that I loftily described as my 'systems'? Don't you remember you used to call me the 'fair philosopher'? Well, the philosopher has since felt, wept and suffered – all the essential ingredients for a good education. What better lesson could one have than to weep? Pain is an eternal truth, which endures while all theories die. You cannot imagine how much I have learned of life since unhappiness struck! You cannot imagine how many true and necessary ideas emerge from our incoherent tears.

That is why I no longer believe in 'the inevitable', which women use in order to shuffle off responsibility. I no longer believe in what we theatrically call Fate. The Will is everything, as vital a principle as the Sun, upon which Fate, fevers and the ideal burst like soap bubbles.

They come running to me, crying: 'It was Fate!' For goodness sake! Let's take an example. The trivial, or commonplace affair; what one might call the 'archetypal affair', the kind we see every day, in every street, at every house number, odd or even. The affair that jostles us on the Passeio Público, that eats a sorbet with us in the Confeitaria Italiana, and is buried beside us in the cemetery at Alto de São João.

The scene is simple, consisting of only three characters. I'll take the part of the woman. My husband is an honest, hardworking man. He gets tired, he struggles, he wears himself out. Early in the morning, he leaves for the office or the newspaper or the workshop or the ministry. He doesn't sleep enough, he lunches in a hurry, cuts short his siesta. He is all concentration, watchfulness, work, sacrifice. To what end?

So that our children can have white pinafores to wear and a uniformed nursemaid; so that my chairs are upholstered and not plain wood; so that I can wear silk dresses made by Marie, rather than making my own from cheap printed cotton, stitching away at night, by the feeble light of a lamp.

My husband is an honest fellow, kind, serious, good-natured. He doesn't use rice powder or brilliantine, nor does he wear showy ties or dress as if for the bull ring; he doesn't write serials for the press; he just works, works, works! With his long hard hours of tedium and fatigue, he earns his daily dinner and his yearly clothes. His one consolation is me. I am the centre of his life, his ideal, his absolute! He doesn't write romantic poems, because I am his poem, the muse of all his sacrifices; he has no affairs because I am his wife. He does not make remarkable journeys across deserts nor does he enjoy the prestige of the widely-travelled, because his world is no larger than the space filled by the sound of my voice. My husband didn't win the Battle of Sadowa, yet he wins the fierce but unsung daily battle to earn his children's daily bread.

He is fair, he is good, he is dedicated. He sleeps soundly because he deserves his rest; he likes to relax in his dressing gown because he has worked all day. He feels no need to wear a flower in his buttonhole because he always carries my image in his heart.

So what do I do?

I grow bored.

As soon as he goes out, I yawn and open a novel, find fault with the servants, comb the children's hair, yawn again, open the window and gaze out.

A young man walks past, handsome or strong, blond or dark, imbecile or halfwit. We exchange glances. He has a carnation pinned to his lapel, a complicated cravat. His hair is nicer than my husband's, the cut of his trousers is perfect, he wears English boots, he boos the dancers at the theatre.

I am captivated! I smile at him. He sends me a letter that lacks wit and grammar. I become infatuated; I hide the letter, kiss it, re-read it, and feel only scorn for the life I lead.

He sends me poems – poems, Lord help me! – and so I forget about my husband, his sacrifices, his goodness, his work, his kindness; I care nothing for the tears and despair to come; I abandon respectability, modesty, duty, family, social niceties, relationships, even my children, everything – all because I have been vanquished, seduced, mesmerized by an error-ridden sonnet copied from some treasury of poems!

Really! That, my poor friends, is what you call 'a fatal passion'!

And, in the meantime, how does *he* react to my awful sacrifice?

He cannot conceal his delight at having a mistress; he puts on mysterious, provocative airs; he compromises me; he leaves me alone and goes off to wait, in highly disreputable company, for the bull fight to start; he leaves my letters for anyone to read on a café table beside a bottle of cognac; he swears to his chums that he doesn't love me, that he's merely amusing himself. And if my husband were to horsewhip him in the middle of the Chiado, he – the lover – being a vile, cowardly, vulgar imbecile, would immediately go and register a complaint at the Boa-Hora police station!

And there you have your Don Juan!

No, we must demolish this despicable type – this so-called *conquistador*, this conqueror of women – through ridicule, caricature, horsewhipping and the police. As a type, the *conquistador* has neither allure, beauty, quality or greatness; and as a man, he has neither breeding, honesty, manners, wit, elegance, skill, courage, dignity, hygiene or spelling...

Please excuse this tirade, cousin. I'm in a very excitable mood; I am, as the saying goes, getting carried away by my own words. I sometimes forget my very modern sorrows and recall my old-fashioned indignation.

And do you suppose that, by condemning these trivial affairs, I am vindicating myself? Not so. Despite having loved a man who was excellent in every way, whose perfect superiority of mind you yourself knew and admired; even though our affection existed in such a refined, noble, proud setting, despite all that, I judge myself to be as reprehensible as those women of whom I spoke, and having no need of a court of law to condemn me, I do penance before the whole world.

IV

I suffered so much in my modest life, alone with my secret. How I wished I were a humble seamstress going for a walk with her child, hand-in-hand!

As I drove away from the theatre in my carriage, sitting on perfumed silk cushions, wrapped in a cashmere shawl, with a sable-skin rug for my feet, how I envied ordinary bourgeois women leaving their seats in the gods, bundled up in shapeless cloaks and picking their way through the mud of the streets.

On the days when I received letters from him, I would escape from Lisbon into the countryside! I would take them with me, crumpled and stained with kisses, to the Quinta de..., where I would plunge into the dense shade of the garden and stay there, immersed in the warm sunny air, lulled by the constant, calm rustle of leaves and the murmur of the fountains.

What a sweet life it is, that of trees and plants! The passivity of grass, the irresponsibility of water, the quiet sleep of moss, the gentle repose of shade! How often you consoled me and taught me to suffer in silence! How often I envied your stillness!

It was there, alone, re-reading those cruel letters, that I felt his love slipping away from me just as water from a stream slips through your fingers.

What would be left to me then?

Could I return to the serene life of the legitimate wife? Alas, no, I was for ever exiled from the peaceful paradise of the family, from the safe, chaste shade of respectability. Should I rebel and throw myself into a life of endless affairs? Heaven forbid! The idea was as repellent to me as the touch of some slimy creature upon my breast.

I was left, then, with no position in life. I belonged to no particular place. I had joined the sad, wretched brigade of abandoned women.

The only honest thing to do would be to hold fast to that love. My only absolution lay in the truth of my love. The more I cut myself off from the world and gave myself to my love, the more dignified my situation. There is always an honest side to such stark, clear-cut cases, and any kind of hypocritical compromise is repugnant to one's chaste instincts. All that remained to me, as regards position, duty and virtue, was to be Rytmel's, his alone and forever, and yet I could feel that he was slowly drifting away from me, just as I was drifting away from my husband.

Thus began my path to expiation.

With such affairs of the heart, it is not only society that punishes the lover; the situation itself contains the elements of a cruel justice. The heart is the first to be castigated by its own passion, while punishment for defiling one's honour is handed down later by men.

I was faced by the greatest moral dilemma that a woman in that unhappy situation can encounter.

I loved Rytmel, but Rytmel wanted to marry someone else.

What should I do? Should I, in the name of my love, divert that man's life from the natural, simple, human path that leads to marriage, family and duty?

Should I prevent him from marrying? But would that not be tantamount to blocking, to stifling the legitimate development of his life? Would that not be denying him the fruitful, serene joys of the family, by holding him captive in the sterile toils of a romantic passion?

Did I have the right to keep that man for the exclusive

use of my heart, to imprison him in a secret and illegitimate relationship where he would grow barren, where his talents and his abilities would grow rusty like useless weapons, and his only social engagement in the world would be to follow the rustle of my skirts? Did that not make my feelings look like mere brute selfishness? Did that not remove from my love its finest quality: the virtue of self-sacrifice?

Could I deprive him of one day having the children who would be the continuation of his existence, his immortality? Could I deprive him, in the name of my ideal love, of the presence of that sweet, silver-haired companion beneath whose mild gaze the good man tranquilly awaits the noble moment of his death?

And it wasn't only that. Can anyone honestly believe that these exalted loves will last, composed, as they are, of high emotions and tribulations, and with deceit, not duty, as their basis? And for the two or three years that this affair might last, had I the right to ruin the future of that other woman, poor girl, who loved him, who was building her life upon his heart, who was preparing herself to be a constant gracious, conscientious presence in his home? Again, no, that could not be.

On the other hand, was it fair that I, having sacrificed everything for him, from virtue to social respectability, should be cast aside like an old glove?

Would I, who meant everything when our love filled his imagination, thenceforth be nothing because it was no longer in his interest? Had I not exiled myself from the domestic paradise for his sake? For his sake, had I not renounced the peaceful joys of life, and the sublime expectation of a dignified death? Since I had sacrificed my husband's honour for him, could he not, for my sake, sacrifice a young girl's romantic ambitions? Was it right of him to have lured me away on false pretences, as if wrapped in a coat of ermine, to have led me blindfolded, spellbound, captive to the rhythm of his footsteps, to a dangerous place, an intolerable situation, and, on arriving there, say to me, 'Right, this is goodbye! I'm off to find happiness. You must stay here, though, because for you there is no way back, and if you take a step forward, you'll plunge into the mire of disgrace.'

No, that's quite wrong. Love is not a literary creation, it's a fact of nature, and as such, it allocates rights and lays down obligations. And I will not renounce the rights of love.

Why should I? For the sake of another woman? Am I expected to show such consideration for tears shed by a pair of foreign eyes, eyes that are two hundred leagues away, while I ignore the tears trickling down my own cheeks and which I catch in my own trembling hands!

'But you're married,' people say. And what of that? Why am I, who have lost most, deemed to be deserving of less sympathy? I, who live almost outside society, with no connection now to any of the superior things that support our lives, suspended above death by the slenderest of threads, by my love, must I now snap that thread with my own hands and destroy that love?

Is there some human obligation that demands this of me? Can any pity deserving of the name look upon my plight with a cold eye? Can any conscience justify it? If so, that conscience could teach the rocks in the sea to be hard!

But, cousin, all this will go no further than the paper I am writing on, because, in reality, I could never have done battle with *her*! She was the English 'Miss', destined to be a wife and mother – she was invincible! It placed her above past affections and above old mistakes, like those paintings of the Virgin standing on a globe of clay and mud around which the serpent coils.

I did not even try to fight!

It was around this time that I received a letter in which he said, 'I am leaving for Portugal.'

What was he coming here to do? What? To say goodbye to me? Was he coming to witness my pain? To comfort me? To convince me? Was he coming to surrender once more to my love? He was coming. Even he knew no more than that.

V

Rytmel arrived. The first time I saw him was at my house.

The count was in Brussels. It was the evening, and a number of friends were gathered in my music room: the Marchioness of..., an old absolutist, who had charmed the rather wild court of Dom Miguel; the Viscount of..., an insignificant fair-haired youth, whom I welcomed warmly because his late sister had been a close friend and my confidante at school.

The Viscountess of... was there too, a tiny, brazen, undistinguished creature, who coupled the virtue of being twenty years old with the misfortune of not knowing how to act her age, and whose speciality was trying to appear wildly unorthodox, when she was in fact merely banal. But beside me, lounging with oriental abandon on a sofa, was a truly original and superior man, a well-known name – Carlos Fradique Mendes. Many considered him to be merely eccentric, but in fact he had a very fine mind. I had the highest regard for his faultless character and for the violent, almost cruel, nature of his talent. He had been a friend of Baudelaire and had the same cold, feline, magnetic, inquisitorial eye. Like Baudelaire, he was clean-shaven, and, again like his poet friend, he dressed with originality and flair, so much so that his clothes were almost a work of art, at once exotic and proper. There was about him something of Ary Scheffer's romantic image of Satan and, at the same time, the cool exactitude of an English gentleman. He played the cello admirably, was a redoubtable swordsman, had travelled in the Orient, visited Mecca, and claimed to have been a Greek pirate. His mind had unexpected depths, and he often came up with thought-provoking ideas.

He it was who said of the pale Duchess of Morny: 'She has the melancholy stupidity of an angel'. The emperor often quoted this remark, as being simultaneously a profound criticism of both face and character.

Carlos Fradique was a sincere and dignified friend to me. He called me 'his dear brother'. He had known me since I was a child and had carried me in his arms. In Paris, he became quite the celebrity; he was what you might call a 'boulevard philosopher'. He had been *l'ami de coeur* of the dancer Rigolboche, and when she threw him over for Victor Capoul, Carlos Fradique wrote her some almost sublimely cruel, disdainful and comically lugubrious verses, a kind of funeral chant – a *Dies irae* – for dandyism. In them, he promised Rigolboche that when she died he would watch over her, so that even in her tomb, she would be able to keep up with chic, Parisian life. He translated some of the lines for me and when, later, he published the poem, they proved both sensational and influential:

> *I, who still love you, O pale-faced slut!*
> *I, who am kind, not proud,*
> *Will make quite sure they bury you*
> *In a made-to-measure shroud!*
> *And I'll come each night with Marie Larife,*
> *That Venus of the street,*
> *To remind the dust on your poor coffin*
> *Of the cancan's dancing feet.*
> *And when it's time for the summer races,*
> *– this I swear to your face –*
> *I'll tell your putrefying self*
> *If* Gladiator *wins the race...*

It was ten o'clock. In an impassive, almost languid voice, Carlos Fradique was in grotesque vein that night, recounting the monstrous but oddly mystical affair he had once had with a black cannibal woman.

'The poor soul,' he said, 'used to anoint her hair with rancid oil. I could tell where she was by the smell. One day, in the heat of passion, I went to her, rolled up my sleeve and offered her my bare arm. I wanted to make her a gift of it! She sniffed it, took a bite, tore off a long strip of flesh, chewed it, licked her lips and asked for more. Trembling with love, enraptured and happy to suffer for her, I gritted my teeth, and held out my arm again.'

'Oh, Senhor Fradique!' everyone cried out in horror at this gruesome tale.

'Then she took another bite,' he continued gravely. 'Again she liked it and again she asked for more.'

He was smiling almost beatifically as he spoke. We were all just about to rebel against the repellent absurdity of this whole story, when I saw my maid, Betty, standing at the door of the music room; she was beckoning to me, trembling, her eyes filled with alarm. I went over to her. She took me by the hand and led me into the corridor, where, spreading her arms wide in consternation, she whispered in my ear:

'It's him!'

I leaned, swooning, against the wall, feeling as if my heart would stop.

Betty tiptoed to the door of my dressing room and opened it. I went in. Rytmel, looking extremely pale, was standing beside a table. I pressed my hands to my breast and stood motionless, waiting. He came towards me with his arms outstretched, ready to embrace me. I fell to my knees at his feet and silently kissed his fingertips. He had knelt down too, and thus, with fingers interlaced, we gazed into each other's eyes and wept. Through my tears I could only murmur:

'It's been such a long time!

'Madam, my dearest child,' said Betty from the door, 'your guests, what will they be thinking?'

I was not even listening. It was he who said, smiling:

'You're quite right, Betty, quite right! We must join them immediately.'

And he gave me his arm. We went in, he grave-faced and I distracted and almost fainting, my eyes filled with tears and with a vague smile on my face.

I introduced Captain Rytmel, referring to him as one of the Count's old friends. I noticed the hint of a smile on the marchioness's face.

Then, turning to Rytmel, I said: 'This is Senhor Carlos Fradique, a former pirate.'

The two men shook hands.

'The countess flatters me. I was merely a privateer,' said Carlos.

To escape, I sat down at the piano and began to play. That way I could see Rytmel clearly. He was bathed in light. He seemed paler and his face graver. His brow was no longer innocent and unlined, but marked by a single deep furrow.

Fradique was still talking. He was now expounding on the virtues of northern women.

'The Irishwoman,' he was saying, 'has more grace than any other. Especially those Irishwomen who live beside the lakes! The best religion, the best morality, the best science for the female temperament is a lake. The still water, blue, pale, cold, peaceful, gives the soul great calm, a thirst for justice, the habit of seclusion and contemplation, a love of modesty and privacy, the secret of cultivating infinity through monotony, and the gift of forgiveness. I shall insist that any woman I marry must have rosy, polished fingernails and have lived next to a lake for at least a year!'

I saw Rytmel redden slightly and nervously twirl his moustaches.

With the lucid instinct of love, I knew at once that there was a connection between that glorification of lakes and Rytmel's private thoughts. It took me back to the military parade at Longchamp and Miss Shorn's blonde Irish curls. I turned to Carlos Fradique:

'My dear friend, won't you play the cello for us?'

The room gave onto the gardens, and the gentle breath of wind filled the billowing curtains. Carlos Fradique began to play a singularly sad ballad from the shores of the North Sea. You could hear the sighing waters, the magical rhythm of the waves, the measured beating of the oars of a Viking ship, and see the cold moonlight. I had gone out onto the verandah with Rytmel, and as the melody issued forth from the strings of the cello, I recalled the history of my love: the *Ceylon*, the silent nights when he swore he loved me truly, and when the voice of the sea seemed endlessly to affirm his words; I recalled the terraces of Valletta bathed in moonlight, the rose bushes at the Clarence Hotel, the soft meadows of Ville d'Avray. I saw him wounded, his face ashen against the pillows; I saw him aboard *The Romantic*, the master of our escape together, weeping over the disasters of love. These memories came and went in my mind, interwoven with the music of the cello.

VI

The next day, I was due to meet him at that fateful house. I went there, as always, dressed entirely in black, hidden behind a large veil. I was deathly pale, and my heart was pounding furiously. It was a moment of crisis. I had made up my mind to have a clear, definitive, unequivocal discussion with Rytmel. If he were to say so much as one sharp or indifferent word or make an impatient gesture, I would consider myself as having been abandoned, exiled from life. I would retire to a chalet in Switzerland or to Jerusalem or to the melancholy of a cloister in the South of France. That, I had decided, was the only solution to my predicament.

When I arrived at the house, he had not yet arrived. For a long time, I sat motionless in an armchair. The noises from the street seemed to rise up from the depths of a dream. The room was lit by the subdued light entering through the opaque glass windows. I was filled with the indefinable feeling that overtakes you when you have spent too long in some quiet, sad place watching the silent falling of rain.

Suddenly the door creaked open and he came in.

He had been in the countryside and brought me a bunch of tiny flowers picked from the hedgerows. He came and leaned on the back of my chair and dropped the flowers into my lap.

Then, speaking very softly, his face next to mine, he said:

'I've been thinking of you all day as I wandered across the fields.'

I made no response, and with my eyes fixed on the coloured pattern of the carpet, I cruelly pulled the petals off those little meadow flowers. I took a kind of bitter glee in destroying those delicate things, which had come from him and which, it seemed to me, had learned from him how to lie.

'You were in my thoughts all the time, and the walk itself was enchanting,' he repeated in a gently insistent voice.

I raised my eyes to him.

'Tell me: do you know how to lie?'

'Goodness,' he said, drawing back, 'you don't seem to like me very much today!'

Again I said nothing, but my lap was full of mutilated flowers.

He knelt down beside me and, taking my hands and gazing into my impassive eyes, he waited, with loving, patient concern, for me to break my silence. I felt my whole being, body and soul, drawn helplessly towards him, but managed, nonetheless, to control myself. In the end, he got slowly to his feet, flung himself down on a sofa, where he remained, as though seeking refuge there, leafing through a volume of Musset's poems he found lying on the table.

I stood up and snatched the book from his hands.

'The problem is this. I don't understand the situation, and you have to explain it to me, frankly and clearly, syllable by syllable! You don't love me, that much is obvious. Please don't deny it. I could tell from the tone of the very first letters you wrote to me from London. And now I can see it in your eyes, your words, your silence even. There's something there, I don't know what, but there is. The truth is that you're leaving me, you don't love me. You have to explain. It can't go on like this. I'm in such pain. If you only knew! I cried all night…'

And I promptly began to cry again, sobs shaking my whole body. He had taken my hands and begun to speak to me in the sweetest of terms, with all the tenderness of a lover and the solace of a friend. I pushed him away and, holding back my tears, said:

'No, no, you need to tell me everything. I don't know what it is exactly that I want to ask you or perhaps I don't dare. But you know what you need to say to me. Tell me the truth.'

Folding his arms, he answered with great composure:

'My dear friend, the fact is that your imaginings are our misfortune. It's not your fault, I know: it's part of being female. Women cannot bear serenity. If they have a quiet life, they look for romance, if they're involved in a romance they look for sadness. Those small, lovely craniums of yours are always harbouring a storm. So, what can I say? Didn't I come to Portugal of my own free will? Hasn't my love always been by your side, like a faithful dog? What more do you want? You say you find me reserved. But if I raged like an Othello, you would doubtless find me ridiculous. Besides, you know perfectly well that I love you! I say it to you now, sitting here on this sofa, in my tailcoat, in an ordinary house with a street number, and from which I will set off shortly to dine, perhaps to play chess, and to don – who knows? – a dressing gown! That's all very regrettable, I know. But is that why you have no confidence in me? Tell me candidly, then: if I were to go into paroxyms of passion like Mark Antony, or were to put on a Venetian costume, or if this were a feudal abbey, or if I were setting forth from here to conquer Jerusalem, tell me – would you be more inclined to trust me?'

'That's all meaningless nonsense...'

'Oh, my dearest...'

'Your dearest,' I said, interrupting, 'asks only an honest, loyal heart. So it's all in my imagination, is it? There's nothing to keep us apart? Well then, I am going to say something, and I swear that my decision is binding and I say it calmly, coolly, unemotionally, having thought it through from every angle.'

'For God's sake, tell me, what is it?'

'You accept this resolution of mine?'

'A resolution? What does it involve?'

'It involves the only thing that will make me believe in you to the same degree that I believe in myself. Do you accept?'

'How could I not?'

'Well then,' I began, and taking his hands, my lips close to his face, I said in a voice as ardent as a kiss:

'Let us elope tomorrow.'

Rytmel turned slightly pale and, slowly withdrawing his hands from mine, said:

'You do realise that there can be no going back afterwards?'

'Yes.'

He had sat down, his eyes fixed on the carpet, while I, standing beside him with my hand resting on his shoulder, was saying to him in a dream-like murmur:

'I've been thinking about this for a month. Let's go to Naples. Let's go wherever you would like to go. I adore you… I'm like someone sliding into sleep. I adore you and I want to be with you…'

I placed my hand on his brow and tilted his head back in order to see the answer in his eyes; they were filled with tears.

'But Rytmel, you're crying!'

'No, no, my love! I was thinking of my mother, whom I may perhaps never see again. But that's nothing. I love you, I love you… so *avante*!'

And he folded me in a passionate embrace, as if sealing an everlasting pact.

VII

I immediately returned home and summoned Betty.

'Betty,' I said, closing the bedroom door. 'Come quickly, Betty, I need to tell you something. You're not to say No.'

'Lord almighty! Calm down, my dear child, calm down! Goodness, how pale you are!'

'Betty, there can be no going back now… it has to be. I made the decision quite calmly. See how relaxed I am, not agitated or nervous or anything. It's a good decision. Betty, don't say that it isn't!'

'But my dear lady…'

'There's no turning back. Besides, I'm so happy, so very happy!'

'Are you really?'

'Yes, madly. And if it were not to be, I would die.'

'So what is it?'

'Tomorrow we're going to elope.'

Betty shuddered from head to toe. She fixed me with a long, tear-filled gaze and said in a choked voice, her hands pressed together:

'And what about me?'

I flung myself into her arms.

'You don't think I would leave you behind, do you, Betty? You're coming with us.'

And I ran about the bedroom, opening wardrobes, throwing clothes onto the bed, clapping my hands and shouting:

'Come on, Betty, pack. Quickly now!'

I ordered the carriage to be made ready. It was four o'clock. I went down to the Chiado. I was carefree, triumphant; my

The Mystery of the Sintra Road

life seemed to me large, full, splendid, dazzling. I went into dressmakers' shops, I looked and chose and bought with the eagerness of a bride and the circumspection of a conspirator. I greeted various female friends.

'Are you going away?' they asked me.

'Yes, to France.'

'When there's a war on?'

'There's no war. But if there was one, don't you think it would be interesting to see Prussians being killed?'

At the door of Sassetti's I met Carlos Fradique.

'I'm going away tomorrow,' I said.

'I'm going away today,' he replied. 'I was just coming to see you to say goodbye.'

'Well, that's a surprise! You're going to France? What for?'

'To see the battlefields by moonlight or torchlight. I'm sure that people die in the most interesting positions.'

'But you're going there in vain,' I insisted. 'The war hasn't started. I'm sure of it. That's why I'm going to Italy.'

'To Italy! But then... ah! So you're off to Italy? My poor friend, who knows how this will end! Well, whatever happens and wherever it happens, be it joyful or sad, I'll be there to comfort you or make up a trio with my cello. I am yours, *adesso e sempre.*'

He shook my hand. I don't know why, but his words had dampened my spirits.

I wanted to go down to the Aterro. Evening was coming on. The river was still and luminous, and the hills on the far side were wrapped in a soft blue haze. Tawny-coloured clouds hung above the water, like a halo. A few boats were passing, their sails coloured by the rosy light.

I was feeling somewhat downcast. The river, the trivial little houses, all the familiar things that had, until then, seemed almost inexpressive, took on a kindly appearance now that I was seeing them for the last time. I felt sentimentally attached to them. I would have liked to smile, to joke, but all those entirely alien things, the landscape, the dull Hotel Central, the terrace of the Bragança Hotel, even gloomy, vulgar Rua do Arsenal, unexpectedly awoke in me an instinctive desire for tranquillity, for family, for quiet times; they made the adventure I was about to embark upon stand out stark and black in my life; like a gathering of familiar friendly faces come to wave me off, they evoked irrevocable things – exile and death!

My carriage trundled slowly up steep Rua do Alecrim. The streetlamps were already being lit. The sky was still light.

I passed a lady walking down the hill, leading a child by the hand; she was a distinguished-looking young woman and seemed very contented. The child, golden-haired, chubby and laughing, was chattering away in that sweet, mysterious language, which is all that remains of Heaven's alphabet.

How lovely to be so at peace with oneself, neatly dressed, one's heart quietly beating, immersed in the good things of life, and holding a child by the hand! If I were her, I would be cheerful and amiable, I would go for walks, give my little man sweeties and dress him in pastel colours, with a flower in his sash; I would talk to him and, when we got home, weary from our walk, I would embrace the peace and serenity of my life. He would fall asleep on the sofa. The window would be open. Large white moths would flutter round the lamp, and kneeling, I would try to get him ready for bed without waking him and softly, secretly, sing him one of Mozart's lullabies. Meanwhile in a corner, his father's quill would be scratching away on some paper. Ah, the perfumed paradises of life, how very far away I am from you!

My mind was still full of all these things when I arrived

home. In the middle of my room my closed trunks, straps buckled, were stacked one on top of each other. Nearby a large fur had been rolled up into a bundle and secured with a strap. Everything was ready, we were leaving the following morning. My nostalgia for the uneventful life immediately vanished.

I felt instead a pressing need for freedom, for the open sea, for vast, distant lands that one could either cross at speed or at the leisurely pace of a wagon. It was night. I did not call for a lamp. The light from the moon was filtering in through the branches of the trees in the garden. I sat down at the window.

My future appeared to me then to have all the charm of a beautiful novel. A thousand imaginings and fantasies were singing inside my head. I felt I was entering upon a life of dangers, ecstasies and glories. I saw myself on the deck of a steamer at risk of shipwreck; or somewhere high up among moonlit mountains with a band of smugglers singing to the Blessèd Virgin; or in the silence of a camel train escorted by Bedouins, camped outside Jerusalem on the Mount of Olives. I would criss-cross Italy, galloping into cities as the lamps were being lit and the crowds were filling avenues flanked by lofty Renaissance palaces. I imagined myself in Naples, on the calm, moonlit bay; sleeping beneath the vines in Ischia, or resting in the cool grottos of Posillipo, where it is said the Naiads still weep… Suddenly, the door opened and a servant entered, bearing a letter. I did not see the handwriting on the envelope, I didn't even look, but I knew. A lamp was brought in. Yes, it was from Rytmel! I held it in my hand for a long time, uncertain and trembling. Then I put it down on a marble-topped table and went to look at myself in the mirror. I was terribly pale. Meanwhile, I could feel the letter calling to me, it seemed to glow on the white marble. I picked it up, weighed it in my hand, smelled its perfume, and slowly, uttering a weary sigh, with my arms bent beneath its weight, I slit it open.

VIII

I transcribe below the whole of that dreadful letter:

My Darling,
My luggage is here in my room, packed and ready to go. I have my passport... Oh, make sure you have yours. I have written to my mother. And I have written to a close friend who knows the innermost secrets of my life. So, as you see, I am holding firmly to your resolution. I am alone. I hold my fate captive in my hand, like a bird – or like a glove: I can set it down on the deck of a mail-boat, place it on a card on a gambling table, attach it to the point of a sword, or close my hand around it and give it to you. But you, because of your social position, have a defined place in the world, limited and circumscribed. You are confined by a wedding ring to a particular order of things, to certain laws, and you are, in life, like a ship at anchor upon the sea. That is why it is only proper, before you wrench yourself away from your legitimate centre, that I, who have experience of misfortunes, journeys, and the way of the world in general, should say a few words to you, which, while they may not warm your heart, will garner for me the respect of your good nature. You trust too much to love, my sweet friend! Forget for a moment my honour and my faithfulness. I speak of love, that law, mystery or symbol, that natural force or literary invention. You trust too much to it! Love, that best of refuges, that solid, protecting buttress in life, for which everyone in the world longs, and which some find in the family, some in science and others in art, you seem to want to find only in passion, and I don't know if that is fair or even feasible!

The Mystery of the Sintra Road

I believe you put too much store by love! It builds nothing, resolves nothing, compromises everything and takes no responsibility for anything. Love is an imbalance of the faculties; it is a momentous but ephemeral surrender to sensation, which means that one cannot entrust one's fate to it. It's a limitation of freedom and a diminution of character; it defines and circumscribes the individual; it's a natural tyranny, the cunning enemy of discretion and choice. Do you want to base your life on that? Do you believe that love can never falter? Yes, that's possible for as long as it lives on the unforeseen, on romance and on obstacles, for as long as it needs carriages with drawn blinds; but as soon as it becomes a normal, regular, permanent situation, becomes organised and managed, it burns out; and when it does try to linger, it resembles the pathetic painted flames on a theatre backdrop depicting Hell. And once love disappears, what reason would there be to exist and how could you justify your incoherent fate? You would have no position in society, everything would be forbidden to you, either by the force of social custom or by your own personal standards. To repent and retreat into a legitimate existence would be impossible. Forgiveness exists in the church, but not in society! To persist in living for love alone would be a hypocritical mistake and could one day find you living in debauchery.

Today, you imagine love to be the sole direction, the sole purpose of your life. That's not true: it is merely the dominant feature of your personality. There are other demands that you cannot hear clamouring inside you at the moment, because they have been fully satisfied by the milieu in which you've been living; but later on, when you have withdrawn from everything and shut yourself up in love, as if in a shell, you will sorely miss that 'something', which is society, other people's

The Mystery of the Sintra Road

opinions, friendship, status, the matchless joy we get from the high regard in which we are held by our peers. Being deprived of your usual elegant, velvet, feathered, garlanded place in society will leave you feeling abandoned. And the consolations that love might offer in compensation for that lack will seem, in your eyes, as tedious as the consolations society might offer for a lack of love. The only place left for a woman who elopes with her lover is the demi-monde or, if she's famous for some particular talent or art, she might find equivocal acceptance in certain artistic salons. But you wouldn't want to go to Italy and visit Madame de Salmé in Naples, would you? Or sing in the theatre or have to go to the trouble of writing a book. To live modestly, you will have to live sadly. To live openly, you must expect humiliation. And do you think that, even for a year, you could live in absolute privacy and secrecy?

The secret, the refuge, the perfumed love-nest on the fifth storey, are all very nice when one can continue to live in society and in the world; the official, public nature of our lives lends a curious charm to those moments of mystery. But if the mystery were to become eternal, then it would be like the legendary torment of eternal beatitude. Imagine two individuals being obliged by circumstance to live entirely with and for each other, constantly immersed in each other's lives, not two of Swedenborg's disciples or two starving wretches marooned on Robinson Crusoe's island, you understand, but two energetic people brought up during the time of the Second French Empire, accustomed to a life of luxury and living in a noisy, lively city. That, believe me, must be a very bitter end.

Just think, our life together will drag on glumly from country to country, with no circle of friends, no family, no end. We will never enjoy the peace of the just during our lifetime nor at the solemn moment of death. Our life will be like that of those romantic shades Paolo and Francesca da Rimini borne along on the contradictory winds. In the end we will die, two sterile individuals, who created nothing and left no one on Earth to inherit their character; and when everyone else, through their children, achieves the only true immortality, we alone will be merely mortal, and for us, far more than for others, the idea of dying will be unremittingly bleak! Forgive my writing to you in this way, but I have done my duty. And now I can freely – and surprisingly – say that I am happy, and that the moment tomorrow, when we see the land disappearing and find ourselves alone on the infinite sea, will be so beautiful, I will feel that it alone justifies my life.'

When I had finished reading Rytmel's letter, I sat down beside my luggage, staring into space, my mind a blank. I opened a drawer, took out some small lace knicknack, and grimly, automatically closed the drawer again. Then I called to Betty:

'Betty, what time is it?'

'Eleven, Madam.'

'Bring me some water, will you, I'm thirsty. Bring me some water with lemon.'

When she went out, I got up and leaned my head against the window, watching the slow, gentle swaying of the dark branches. The moon seemed frozen in the sky. Betty returned.

'You know, Betty,' I said in a faint voice, 'I'm frightened of dying mad.'

She looked at me and seeing my distraught face, said:

'What's happened, what's happened? Cry, my precious child, cry…'

'I can't, I can't. I'm dying… Come here, Betty!

'What is it? Would you like to lie down? Say something!'

And raising her eyes and hands to heaven, in a prayer of

anguish and desperation, she exclaimed:

'Ah, Madam, none of this would have happened if your Mama were still alive!'

She began to cry. I looked at her in great distress, felt my eyes fill with tears, my sobs choking me, and throwing myself into her arms, I cried, cried bitterly, cried savagely, cried for what I had lost and for how I had been betrayed, I cried for my respectable past, I cried for my delicious sins, cried simply to feel that I was crying.

IX

I grew calmer, and lay exhausted, silent and as if dead on the chaise-longue. I gazed blankly at the flickering lamplight.

'Betty,' I said, 'go to bed. I'm all right now. Off you go.'

She left the room, still weeping. The room was barely lit. Through the window, I could see the branches of the trees in the garden, silhouetted dark against the pale, moon-bright sky. I sat for a long time, staring unthinkingly into space. Slowly, if I remember rightly, my mind turned to things other than my own sorrow: I remembered the cut of a dress that I had sketched for Aline to make for me.

At last I got up and, for a long time, paced up and down in my room, and that movement brought home to me the nature and reality of my troubles. I tore a page out of a notebook, and, in a frenzy, scribbled: *You are right, you are right. I will see you at the house tomorrow evening at ten o'clock. Until then, I will not tell you that I love you, only how I suffer.*

I myself went out into the corridor, and from the top of the silent staircase, lit by the frosted globe of a large lamp, I called André, a dim-witted, but discreet servant, and threw the sealed note down to him, saying:

'Deliver this immediately. Take a cab.'

And I told him how to find my cousin's house, where Rytmel was a guest.

I went and sat at my bedroom window; a sweet perfume drifted in from the garden; and there was something romantically, sadly restful about the moonlight and the vast shadows. Gradually, my misfortune began to appear before me in its entirety, clear in every detail, as if it were a map.

The Mystery of the Sintra Road

I had been betrayed! At twenty-three, in the grip of passion, seduced by the delicate charms of love, I had been betrayed! I felt then, for the first time, the pangs of jealousy, that fearsome creature, so often found in epic verse, so often dragged onto the stage, so familiar to the police; so cruel, so ridiculous, but so real! I could see him! I had met him! I found him irritating and corrosive; his reasoning was petty, Jesuitical, implacable and cruel, in short, he was everything that can turn even the purest heart into the filthy lair of a wild beast.

I felt the very worst of jealousies: the one that describes our rival, tells us her name, sketches a profile, shows her to us, arms us and obliges us to attack. I had a focus for my jealousy: *her*. It was *her*, the *other woman!* I had a vague recollection of her: fine, abundant blonde hair, a cloud of spun gold. I had seen her dressed in purple at the military review at Longchamp. She had a candid manner. Men would find in her everything that promised a peaceful future. What secret charm emanated from that slender, fragile body? Was it innocence? Was it intelligence? Was it her knowledge of love? I was burning to meet her! And I knew nothing about her except that she was Irish, and her name was Miss Shorn.

Ah, yes, I knew something else – he loved her!

If only I could get to know her, if only! But how? Maybe through her letters... Of course! She must pour all her most personal feelings into them. She was blonde, she was English, and must therefore be a rationalist: she would write calmly, plainly, without any explosions of passion. In her letters she would probably reveal her heart. I would know her well if I read them! Through her letters I would discover Rytmel's state of mind, the evolution of his love! I had to read them, even if I had to beg, steal or buy them!

Of course, I had no actual proof that he received letters

from her, but I was sure that they existed and that his heart was full of them.

I needed to calm down, to sleep, but when I went to my bed, my poor brain was too tempest-tossed to rest; it was as if it were caught up in one of those storms that brings to the surface of the same wave the flotsam of a shipwreck and a tangle of seaweed. The most serious and the most futile of memories rose to the top of that mental whirlpool, my griefs and my fantasies, my disastrous love and the words from a comic opera! I felt a fever coming on. I called Betty.

'Betty! I can't sleep, I don't know what's wrong. I have to sleep. Tomorrow I need to have all my wits about me. If I don't sleep I'm lost, I'll go mad… Give me something.'

'But what, Madam?'

'Anything. Fetch me that drink you used to give to Mama for insomnia, the one that you yourself take for your rheumatism. Do we still have some?'

'Opium, you mean?'

'I don't know! Opium and water, opium and wine, whatever it may be. The doctor told me…'

'Yes, my child, I have some opium. Just one drop in a glass of water. But what if it harms you?'

'Give me some, will you, the doctor mentioned it to me yesterday. Quickly now.'

I drank it. It was opium in water, I believe. I'm not sure. I seemed to fall asleep at once, and I remember that as I slept, I felt as if I were constantly walking, caught up in a kind of perpetual motion that took every possible form: now slow and leisurely as if I were strolling down a tree-lined avenue; then quickly, as if I were dancing a waltz by Gounod; then solemnly and sadly as if I were accompanying a funeral cortège; then swiftly and glidingly as if I were in Paris, in winter, and skating over the snow.

In the morning, I woke feeling serene and resolute. I sent for the carriage and went out. At two o'clock in the afternoon, I stopped in Belas outside my cousin's house. I had known from the previous morning that Rytmel was staying with him. I went up the steps to the door. Luís, a Portuguese servant, appeared. I knew him, he was a fool, always after money, and discreet only out of fear.

'Is Captain Rytmel in?'

'He has gone out, countess.'

'And Jacques?'

'He went with him, countess.'

Jacques was Rytmel's long-standing servant.

'Luís, take me to Captain Rytmel's room.'

When he opened the door to the room, I shrank back. I felt humiliated. Nevertheless, I hurried over to the desk, rifled through the drawers and in the bureau. There were no letters, or only ones of no interest to me. Annoyed, I opened the dressers, rummaged through his clothes, searched suitcases and trunks, felt in his pockets and under his pillow. I was shaking, breathless. It was like an inquisitorial search, frantic, desperate, shameless!

'Luís,' I said quietly. 'I've already given you twenty *moedas*. How would you like fifty?'

'But, countess...'

'Where does the gentleman keep his letters? I'll give you more. I'll give you everything, you idiot... Where are his letters?'

'I don't know, madam,' said Luís in a plaintive voice.

'You must have seen them. Isn't there some other desk or bureau or perhaps a wallet?'

'Yes, he has a morocco leather wallet, but he will have

The Mystery of the Sintra Road

taken that with him. It's full of letters. He took it, I'm sure. He never leaves it behind.'

I left, running down the stairs, fleeing from that shameful, bungled, brazen search. I leaped into the waiting carriage.

'Home!' I cried.

I had drawn the blinds and was sobbing, and yet I shed no tears.

'Betty! Betty!' I called as soon as I arrived.

'Betty,' I said excitedly, closing the door of my room. 'Tell me, that mixture of opium and water, can it do any harm?'

'Why? Do you feel unwell?'

'No. I'm fine. It is harmless though, isn't it?'

'Yes.'

'Do you swear?'

'Yes, I swear, but…'

'Do you swear on the Bible?'

'But why, madam? Yes, I swear, but why?'

'Give me all the opium you have.'

'Do you want to sleep?'

'No.'

Betty looked at me and turned pale.

'But, Madam, what do you want it for?'

'Come now, Betty, give it to me. Do you really think I want to kill myself?'

She made no reply.

'Don't be so silly!' I said, laughing. 'If I wanted to kill myself, I wouldn't ask you for it. But I'm quite happy now… Certain things have happened, you see. I won't tell you what just yet, but I'm happy. And do you know what? Very soon I'm going to meet him.'

And in a quieter voice, as if embarrassed, I added:

'I'm meeting him at ten o'clock, you see. And I want to

sleep away the hours until then.'

'In that case, madam, no, it won't do you any harm! I'll prepare it for you myself. The bottle is here in the drawer of the washstand. No, no, it won't hurt you!'

'Of course it won't, Betty! It's in this drawer, you say. Good. You just add one drop, is that right? I'll be fine. I'm so happy that I'm not sure I want to sleep now. Stay here and talk to me. It's five o'clock. It won't be long till ten. I can easily wait. The bottle's in that drawer, is it? Good. Do you know something, Betty? I'm so happy, I don't want to sleep. Tell me a story.'

Seeing me so cheerful, the poor woman smiled. I, meanwhile, had my eyes fixed on the drawer in the washstand. And Betty talked and talked! I listened to her without understanding a single word, as if I were listening to a babbling stream.

X

Meanwhile, evening was closing in and I was feeling increasingly uneasy and anxious.

Cousin, I'm not sure I can tell you exactly what happened that night. And you won't demand that I do so, will you? Nothing could be more terrible than to have to set out my crime in vivid detail. Forgive my confused words and my unsteady handwriting.

It was ten o'clock at night: I went to the house. Rytmel had already arrived. He looked pale, I thought, and a shiver instinctively ran through me. We talked. While he was speaking, I watched him keenly, trying to spot where on his person he might keep that wallet containing all those letters. At the same time, with my hand damp with perspiration, I kept feeling the glass bottle in my pocket: the bottle of opium. It was a green cut-glass bottle with a metal top. Rytmel's words that night were exceptionally sweet and loving, still full of passion as he tried to explain his letter. Did those words really come from the depths of his heart, I wondered. Or was it just empty rhetoric, as false as a theatre backdrop? How could I know? Only his letters could reveal that to me, and he had them there in his pocket! I could see the shape of the wallet now in his breast pocket! Therein lay the verdict on my life: endless grief or a future of boundless peace! How could I possibly hesitate? Rytmel was still talking. I was trembling all over. Now I could not take my eyes off a glass that was there on the table beside a carafe of water. The curtain to the bedroom was drawn; it was dark.

Betty, who had come with me, had remained elsewhere in

the house, in a room that opened onto a plot of vacant land.

'What if it all goes horribly wrong?' I thought. 'There are people who have succumbed completely and whose sleep has ended in the cold grave.'

But all the time, the knowledge that his wallet was there within my grasp kept luring me on like some splendid, living thing. Perhaps I could go over to him, seduce him with the ardour of my words, and then stealthily, slyly, seize the wallet from him and run away, leap into my carriage and escape. But what if he were to resist? What if he forgot his dignity and my frailty? What if he were to subdue me violently and snatch back the letters?

No, that wouldn't work. He had to be sleeping soundly. If the letters were innocent, unemotional and cool in tone, then how I would kneel beside his sleeping body, how I would wait for him to wake! What a sublime dawn he would find in my eyes when he opened his! But what if the letters spoke of guilt, treachery, abandonment, what then?

I stood up. Rytmel had a glass of water beside him, from which he sipped as he smoked. I let him continue to smoke. However, I didn't know how best to find a moment long enough to put one drop of opium in the glass.

I invented a feeble, trivial excuse.

'Rytmel,' I said, in a ridiculously cheery voice, like a character out of one of Scribe's comedies, 'go and tell Betty that she can go home, if she wants. The poor thing has hardly slept, she's not well.'

He left the room, and I got to my feet. But when I went over to the table and stood looking at the glass, I froze, unable to move. I remained like that for what seemed like an eternity, but which could only have been a matter of seconds, with my hand gripping the bottle in my pocket. But it had to be done.

I could hear his voice, he was coming back, I could hear his footsteps, he was about to come into the room... Biting my lip so as not to cry out, I hurriedly took the bottle from my pocket and emptied it into the glass.

He entered. I dropped onto a chair, trembling, bathed in sweat, and at the same time, I'm not sure why, I was filled with a great tenderness for him. Smiling and almost in tears, I said:

'Ah, I love you so much! Come and sit beside me!'

Rytmel smiled. And – oh dear God – he came towards me, still smiling, I think, and he picked up the glass, and with the glass in his hand, he said:

'No one knows that better than I. If it weren't for your love, how could I live?'

He still had the glass in his hand. I sat as if under a spell. I could see the water glinting; it seemed to have a greenish tinge to it. I could see the light sparkling on the cut-glass surface.

Finally, he took a sip!

From that moment I was terrified. My God! What if he died? But why should he? Don't we give opium to children, to the sick? Isn't it the merciful solution to pain? There was no danger. When he woke, I would be extra tender, extra loving, to absolve myself from that imprudent adventure! Even if he is guilty I will still love him, I said to myself. The poor man. Wasn't it punishment enough for him to have to be lured into that heavy, unnatural slumber? Yes, I would still love him if he was guilty. I would still love him if he had betrayed me!

For now, though, he lay silently on the sofa with his head back. Suddenly, he seemed to turn very pale, to wince or to smile. I don't know what happened next. I don't remember whether we spoke, whether he quietly fell asleep, whether he was seized by convulsions. I remember nothing.

It must have been midnight when I found myself kneeling

at his side. He was lying motionless on the sofa. Two hours had passed. He felt cold, his face was ashen. I didn't dare call Betty. I paced back and forth in wild distraction. I spread a shawl over him.

'He is going to wake up,' I kept repeating to myself.

I gently smoothed his slightly dishevelled hair. Suddenly, the clear and terrifying idea came to me: he was dead! I felt as if everything had ended. But gently, sweetly, I called to him:

'Rytmel! Rytmel!'

And I tiptoed around so as not to wake him! I stopped abruptly, looked at him with frantic eyes, then flung myself on his body, sobbing:

'Rytmel! Rytmel!'

I raised him up: terror gave me sudden strength. His head hung lifeless. I untied his cravat and cradled him in my arms. At that point, my hand touched the wallet in his breast pocket. I had forgotten about the letters. And I had done all this just so that I could read them. I took off his jacket, with some difficulty, because his muscles were already growing stiff. Along with the wallet there were other papers and a bundle of banknotes. Some of the papers and letters fell to the floor. I gathered everything up, wrapped it all in his white cravat and stuffed it in my pocket.

All this was done in a blind, unthinking panic. Then my eyes met Rytmel's, and for the first time I saw his dead face. I called his name. I spoke to him. I was in a frenzy! Why didn't he wake up? I shook him, got angry with him. Why was he doing that? Why did he want to upset me so? I felt an urge to slap him, to hurt him.

'Wake up! Wake up!'

No response. Nothing! He was dead!

I heard a cart rattle by along the road. At least someone

was alive!

Suddenly, I don't know why, I realised that I had emptied the whole contents of the bottle into Rytmel's glass! It should have been just one drop! He was dead!

'Betty! Betty!' I shouted.

She came in, and I threw myself into her arms. I cried. I went back to him. I knelt down. I called to him. I wanted to kiss him. I pressed my lips to his forehead. It was cold as marble. I screamed. He filled me now with horror. I was afraid of his ashen face and his icy hands.

'Betty, Betty, we must leave!'

Conscience, willpower, reason, shame, all fell away from me. I was left only with fear, a vile, base fear.

'Betty, we must leave!'

I don't know how we got out.

From the front door, I could see a light approaching from the far end of the street. It was coming closer, getting larger. Someone dressed in red was carrying it. To me, that red looked like blood! The light grew larger. I waited, trembling. It was coming towards me. I shrank back into the doorway, into the shadows, feeling as cold as stone. The light drew level with us. Now I could see that it was a priest, accompanied by another man wearing a red surplice and carrying a lantern. They were on their way to administer the last rites to someone.

I leaned on Betty's arm and I began to walk, with no idea where we were going, as if I were mad...*

*Here follow some lines in which the countess describes her encounter with me. I have omitted this passage because it describes events that appear in my own account and that are, therefore, already known to you. A.M.C.

The Concluding Revelations of A.M.C.

I

Invited to explain what she knew, the countess told in her own words, humbly and bravely, the reason why and the manner in which she had unintentionally killed Captain Rytmel.

'Here are the letters and the money he had with him,' she concluded, placing on the table a packet of papers bundled up in a white cravat. 'I have written my will. Do with me as you choose. Impose upon me the punishment I deserve.'

We all stood in silence. F. moved to the centre of the room and said:

'To punish is to usurp the power of Providence. Human justice, when applied to criminals, does not have society's revenge as its purpose, but the need to protect society from the contagion and infection of crime itself. All crime is a disease. The courts' jurisdiction over criminals ends when a cure has been achieved. Locking up those from whom evil has been shown to be expunged does irreparable harm to society, and is, besides, monstrous and cruel. Everything that is not harmful is necessary and indispensable to our understanding of human emotions, ideas and acts. The nature of the action we are considering, the determining factors, the extenuating circumstances and the underlying intention, all of these things convince us that allowing this lady to go free cannot possibly constitute a danger to society. Incarcerated and delivered over to the courts, she would become the subject of an interesting, scandalous, contentious case. Left to herself, she will be an example, a lesson.'

And going over to the door, he turned the key, flung the door wide, and addressing himself to the countess, announced in a grave, respectful voice:

'You may leave, madam, you are entirely free. Official justice might disagree, but the right-thinking men who were called upon to judge your case will not stand in your way. Your future, so deeply marked by misfortune, is not that of a criminal, but of a poor unfortunate wretch. Take to your fellow wretches, then, the melancholy lesson of your own bitter disappointments, and may God, in His supreme judgement, find that the obscure and unacknowledged kindnesses you scatter about you will make up for past transgressions. The evidence of your guilt will remain buried in this house.'

We stood aside for her to leave. Pale as death, the countess swayed; her strength failed her; she could barely stand. The Tall Masked Man gave her his arm. She made as if she were about to speak; her face took on a pained expression; she hesitated for a moment; finally, she pressed a handkerchief to her lips and left, either stifling a word or choking back a sob.

Moments later, we heard the carriage moving off, carrying with it the person who had, in the world, been the Countess of W.

*****

We had already agreed on a means of concealing the body, which was made all the easier given that no one knew of Captain Rytmel's presence in Lisbon.

We took the stairs to the ground floor of the building and went down four more steps to a kind of cellar room located below street level. It was late afternoon. No daylight reached the room and so we were lit by candles. A deep grave had been dug there. The freshly turned soil gave off a dank and acrid smell. Two of the men to whom I have referred as 'the masked men' were carrying a candelabra, each holding five pink candles. From the dark beams hung grey, silvery cobwebs, broken by the weight of dust.

We unwrapped the bundle we had laid beside the grave and contemplated for the last time the face of the dead man lying on his travel rug.

His white cravat had been neatly tied, his waistcoat buttoned and he had on his gold-buttoned blue tailcoat, with a faded rose in its lapel. In the dim light, his face had taken on an ideal beauty. With his still, closed eyelids he resembled one of those blank-gazed ancient statues. Beneath the arc of his moustache, a slight smile seemed to hover over his parted lips. His hair, dishevelled by contact with the rug in which his body had been wrapped, stood out against his pale features like gold on ivory.

A profound silence reigned. We could hear the ticking of our pocket watches and the buzz of the flies hovering around the dead man's face. Gazing at him with tear-filled eyes, my mind was filled with melancholy thoughts.

Poor Rytmel! At this solemn moment, when your body waits at the graveside for its eternal rest, your funeral may lack the pomp proper to your rank; you may not have been escorted here by a cortège of gold-braided uniforms; you may not even be accompanied to your final resting place by a holy candle and by the prayers of a priest, but you do, at least, have the blessing of friendship! The young, intelligent, handsome scion of an aristocratic family, beneath whose feet bloomed all the flowers that perfume life, the star that presided over your birth has suddenly been snuffed out, and you tumble, like the most despised of beings, into an unmarked grave, in the very house to which you came in search of the ultimate expression of your happiness, and by the light of the same candles that lit your last kiss! At least the place where other unfortunates are buried is known to those who loved them, who can go there to weep. Your fate is far more cruel; you die and disappear! The sad trees of cemeteries will never shade your grave. The birds in the sky will never swoop down to drink the water that the rains have left in the urn by your tomb. The moon, gentle friend of the dead, will never shine through the dark branches of the cypresses and kiss your white headstone. The morning dew will never drop upon the flowers that adorn your burial place. No bees will buzz around the roses planted in the soil that covers you. White butterflies will never flutter about whatever essence of you might burst forth from the bosom of the earth into the dawn light in the form of scent from jasmines and gillyflowers. Your mother, wan and pensive, will search in vain for the rails surrounding your grave to which she can cling as she kneels and raises questioning eyes to Heaven, a gaze in which the remembrance of dead children is always wrapped as if in the luminous robes of a resurrected Christ.'

The Tall Masked Man bent over Captain Rytmel's corpse and took it firmly by the shoulders. We all helped lower the body into the hole. The Tall Masked Man then knelt down and covered the dead man's face with a handkerchief, saying, as if he were speaking to a sleeping child:

'Rest in peace! I will tell your mother where your body lies and I will come back to kneel beside this tomb after I have received on my own breast the tears she sheds for you. Farewell, Rytmel! Farewell!'

Then he shovelled a large portion of the earth piled at his feet into the hole. It fell with a soft, muffled thud onto the corpse.

II

Afterwards, we examined Rytmel's papers with the idea of settling his business affairs. There were the £2,300 in notes. Of the letters, not a single one was from Miss Shorn.

None of us was in a sufficiently calm frame of mind to feel able to return at once to life's trivialities. We decided to stay at the house for a few days, to allow a little time to elapse after the tragedy to which we had been witness.

The house was subsequently bought by Rytmel's mother, and it became a repository for all the objects that had belonged to Rytmel. An iron casket inlaid with gold and intended to receive the ashes of the deceased was placed on top of his grave.

The countess's cousin was on the point of leaving for London when we learned about the publication of the doctor's letters in this newspaper. The countess vowed that she would hand herself over to the police if we did not refute Z.'s suspicions about the doctor's probity and if F. did not unreservedly retract the slanderous comments made about us in his inopportune letter to the doctor, delivered through the intermediary of Friedlann. The countess authorised us to make her story public, saying that she had ceased forever to belong to the world, to whom her confession might serve as a useful example.

It was then that we decided to provide you with the full details of these painful events, concealing or altering the names of the people who took part in it, and leaving to society the possibility of unmasking them and the right to condemn or absolve them.

The Mystery of the Sintra Road

The countess decided to enter a convent, which she herself chose after making careful enquiries. Her cousin escorted her and I went with them to a town in the province of Minho, where there still exists an old convent of Discalced Carmelites, ruled with the full ascetic rigour of the order and inhabited by only five or six nuns. These frail old women hold firm to their vow of poverty, living lives of prayer, meditation, penitence and fasting with the same mystic exaltation, the same Catholic fervour, as when they first became brides of Christ. They go barefoot and wear coarse woollen habits, never linen or cotton. No meat is permitted at their meals. They eat together in the ancient refectory, with the sisters taking it in turn, in accordance with custom, to prostrate themselves at the entrance to the room, so that the others can walk over them as they enter or leave. They have no property of any kind, nor any other income apart from that earned from the work that they do. Removed from all contact with the outside world, they live a strictly cloistered existence and in the utmost poverty. Once those women enter that place, they are never seen again. When they die, they are buried in the cloister by their fellow nuns and covered with a stone that bears neither name nor date. No inscription or other marker distinguishes those who have ceased to exist. Death begins when they cross the convent threshold. Inside, everything is a tomb. Death is simply a change of cell.

This was the place the countess chose as her refuge, to live out the rest of her days. From the outside, the building looked gloomy and mysterious, encircled as it was by a high wall separating it off from the rest of the world and protecting the quarters inhabited by the nuns from prying eyes. The sombre, grey wall, four storeys high, was blotched and stained like a hermit's cowl or like a winding-sheet fashioned for a deceased building. At one point, this stone barrier shrank in on itself, forming the courtyard where visitors could enter; the heavy studded convent door was located at the far end, just visible behind the thick bars of a metal grille. Like rude, unruly tufts of hair, clumps of nettles sprang up between the uneven flagstones paving the courtyard. In the middle stood the shaft of a well, its bucket dangling from a rope attached to a post. The impoverished women who lived nearby did their washing there, and their ragged clothing lay spread out on the ground to dry, alongside the torn and rotting straw mattresses from their children's beds. In one corner hung a metal bell pull. When the bell was rung, a wooden cylinder set into the stonework began very slowly to revolve, its convex face rotating inwards to be replaced by a hollow interior. It was like a mute monster turning its head to reveal an eyeless socket. This device was known as the *roda* or foundling wheel. The countess spoke one word into it and, in response, received what sounded like a kind of groan. Then she went to wait by the dark convent door at the rear of the courtyard.

When the door opened and the countess's cousin shook hands with her for the last time, the tears which, up until then, he had managed to hold back, started to his eyes.

'You find it horrifying, don't you?' she asked him with a smile filled with the strange light of resignation one sees in paintings of martyred saints. 'What would you like me to do, my dear friend? Kill myself? Slip back into society life as if nothing had happened, thus prostituting my heart? I cannot. I lack the courage to risk the salvation of my soul for the sake of my present unhappiness and, needless to say, I also lack the necessary audacity to sacrifice my chaste heart for the sake of a life of ease. As you see, I have chosen the gentler solution. Poor man! How my sad fate pains you! Don't worry. I promise to die very soon, unless I suffer the misfortune feared by St Teresa of Ávila, and the pleasure of feeling myself to be dying only further prolongs my life.

She handed him her cashmere cape and shawl.

'Farewell, cousin, farewell,' she said, allowing him to kiss her on the forehead. 'Pray to God to forgive me and ask the living to forget me.'

As soon as she had taken a few steps inside the door, it closed as it had opened, as if by an invisible hand, having first briefly revealed a dismal hole, as deep and dark as the mouth of an abyss, and thus Rytmel's lover entered the cloister. The various bolts inside juddered home, with a sound like that of stuttering sobs torn from an iron throat.

The countess's cousin and I spent part of the night in the town, waiting for the one o'clock mail-coach. As we were climbing on board, we heard two bells ringing what sounded like an alarm. We enquired as to its purpose. The district deputy, who was travelling with us in the coach, tossed the match with which he had lit his cigar out of the window, and explained:

'It's the Carmelites. They're calling for alms, because they have nothing to eat.'

The coachman cracked his whip, and the ancient coach set off at a gallop, drowning out the doleful clamour of the bells with the racket its wheels made on the narrow, winding, cobbled streets.

I have little more to say.

In Brussels, the Count of W. received a letter from his wife containing these lines: 'I voluntarily divest myself of my position in society. Of all the rights I might possibly demand, I ask that only one remain uncontested: the right to die. I beg you to allow me to disappear, and for that, please accept my sincere and eternal gratitude.'

The doctor, as he said he would be, is working in the field hospitals of the French Army.

Friedrich Friedlann left suddenly on the day he posted F.'s letter, to join the militia in his home country.

For some days now, Carlos Fradique Mendes and F. have been staying at a country house just outside Lisbon, sitting under a shady tree or lounging on the grass, and collaborating on the writing of a book, in which—or so they have promised to burgeoning Mother Nature—they will strike a blow for the inviolable freedom of the mind, which Portugal's literati have, for far too long now, sought to trammel with convention.

And lastly, if I may be permitted to speak of myself, I now live in a small house in the provinces. Do you remember Teresinha? Well, then, it will come as no surprise to you to learn that we were married a few days ago. My heart was crying out for the peace of a tranquil home. Being witness to such profound emotional turmoil is like witnessing a terrible shipwreck. One feels the consoling need of peaceful things. Then, more than ever, one recognises that our only happiness lies in having done our duty.

A.M.C.

The Final Letter

To the Editor,
Diário de Notícias

Sir,
In case there should be any doubt among readers of the story that your newspaper has been serialising for the past two months, we duly state that it contains only false names and hypothetical places, and hereby authorise you to date the dénouement of said story as follows:
Lisbon, the twenty-seventh day of September, 1870, and to sign it with the names given below.

Yours faithfully,
Eça de Queiroz
Ramalho Ortigão

Afterword

At the south-western corner of central Lisbon, Rua do Alecrim climbs straight and steep from the waterfront area around Cais do Sodré up to the Chiado. Most of the stone-built shops and offices that line it are old enough to remember the days when coaches bearing characters from the novels of Eça de Queiroz used to rattle past their doors. A short distance from the top end of Rua do Alecrim is Largo Barão de Quintela, a small square with, in its centre, a grassy hummock, a clump of palm trees and a statue of a bewildered man.

His reaction is not without cause, for he seems to have found himself unexpectedly clasping a woman, naked above the hips and diaphanously veiled below, who leans back and gazes up at him with a quietly triumphant expression.

The man is Eça de Queiroz, and the usual interpretation of the statue is that the naked represents truth, i.e. Realism, and the covered represents fantasy, i.e. Romanticism, the two poles of the literary dispute that played such an important role in his career.

Throughout the nineteenth century, the publication of novels in serial form in newspapers or magazines was common practice in Western Europe and the United States. In some countries the serial was a more frequent road to readership than individual publication.

Portuguese readers avidly embraced foreign, especially French, serial publications *(roman-feuilletons)* and by 1870 had become aware of a new style: the crime and detection novel.

Afterword

In the summer of that year, José Maria de Eça de Queiroz and José Duarte Ramalho Ortigão, aged 24 and 33 respectively, decided to try their hands at just such a novel, to be published as instalments in the newspaper, *Diário de Notícias,* with the intention of stirring up Lisbon, which they saw as a city overcome by inertia, and showing its people how literary styles were changing. The two had met several years previously and shared a passion for a move away from classical romanticism and towards modernist realism. Neither had previously written a novel but both had experience as journalists. At the time they discussed their plan, Ramalho was on the staff of the Academy of Sciences in Lisbon, and Eça had been appointed Administrator of the Municipal Council in Leiria, a full day's travel from the capital.

Eça and Ramalho lost no time in calling upon Eduardo Coelho, editor of the *Diário de Notícias*. As well as being its editor, he had founded the paper himself only six years before, and, as one would expect, he readily agreed to take part in a project that would boost circulation.

Eça was not an unknown quantity. He was well enough connected through his father to have been sent by Eduardo Coelho to accompany the Count of Resende to the ceremonial opening of the Suez Canal in November 1869, and to write news chronicles for publication on his return to Lisbon. The four reports that Eça brought back show that Coelho had chosen well. Eça clearly had a talent for telling a colourful story, and the experiences he had, along with the images he retained in his mind, were now forming themselves into aspects of a novel. *The Mystery of the Sintra Road* contains phrases that are hardly changed from the Suez Chronicles.

Out of whatever arrangements Eça and Ramalho made came *O Mistério da Estrada de Sintra (The Mystery of the*

Afterword

Sintra Road). It was unlike any serial novel that had been published. In most cases, instalments were printed monthly, though a few appeared weekly, and unless the author had an established reputation, they were chapters of a completed work. *The Mystery of the Sintra Road* appeared daily, and its superbly confident authors wrote the instalment the previous day with clear ideas as to style but only a vague idea as to where the plot was heading.

*****

Eça de Queiroz was born on 25 November, 1845, in Póvoa de Varzim, north of Oporto. His parents, both from influential families, were not married at the time of his birth. Eça was nearly four years old when they finally married, and he did not live with them until he was twenty-one.

Ramalho Ortigão was born in Oporto on 24 October 1836. He was privately educated at his grandmother's estate by his great-uncle and godfather. Ramalho briefly attended the course in Law at the University of Coimbra before he decided to take a position as a teacher of French at the Colégio da Lapa in Oporto, where his father was head-master. There, his work brought him into contact with Eça de Queiroz who was a boarder at the Colégio from 1855 to 1861. For at least some of that period, Ramalho was Eça's French master. At the same time he began to submit copy to the newspaper *Jornal do Porto*.

Literary Lisbon during the 1860s was a kaleidoscope of ideas and theories, a city where quickly printed pamphlets and more substantial newsletters circulated, and meetings – often rowdy and inconclusive – were commonplace. Ramalho Ortigão briefly became the centre of attention in 1865 when he challenged a friend and fellow-poet to a duel with swords for calling him a coward. Honour was satisfied when the first blood (Ramalho's) was drawn. In the same year he published *Literatura de Hoje* (*Today's Literature*), a polemic aimed at the conservatism of the older writers and the disrespect of the young.

In 1866, after graduating in Law at Coimbra, Eça de Queiroz went to Lisbon intending to practise both law and journalism. An assignment as a lawyer found him on his way to the provincial city of Évora. Once there, he took the opportunity to distribute the first edition of what he intended to be a bi-monthly political newsletter. At the end of the case, he abandoned the newsletter and returned to Lisbon to write for the *Gazeta de Portugal*, the periodical in which his first published work had appeared.

The following year, Ramalho temporarily left his family in Oporto and moved to Lisbon, where he and Eça renewed their acquaintance and a lifelong friendship developed.

All this time, the *Questão Coimbrã* (Coimbra Debate) – an amorphous movement to discuss social changes and trends in literature – continued to ferment in the background. It had been bubbling since 1862 as former Coimbra students tried to perpetuate their salad days by taking their theories to Lisbon. The two men became vital members of groups of like-minded others who argued the concerns of the *Questão*.

*****

On Sunday 24 July, 1870, a lengthy letter to the editor appeared in the *Diário de Notícias*. It was apparently from a doctor who had been kidnapped at pistol-point, blindfolded, bundled into a coach and taken to the site of what looked to be a serious

Afterword

crime. He had been released unharmed, but through fear of retribution for having written to the newspaper, he had not dared to sign his letter.

It was not an authentic letter; it was the first instalment of the *Mystery of the Sintra Road*, and it made an immediate impression on the public. Further instalments appeared in the *Diário de Notícias* every day until 27 September, 1870. In all, there were sixty-seven including 'The Final Letter' that formally identified Eça and Ramalho as the authors of *The Mystery of the Sintra Road*. Evidently, the instalments used for the newspaper serial were consolidated into the 49 sections and chapters of the book version.

*****

From the day the truth came out as to the authors of the serial, controversy surrounded the question of 'who wrote what'. Eça de Queiroz's standard response when the question was put to him, seems to have been (no first-hand instances can be quoted) that they took it in turns.

The received wisdom, based on a study by writer and philosopher José Sampaio Bruno in 1885, was that Ramalho Ortigão wrote only three chapters: F.'s letter to the Doctor and A.M.C.'s two separate contributions. Sampaio based his conclusions on an analysis of the two writers' very different styles, describing Ramalho Ortigão's as 'stiff' and 'dull'.

To state categorically that Ramalho wrote just three chapters is to over-simplify the matter, and seems intended to denigrate Ramalho's role. It is a rare duo whose members play equal parts.

From the point of view of the translators of this book, we certainly noticed differences of style and vocabulary in those

Afterword

three chapters, and in other places such as the soliloquy on the death of Carmen, and the 'dreadful letter' that Rytmel sent to the Countess, but we both agree that Eça dominated the project and left his mark on every page.

Within ten years, José Maria de Eça de Queiroz had developed a literary style that blended Realism and Romanticism, coloured with social satire and ironic humour, and he was being taken very seriously indeed, having published *The Crime of Father Amaro, Cousin Bazílio* and *The Mandarin*, as well as serving as Portuguese Consul in three countries. Later works included *The Relic* and *The Maias* (considered to be his finest novel). In all, Eça published six novels/novellas during his lifetime, and a further seven were published posthumously. On his death in 1900, he was honoured with a state funeral as Portugal's greatest nineteenth-century novelist.

Ramalho Ortigão became one of the principal figures in the so-called 'Generation of the Seventies' which was dedicated to bringing the culture of an underdeveloped Portugal into line with that of the more progressive European countries – and then back-pedalling for fear the pan-European approach would rob Portugal of its individuality! Ramalho died in 1915 after a successful career as a poet, journalist and political writer.

After appearing in the *Diário de Notícias* to great public acclaim in 1870, *The Mystery of the Sintra Road* was twice published in book form during the years immediately following, and for a third time in 1884. It is still in print.

Despite certain defects that come from the breakneck speed of its writing and publication, *The Mystery of the Sintra Road* is an entertaining story with a good measure of ironic humour and social observation. We cannot accept the authors' (doubtless tongue-in-cheek) description of their work as 'atrocious'. Deliberately clichéd at times, it is perceptive and

Afterword

moving at others. It is also an important part of the Eça de Queiroz canon.

Nick Phillips

Two Authors : Two Translators

One December morning in 2011, one of us had the idea, quickly sent to the other side of the world, of *doing something* about the one that got away – *The Mystery of the Sintra Road* – the almost forgotten novel that Eça de Queiróz wrote in collaboration with Ramalho Ortigão. And the *something* we ought to do was to collaborate on a translation.

To that end, with no experience of working together, but with the support of Mr Eric Lane of Dedalus Books, we began the translation, one of us in England, a well-known translator of the works of Eça de Queiroz; the other in New Zealand, an obscure enthusiast for the Portuguese language, each of us with a computer and a store of optimism and patience.

As for who translated what, we can truthfully say that every page has felt the hand of us both.